Sand Dollar

A STORY OF UNDYING LOVE

"If someday you should ever think of me and miss me,
know in your heart that I'd want you to find me once again.
No matter how distant in time or space... FIND ME."

Sebastian Cole

Sand Dollar
A STORY OF UNDYING LOVE

Sebastian Cole LLC
PO Box 8909
Warwick, RI 02888

Please visit our website at www.sebastiancoleauthor.com

Library of Congress Control Number: 2012904626

Paperback ISBN 978-0-9851156-0-9
eBook ISBN 978-0-9851156-1-6

First Printing: May 2012

Printed in the United States of America

Cover pastel drawings by Deborah DeWit | www.deborahdewit.com

Cover & Interior Design by Scribe Freelance | www.scribefreelance.com

This book is dedicated to our loving parents. We are grateful for everything you've done for us throughout our lives. By giving us love and support, honesty and integrity, we are who we are today thanks to you. And we love you for it.

Prologue

Of all the guests congregated inside Touro Synagogue, no one was more delighted than Miriam Hartman, mother of the groom. She was sitting in the front row with tissues in hand, her husband to her right, the bride's mother — a close friend — to her left. *If only Noah had married a nice Jewish girl like Sarah all those years ago,* Miriam thought, *his life would have turned out perfect, just the way she had planned. Instead, his life was ruined by that shicksa Robin he had insisted on marrying against her wishes. She and Jerry tried to nip it in the bud before it was too late, but Noah was stubborn, some nonsense about butterflies and the way she looked at him. For the life of her, Miriam could not understand why Noah never listened to his mother, because after all, she only wanted what was best for him. And at this point in Noah's middle-aged life,* Miriam concluded, *Sarah was best for him. With all the bad decisions he had made throughout his life, proposing to Sarah appeared to be the only redeeming one.*

Relishing in subdued victory, there was no need for Miriam to ever take credit for the role she had played in getting the two of them together. For all Noah knew, running into Sarah at the premiere of **Sand Dollar** happened by chance, or perhaps even divine intervention — if you believe in that sort of thing. However, there was nothing divine about it — not that time anyway — because Miriam had secretly planted her there.

Miriam was wearing a wide-brim chapeau with beige satin sash, tulle, and rose clusters. She had on a brown silk Carolina Herrera gown with sparkling gold beads and lace trim, an exquisite emerald butterfly-shaped broach pinned on the shoulder. A spectacular 22-carat emerald-cut diamond engagement ring eclipsed her finger, and long crystal-shaped emerald earrings dangled beside her slim neck. Sitting beside her, her husband Jerry resembled an eighty-year-old James Brolin, tall and thin, with manicured white hair and a commanding presence. He was wearing a black Brioni tuxedo accessorized by the black cane resting against the side of the pew.

SEBASTIAN COLE

The synagogue was filled to capacity by half the membership of Spring Valley Country Club, all wearing tuxedos and gowns for this black tie affair. It was a who's who of Rhode Island's most prominent Jewish community. Up on the *bema*, two thousand large white rose-heads adorned the white *chupah*. Standing underneath it, the rabbi gave Jerry a friendly nod, acknowledging the temple's most generous benefactor. Just to the right, Noah was standing beside his best man, his brother Scott. They were wearing white formal tuxedos with tails on their jackets, white bowties, and white *yarmulkes* on their heads.

The conductor raised his baton, and the ten-piece orchestra started playing **Canon In D**. Heads turned as all eyes focused on the first bridesmaid walking slowly up the red-carpeted aisle in a wine-colored gown. After all six bridesmaids took their place on the *bema* to the left of the *chupah*, the superlative performance of Pachelbel's masterpiece was concluded, and there was silence.

As the orchestra began playing **Here Comes The Bride**, all heads turned back down the aisle toward the entrance with anxious anticipation. Sarah was a beautiful, young woman, no doubt the most beautiful bride this congregation would ever see.

Fifty pounds overweight with a silver cross bouncing around her neck, Robin rushed through the front door into the synagogue in ripped jeans and a Block Island T-shirt. Stopping dead in her tracks, her eyes scanned the room. All five hundred congregants sitting in the pews were staring directly at her. Turning her head slowly to the right, she suddenly was aware of Sarah standing just a few feet away in a long, white wedding gown, a mortified look on her face behind her sheer, white veil. The orchestra's music came to a grinding halt.

Noah's smile, which had been filled with anticipation, turned to curiosity as he raised his hand above his eyes to see who had just entered, his jaw dropping at the sight of her. He looked at his brother standing beside him, speechless.

With a look of embarrassment, Robin turned around and escaped through the large, wooden front door. The guests started buzzing and heads turned as they tried to make sense of it all. Glancing around nervously, the maestro looked at Miriam for guidance, who motioned with her hands for him to continue. He raised his baton, and, to the tune of **Here Comes The Bride,** Noah ran down the aisle toward the door. "Don't worry," he blurted out to Sarah as he ran past her. "I'll be right back !" With a bewildered look on her face, Sarah pulled off her veil and looked across the synagogue at her bridesmaids. The chatter from the

6

surprised guests grew steadily as everybody stood up and headed for the exit. With a rustle of expensive silk, Miriam fainted to the floor.

Noah ran down the flight of red-carpeted granite steps, past the line of white stretch limousines waiting out front. He caught up to Robin walking quickly down the sidewalk.

"Hey... what the hell are you doing here?" he exclaimed, grabbing her arm.

"I'm sorry, Noah," she said, wiping a tear from her eye, turning to look at him. "I never should have come here. I'm such a fool." Shaking her head, she glanced at the white stagecoach with two white horses. "Go back to your fairy tale wedding," she sobbed, running across the street.

Noah continued his pursuit, dodging traffic and catching up with her on the other side. "HEY !" he yelled, walking briskly behind her, grabbing hold of her again. "You still haven't answered my question. Why are you here?"

She looked at him lovingly. "It's not your fault... There's no reason why we couldn't have stayed married. The medication... the psychiatrist... God, I don't even know where to start," she said, covering her mouth and looking off.

"I don't believe this," Noah said, shaking his head. "Don't tell me *you're* the one who needs closure, because if you do — "

"No... no, that's not it. I made a big mistake... I never should have left you."

"Let me get this straight. You came all the way down here just to tell me you made some kind of big mistake?" She nodded. "A mistake," he repeated, throwing his hands up in the air, looking away. "A mistake?" he questioned, looking back at her, seeking confirmation. "Don't you think I know that already? Huh? I wanted to hate you so bad, but I couldn't stop loving you long enough to hate you. If there were any way I could have erased your memory from my brain, I would have done it in a heartbeat. But not a chance of that... not with my heart refusing to let go. I would have given my *left lung* just to hold you in my arms for one more day, just one day. Thirteen years... and not a day gone by that I didn't pray you'd come back, look into my eyes, and say the words that you just said to me," he said, turning his head away, looking across the street at Sarah and the rest of the wedding party filtering out of the building.

"NO... No, I can't do it. Sarah's a good woman and a good friend. She'd never leave me; she loves me. I'm sorry, Robin," he said, looking back at her. "You're too late. In case you haven't noticed, I'm getting married today," he said, turning and walking away, forcing himself not to look back. Anxious to rejoin his bride waiting for him on the other side of the street, he stopped at the corner and waited for a few cars to pass. Stepping from the curb, he heard Robin shout.

"What did you just say?" he asked, his foot landing back on the sidewalk as she ran toward him.

"I remember," Robin said, out of breath as she reached him.

"You *remember*?" he said incredulously. "What could you possibly remember?" he asked, staring at her, waiting for the answer.

The beauty from within her soul shined brightly through her loving eyes as she looked deep into Noah's now melting eyes.

"I remember — I love you," she said in a soft voice, nervously biting her lip.

There it was... she actually looked him in the eyes and said it. As Noah heard these words coming out of her mouth, tears formed in his eyes. After all these years, Noah finally got the closure he so desperately needed.

Letting out a scream of anger, he turned and walked straight out into the street in front of a taxicab coming to a screeching halt, almost hitting him.

"GODDAMN YOU !" Noah screamed at her, slamming the hood of the taxi with his fist.

"HEY !" yelled the taxi driver out the window.

"How do you do that?" Noah asked her. "How do you just stand there and tell me you love me? Like... like the last thirteen years never existed. Like you somehow traveled back in time to when I last held you in my arms, and... and everything's still the same, just the way you left it. What do you expect me to do, Robin? What do you — " The lump in his throat prevented him from saying anything further. He shook his head and looked away, a tear rolling down his cheek as Robin opened the taxi door and jumped in.

Cars were beeping their horns, blocked by Noah standing in front of the taxi in the middle of the road. He looked over at his bride on the other side of the street, and then looked back at the woman he truly loved, crying inside the taxi.

Now what? he thought.

FRAGILE:
Handle With Care

*L*ook at me. Not too shabby for an eighty-year-old man, huh? I'm feeling pretty good, although I can't seem to remember how I got here or how this bandage ended up on my forehead. I hope I get out of here soon; I'd like to go home. After all, today's our anniversary.

I lean closer to the mirror, turning my head to the side and touching the edge of the white medical tape holding the square gauze to my forehead. Let me just pull the tape up a little bit over here and see what this looks like. I hear a knock at the door. Better get back in bed.

I scurry out of the bathroom and run back to my hospital bed, jumping in with relative ease. There's a second knock, this time louder. "Come on in," I say, pulling the white cotton sheet up over my hospital gown.

An orderly in blue scrubs enters my room pushing a cart full of folded, white linen robes. He looks about sixty-five, with dark skin, gray hair, and a five-o'clock shadow. A pair of glasses and a photo ID card hang down around his neck.

"Noah Hartman?" he asks, putting on his reading glasses to check the name on the clipboard.

"The one and only."

He pushes a table on wheels over my lap and places a tray of food on it from beneath his cart. I sit up to take a look as he removes the lid, revealing a nicely prepared dinner.

"Mmmm, smells great." I'm hungry, so I take a bite. "Now *that's* good," I say, pointing at the food.

"I'm glad you like it. I made it myself," he says proudly in a deep, soothing voice, hanging the clipboard back up on the side of his cart.

"Hey, how'd you know what I wanted, anyway?"

"You filled out a meal card, remember?"

"No, not really..." I think to myself, trying to put the pieces back together. "The last thing I remember, I was standing in the ark... something important to tell her. But after that, everything's just a blank," I say, taking a sip of wine from the plastic cup. "So, you must be the cook here at the hospital."

"Who, me? Nah... I work second shift doing whatever's asked of me. Right now it's serving dinner and passing out these robes to the patients."

I try to hold back a sneeze, but it's no use, I sneeze anyway.

"Bless you."

"Thanks," I say, accepting a box of Kleenex from him. "You look familiar. Do I know you?"

"I get that all the time. Got one of those faces, I guess. But I have been known to volunteer at the Hartman Foundation from time to time. Maybe you've seen me there, although I doubt you'd ever recognize me if you saw me. I've got to tell you, Mr. Hartman, you've done a wonderful job down there."

"Eh, it was nothing, really. And please... call me Noah."

"*Nothing?* Don't be so modest. The Foundation has helped thousands of families in need. I wouldn't exactly call that *nothing.*"

"Like I said, you do look familiar..." I say, staring at him. "So, what'd you say your name was again?"

"Josh... Josh Numen," he says, extending out his hand.

"Nice to meet you, Josh."

"The pleasure's all mine," he says, smiling with warm eyes. I return the smile. "Oh... before I forget, I believe this is yours," he says, handing me a delicate photograph, being careful not to tear it. "Careful, it's a little soggy. They found it in one of your pockets. Don't know if it means anything to you."

Mesmerized, I stare at the old photograph, the impression of the sand dollar stamped in my mind like it happened yesterday. "My wife took this with one of those disposable underwater cameras forty years ago, back in ninety-six. See what I'm holding in the picture?" I say, turning it around. "Take a good look, because you'll never look at it again quite the same way. We were snorkeling on our honeymoon in the warm, tranquil water..."

A forty-five-foot catamaran dropped its anchor in a secluded, horseshoe-shaped cove. Steep cliffs rising up from a private, white sand beach painted the backdrop to this tropical island paradise situated in the Leeward Islands of the Caribbean.

Noah was a good-looking thirty-eight-year-old man with dark hair, blue eyes, and a chiseled body. He was wearing navy Nautica trunks as he floated effortlessly on his stomach, snorkeling in the crystal clear turquoise water. Robin was a beautiful twenty-eight-year-old woman. Her red bikini showed off a silver bellybutton ring on a trim waist. Her long, red hair flowed freely on top of the water's surface as she took pictures of the sea life with an underwater camera. The clarity of the water was so pure that everything in sight seemed to be within reach, no matter how near or how far. Tropical colored fish in vivid colors glided freely all around them in the boundless sea. In awe of his surroundings, there was no other place on earth where Noah could experience such unsheltered freedom.

He tapped Robin on the shoulder and motioned with his hands, pointing out a lone object sitting undisturbed on the ocean floor below.

"It's a sand dollar. I'm sure you've seen one, probably even held one in your hand, huh, Josh?"

Noah kicked his fins and dove down about ten feet, picking up the sand dollar and resurfacing to get air through his snorkel. From beneath the water's surface, he proudly displayed his newfound prize to Robin.

"No two are exactly the same. Its simplistic design and imperfect form may appear somewhat... well, ordinary. Most people probably wouldn't think twice about it. So why should this seemingly insignificant object capture so much of my attention?"

BOOM ! The precious sand dollar in Noah's hand exploded. In what seemed like slow motion, the sand dollar disintegrated through his fingers into a thousand tiny grains of sand that evanesced into obscurity.

"*Because for me, the sand dollar represents life, and how fragile life really is. What was once so very precious to me, suddenly and without warning, disintegrated and vanished before my eyes. Just like the sand dollar, life holds no promises. Seemingly solid and secure in our grasp, the blessings we have in our lives today are easily shattered tomorrow. The lesson learned: never take your loved ones for granted. And if you're ever lucky enough to find that one person in life who makes you love more than any other person could possibly make you love, you treat every day together as if it were your last. You cherish every moment.*"

"*However, for me, this lesson came too late, for she was already gone, seemingly lost forever. And there was nothing I could do to put the pieces back together. I would spend my life wishing I could somehow travel back, back in time, to the day I first laid eyes on that precious beauty.*"

The precious beauty of Robin's young face was shadowed by sadness as she nervously searched Noah's worried eyes for reassurance.

"*If only I'd known how fragile she really was. If only I'd known her hidden secret. I would have held onto her so differently... never letting go...*"

Snapping out of it, my eyes drift back to the picture as I set it down on the table.

"Wow, she left quite an impression on you, didn't she?" Josh says, picking up the picture to look at it. "You must have really loved her."

"Yeah, I loved her, all right... never stopped, even after she was gone." But why bother Josh with all this? I'm sure he has better things to do than listen to an old man ramble on about the one who got away. "Hey, pass me the salt, will you?"

"So, what was it about her that made you love her so much?" Josh asks, handing me the shaker.

A compelling question for sure. I mull it over while I take another bite. I guess there's no avoiding the subject after all. Besides, I really do need to tell the story to someone. I guess Josh is as good as any. "You mean besides the way she used to look at me... gazing deep into my eyes, my soul, as if I were the only other person on earth?"

"Yeah, besides that," Josh says, laughing, his kind eyes encouraging me to tell him all about her.

"I didn't know it at the time, but I guess you could say I was dead on arrival, so to speak. Then she came into my life and fixed what was broken, opened my eyes to what really matters, you know what I mean? She was full of life, a real free spirit. I gave up everything for her, and in return, she taught me how to live my own life and be free. Made me feel alive."

"Then what happened?"

"She disappeared... vanished into thin air."

"Sounds to me like a story of heartbreak and misfortune."

"Yeah, some people might call it that," I say, looking away. "But that's not what I'd call it. No... I prefer to call it something else," I say, looking back at him.

"What's that, Noah?"

"A story of undying love."

$\mathcal{P}$riorities

"It was four years before that incident in Saint Barts with the sand dollar," I tell Josh. *"I had everything a man could possibly need — or so I thought. The year was 1992 and the place was Jamestown, Rhode Island..."*

$\mathcal{H}$igh on top of a hill rising up from a private, sandy beach sat a gray, shingled Nantucket-style house with six bedrooms, three balconies, and a large deck overlooking the mouth of Narragansett Bay. Scaffolding flanked the house on two sides. Thirty-five-year-old Noah stepped out onto the back deck wearing jogging shorts, a tank top, and running shoes, the sun just moments away from rising over the tranquil sea. He jogged down the numerous wooden steps leading to the beach below and along the vacant shoreline. Seagulls flew out of his way as small waves broke gently against an orange background.

The sun was shining as he made his way back to the house, running by a sand dollar sticking up in the sand, undetected.

Standing on the back deck of his home, Noah was drinking a cup of coffee and peering through an old brass telescope. On clear days like this, he'd scan the bay through his grandfather's telescope, his eyes eventually settling on the old lighthouse that sat on a small half-acre island in the middle of the bay. Built in 1871 and now in disrepair, the lighthouse had long since been abandoned by its keepers. It was a square, white house with a red Mansard roof. Ascending from the roof was a white hexagonal lighthouse tower with a rusted iron catwalk that wrapped around the light. Next to the lighthouse sat a small, white shed that once housed the oil needed to run the light.

Noah went back inside the house, turned off the computer, and put a large stack of papers into his briefcase. He grabbed his suit jacket, briefcase, a set of blueprints, and a bouquet of 24 red roses as he left the house. He opened the trunk to the red 1966 Ferrari 330 GTS Spider parked in the circular cobblestone driveway and put his things inside. With the top down and the engine purring, he donned a pair of large Porsche sunglasses with gold frames and drove away, waving to the painters as they arrived in a white van marked *Hartman Enterprises.*

As he merged onto the highway, he found himself driving next to an attractive woman in a yellow Volkswagen convertible. She had long, dark, flowing hair and an exotic face. The woman looked over at him and gave him a big smile. Noah noticed her, but didn't acknowledge her, smiling to himself as he accelerated, pulling up alongside a school bus. The kids flocked to the windows to gawk in awe at the man driving the fancy, antique sports car. He glanced at the kids briefly and smiled to himself once again. It felt good to be Noah.

Inside the security office of Hartman Enterprises, a black and white monitor showed the Ferrari convertible pulling into a reserved parking space at the front of a crowded parking lot. The sign in front of the car read *Reserved for Noah Hartman.* Parked next to him were a Rolls Royce Corniche, a Porsche Carrera, and a Mercedes sedan, all with reserved parking signs that bore the name *Hartman.* Stan, one of the security guards in the office, watched Noah on the video monitor grabbing his things from the trunk as another security guard talked with a disgruntled employee about the parking ticket she had received.

Noah walked past a large sign that read *HARTMAN ENTERPRISES, National Headquarters,* and headed toward two buildings sitting side by side. One looked new and expensive, with mirrored glass and a sign over the door that read *Executive Offices.* The other was a rundown brick building with a sign that read *Real Estate Leasing and Development.* Built by Noah's great-grandfather at the turn of the century, the old building had never been torn down due to its nostalgic value to the family.

As Noah approached, three executives in dark suits stopped talking to greet him. "Good morning," Noah said with a pleasant smile, shaking their hand and glancing up at the sky, where a whooshing sound was getting louder and louder. Noah waved and headed directly into the old brick building, while the executives, looking at their watches, headed into the nicer, mirrored one — the one with the sleek, black helicopter landing on top of it.

Noah walked into his small, cramped office that had two desks in it: one for him and one for his secretary, Diane. The office was furnished modestly, with wood paneling on the walls and linoleum on the floor. Diane, heavy-set with short hair and glasses, was on the phone trying to track down a shipment of L.V.L.

beams that was delaying a construction project. With a smile, he handed her the roses and hung his suit jacket on the back of his chair.

Smelling the roses, she said into the phone, "Hold on a sec," and looked over at Noah pinning blueprints to the wall. "Now what's this for?"

"Come on now... you don't remember what today is?" he teased.

She shook her head.

"It's our five-year anniversary... working together," he announced proudly.

She nodded. "You know what, Noah? You haven't figured this out yet, but you really are just a kind, regular, down-to-earth type of guy — just like the rest of us — trapped inside an outrageously privileged, white-collared body."

"Yeah, that's what you keep telling me," he said with a mischievous smile, setting his briefcase down on his desk and snapping it open. He removed a stack of papers and set them in three piles on Diane's already overloaded desk. With an annoyed look, she struggled to find the Tenant Occupancy Report buried underneath the new stacks.

A dry-erase board was sitting on the floor facing the wall, concealing what was written on it. Noah picked it up, turned it around, and hung it on the wall, writing on it where he had left off, erasing some things and adding others.

"Thanks for the beautiful roses," Diane said, hanging up the phone and grabbing a large vase off the shelf that was holding a small bouquet of wilted pink carnations. "Don't forget, Russ will be here any minute. Can I get you anything for your meeting?" she asked, dumping the wilted flowers into the trash and replacing them with the fresh roses.

"No thanks, Diane. I'm all set," he replied absently as he continued to write on the board.

Diane frowned at the piles of paper covering her desk. On top of each one was a spreadsheet titled *Prospective Mates*. The header read *SCORE, Name, Handle, Email, Age, Town, Height, Body Type, Number of Kids, Phone Number*. She picked up one of the spreadsheets and studied it, shaking her head in confusion as she glanced up at him.

Catching her look, he explained as he continued to write, "The pile on the left is all of the profiles of the women I want to contact on Mymatch.com. As you can see, I've given each woman a calculated score based on my special rating system. The middle pile is all the profiles of the women who have already contacted me first."

"Already? How long have you been doing this; six months?"

"This site is amazing. I just joined three days ago."

Diane picked up the first pile and riffled through the profiles. Large numbers were circled on each profile, denoting the score that each woman had received — *55, 27, 42, 48...*

"What's with this puny little pile?" she asked, picking up the small third pile.

"Oh... those are the women my parents would like."

Diane looked even more confused.

"The Jewish ones."

Noah's eyes saddened as he stopped writing for a moment, reflecting back on his childhood.

> Six years old and wearing a white tennis sweater and Mickey Mouse backpack, little Noah tramped behind his babysitter into the Mahjong room at Spring Valley Country Club. The room was all green, with green-flocked wallpaper, green upholstered chairs, and green satin drapes. Noah's mother, Miriam, was seated with three other women at one of the twenty square wooden tables, playing Mahjong with small tiles spread out in front of them. With long, black hair and delicate facial features, Miriam always dressed to impress. In a Long Island accent, she thanked the young babysitter and smiled lovingly at her son.
>
> "Hey, sweetie, say hello to my Mahjong partners: Helen, Maxine, and Doris."
>
> Noah looked at the ladies. "Hello," he said politely with a shy, adorable smile.
>
> "Look at this cute, little *bubeleh*," Doris said, grabbing Noah's cheek and pinching it. Noah grimaced. "Don't you just want to eat him up?"
>
> "You know, Miriam, he's turning into quite the *boytshik*," said Maxine.
>
> "Noah, tell my friends what you told me you'd do someday if you ever bring home a *shicksa* who is mean to your mommy."
>
> "What's a *shicksa* again, Mommy?"

"You remember, dear — a girl who isn't Jewish," Miriam reminded him.

"Oh yeah... I'll throw her right out of the house !" he said, swinging his fist through the air.

The women laughed while Noah smiled with pride. Miriam patted her son on the head and smiled quietly to herself, pleased that she had instilled her lofty priorities in little Noah.

Noah stared into space in front of the dry-erase board, a marker in his hand and a sad look on his face. Diane stood up and tucked the Tenant Occupancy Report away in the file cabinet beside him. Looking over his shoulder at the checklist on the board, she observed dryly, "Okay, Noah, now you've *officially* lost your mind."

DATING CHECKLIST
PHYSICAL:
voluptuous — A
pretty — A
young — B
not too tall — B
thin — B
good teeth — C
5+5+3+3+3+1= 20 possible points

PERSONALITY:
easy-going/soft-spoken — A
loving — A
affectionate — A
likes children — B
not Jappy — C
5+5+5+3+1= 19 possible points

BASICS:
no kids — A
doesn't smoke — B

lives nearby — C
5+3+1= 9 possible points

BACKGROUND:
Jewish — A
good education — B
good occupation — C
5+3+1= 9 possible points

OTHER:
likes sailing — A
sexy — B
good kisser — C
5+3+1= 9 possible points

A= 5 points
B= 3 points
C= 1 point
20+19+9+9+9= 66 TOTAL POSSIBLE POINTS

"Voluptuous?" Diane questioned, one eyebrow raised.

Noah shrugged. "Okay, I know it must seem a little shallow, but dating in today's world can be very confusing. It's information overload. By prioritizing the qualities that are most important to me, and generating a total score, I figured it would help me sort through it all. You know... find my best match in those stacks of papers."

"You can't be serious? Love can't be defined by a number. I'm telling you, Noah, when the time is right, it'll just happen."

"And this rating system will guarantee it happens," he said confidently, picking up Stacey's profile and looking at it. "Now take Stacey here, for example. She scored a fifty-five out of sixty-six possible points," he said proudly. "Now you can't tell me that she doesn't have a better chance of wooing my achy-breaky heart over..." he said, shuffling through the pile of profiles, grabbing one, "over Shelly here, scoring a measly twenty-seven points — come on now."

"You just don't get it, do you? People aren't some kind of two-dimensional statistic. They've got souls."

"Yeah I know, but how do I put on a number on that?"

"EXACTLY. You can't."

"I'm telling you, this is a foolproof system I've got here," he insisted, pulling a calendar off a nail in the wall. "Just give me 'til..." turning a couple of pages, "'til Labor Day," he said, drawing a heart around the date. "That's six weeks from now. I just have to do a little weeding out, that's all, and I'll find love — guaranteed."

"Six weeks, huh? Care to wager on that?"

"Okay... okay, I can do that. What do you say the loser buys the winner flowers every week for two months?"

"Nah, I always win that," she said, looking at the wilted carnations in the wastebasket. "Can't you think of something else?"

"Yeah, but this time *I'm* going to win, and you'll be buying *me* flowers for a change."

"Uh huh..." she said, rolling her eyes.

Noah's phone rang.

"Mr. Hartman's office," Diane answered.

"Russ is here," she announced.

"Okay, send him in," he said, lifting the dry-erase board off the wall and turning it around just as the construction manager walked in holding a briefcase and several rolls of blueprints under his arm.

$\mathcal{L}$ife $\mathcal{B}$efore $\mathcal{R}$obin

"Rachel was a complainer," I explain to Josh, continuing with the story, *"always complaining about one thing or another. She complained that I was shallow and self-centered. She complained I never listened to her, especially when it came to having enough chutzpah to stand up to my parents. Let's see, what else... Oh yeah, she complained I was materialistic and loved my boat more than I loved her. Maybe she was right — I don't know. In any case, it didn't matter anymore because my lawyer had called to tell me that my divorce from Rachel was now final, and I could start dating again. But finding the right woman was going to be quite the challenge. I needed to find someone that would love me for me and not for my money. And with Internet dating, finding the right match soon became a full time job."*

"So I started with the Jewish pile first, not because it was important to me, but because it was important to THEM — my parents.

"What was important to me?" I say, repeating Josh's question. *"That's easy... LOVE."*

$\mathcal{T}$he clock read *9:01 PM*. Noah was lying on his antique four-poster bed, talking on the phone to a prospective mate while holding her profile in his hand. They were hitting it off so well on the phone that before he knew it, the clock read *3:03 AM*.

"Wow, I can't believe we've been talking for six hours already. We really do have a lot in common, don't we? Better get some sleep or we'll be falling asleep at dinner later on," he said with a yawn. "Sweet dreams, Stacey," he said, hanging up the phone and writing her name on the calendar below two other women's names that had been crossed off with large "Xs".

That evening, with growing excitement and a long-stemmed red rose on the passenger seat beside him, Noah drove an hour north to Boston to meet his potential mate. "I'm too sexy for my car, too sexy for my car, too sexy by far. And

I'm too sexy for my hat, too sexy for my hat..." Noah sang along with the radio as he traveled up Interstate 95 with the top down and the wind blowing through his hair.

In his brown leather jacket and natty brown tie, Noah looked rather dapper as he pulled up in front of the cozy Italian restaurant in the North End and stepped out of his car. Holding the rose behind his back, he headed toward the woman standing in front of the restaurant.

It took only one glance to crush the excitement and anticipation that days of long emails and phone calls had built up. Noah tried not to let his disappointment show through as he politely greeted the woman who looked nothing like the photograph in her profile, surreptitiously taking in her dowdy floral dress and long, drab brown hair.

The young, attractive hostess smiled at Noah as she seated them at a cozy candle-lit table for two in the corner of the room. Noah returned the smile, more attracted to the hostess than his blind date. Noah and Stacey talked, ate, and drank wine together, capping it off with cappuccino and an order of tiramisu with two spoons. The look in Stacey's eyes and the permanent smile on her face told Noah that she was really into him. Noah did his best to show interest in Stacey despite the absence of physical attraction.

Relieved that dinner was finally over, he walked her back to her car, thanked her for an enjoyable evening, and leaned in with his lips shut tight for a quick peck good-bye. Stacey, on the other hand, had other ideas as she grabbed at him with her mouth wide open. Noah wrestled free from her grasp and walked briskly back to his car, ignoring Stacey's frustrated exhale behind him.

Every night for a month, Noah put on a sport jacket and tie, and drove an hour to meet the next prospect for dinner. Every night, a long-stemmed red rose sat patiently on the passenger seat beside him awaiting its beneficiary. Every night after dinner, he'd cross off one more name on the calendar and call the next woman on the list, talking for hours and setting up his next rendezvous. If one woman wasn't available to fill a particular dinner slot, another woman was. When he was done making his phone calls, he was back online perusing the website again, crossing some names off the list and adding even more to the bottom. It was a tiring exercise in mathematics — addition and subtraction. And in the end, after processing all of those women, not one received so much as a second date. Discouraged, Noah thought that perhaps he was just trying too hard.

"Pretty soon I had gone through the entire Jewish list, all the A's on the master list, and half the B's. Eventually, I stopped writing long letters and having long phone conversations. It was way too much effort to spend on someone I'd most likely never see again. Forget the long dinners, the long emails, the long phone calls; meeting for a quick cup of coffee was much more efficient..."

With no rose in sight, Noah walked into a Dunkin Donuts and shook the hand of a woman. Discretely pressing a button on the stopwatch in his pocket, the fifteen-minute countdown began. When his pocket started beeping, Noah was back on his feet shaking the hand of the woman he'd most likely never see again. This scenario repeated itself dozens of times with an assortment of women. Anything over fifteen minutes would have automatically qualified for a second date — if only there'd been a second date.

Finally, Noah walked into his office one morning with a resigned air. After handing Diane a large bouquet of exotic flowers, he slumped down at his desk and took out his calendar, putting a big "X" through the heart drawn around Labor Day, next to all the other "Xs" going back six weeks. Looking over his long spreadsheet, marked up with so many additions and scratch-offs that it was hard to follow, he stood up and dumped the entire stack of profiles into the recycling bin, shaking his head and wiping the dry-erase board clean.

"It wasn't long before I became overwhelmed with the whole Internet dating thing. The list wasn't getting any shorter. In fact, it was only getting longer. There just wasn't enough time in the day. There had to be a better way. Besides, meeting women the old-fashioned way was much more my style..."

Hip-hop music was blasting as Noah walked into The Art Bar in downtown Providence. After paying the $10 cover, he began scanning the crowd. *What a meat market,* he thought, *and there's lots of meat.* The guys all sported greased-back hair and heavy gold chains, while the women displayed big hair, short skirts, and open blouses. In his brown tweed Brooks Brothers jacket, beige Tommy Bahama pants, and yellow Hermes tie, Noah quickly realized how out of place his conservative attire was in this libidinous crowd.

Handed a Heineken by the bartender, Noah navigated through the swarm of people, weaving in and out in a clockwise motion around the dance floor, eventually arriving back where he started, next to the bar. Noah was on the hunt, circling like a shark in the water. But he was not alone — there were plenty of other sharks in the water too.

After his first pass, Noah turned his attention to the dance floor, where two young men confidently entered the arena and danced fearlessly up to two young women who were dancing together. Turning their backs to them, the women moved to another spot on the dance floor. Unfazed, the two young men danced over to the next closest targets. This new pair seemed unimpressed too, giving them the cold shoulder. But this didn't deter the young men, who were up for the challenge. Their strategy seemed quite simple, really: gyrate their bodies continuously until the women acquiesced; then divide and conquer. Their perseverance appeared to be paying off as the women eventually succumbed, joining the two male specimens in dance. Implementing the final stage to their mating ritual, the females were separated and their dancing grew ever more suggestive.

Noah turned away from the dance floor and scanned the crowd. He knew he couldn't just dance up to women like that; he was shy, and it wasn't his style. And so an hour later, he finally got up the courage to ask an attractive younger woman with long, blonde hair to dance. "I don't think so," she replied rudely, walking away from him to dance with her girlfriend, who was already dancing. He asked another pretty, young woman to dance. "No." He went up to a third young woman and received yet another "No".

Stepping up to the bar, Noah ordered something a little stronger, a Captain Morgan and Coke. Also at the bar, sitting to his right, was a woman with average looks, about the same age as him. He smiled at her, and she smiled back. Things were starting to look up. Asking her politely if she'd care to dance, she replied "No thank you," with a stiff smile, looking away.

Frustrated, Noah looked at his watch. It was already 12:30 a.m., and he hadn't danced all night. Feeling his chances diminishing by the minute, he spotted a woman standing nearby. She was chewing gum and was dressed haphazardly. He walked hopefully over to her, only to receive another "No." Noah couldn't believe his luck. He was now on a mission and wouldn't stop until somebody agreed to dance with him — anyone at all.

"AH-HA !" he said to himself, spotting a not-so-attractive, overweight, middle-aged woman separated from the crowd. *If this woman says "No", I'm leaving*, he thought to himself, approaching her with eyes of the tiger. "No," said the woman, shaking her head as a very large man came out of the bathroom behind her, walking up to her and giving Noah a dirty look.

"I never really liked nightclubs that much either. There was always so much noise, you could barely have a conversation. All you could do was ask a woman to dance and hope for the best. Most of the time, the women just wanted to be left alone so they can dance with their friends and have a good time. To them, I was just some stranger, no better than the rest of the creeps who were hitting on them. If only they knew the real me, they wouldn't have been so quick to dismiss me. Oh, I'm not talking about anything superficial, or anything like that. I'm talking about who I really was inside, what I stood for, my honesty, my integrity, but most of all, my tremendous capacity to love. But who was I to tell them?"

It was now one o'clock, and the club was closing. Masses of people were filtering out of the building into the parking lot as the Providence Police came in to disperse the crowd and send everybody home. It had not been Noah's night, asking ten women to dance and receiving ten rejections. And now he had to stand in the middle of a long valet line waiting for his car, his arms wrapped tightly around his body, shivering without a coat.

As a red antique Ferrari roared around to the front of the building, everyone in line wanted to know just who belonged to the fancy sports car. A couple of women who had refused to dance with him earlier that night saw Noah getting into the car and ran over to him.

"Can you give me a ride?" asked the young woman with long, blonde hair.

"I don't think so," Noah replied, shutting the door on her.

"Hey, wait, where ya goin'?" said the other, chomping on her gum as Noah pulled away. "Why didn't you say you was rich?" she yelled as he turned onto the street, the tires screeching.

The year was flying by, with Noah dating one woman after another. After a couple of months of dating a woman named Debbie, he realized that he didn't want to waste his or her time if it wasn't going anywhere. As nice as she was, she just wasn't *the one.* Breaking up with her would not be easy, but it was for the best, not wanting to lead her on if his heart wasn't in it. After Debbie there was Cheryl, and after Cheryl there was Susan, and after Susan there was Monique. Each woman lasted no more than a couple of months. But there was always something missing, and Noah refused to settle. What that was... he didn't know.

"It wasn't long before I did have a girlfriend. Or should I say girlfriends? For me, I guess it was kind of like trying on different pairs of shoes. You know... until you try them on and wear them for a while, you really don't know if they're going to be a good fit. Oh, don't get me wrong; they were all really nice women. But I wasn't looking for just any woman; I was searching for one in particular — my soul mate. I had no idea where to find her, but I knew one thing for sure: I'd know her when I see her."

Life At First Sight

While **Y-M-C-A** by The Village People was playing at the main dance floor inside the Mardi Gras complex in Cranston, people were lined up outside, waiting to pile into the club. Noah and Scott were handed bottles of Heineken by the pretty, young ponytailed bartender as they stood watching the DJ spin records inside the mirrored booth. Scott resembled his brother, only with glasses, a slightly receding hairline, and an extra fifteen pounds from all the years of his wife's good home cooking. Scott looked tailored, lawyer-like as a matter of fact, with a navy pinstriped suit, white shirt with gold cufflinks, and blue tie. Noah, on the other hand, was dressed more casually, wearing a blue sport shirt and tan pants.

"Thanks for coming," Noah said as they stepped away from the bar. "The last time I came to a place like this, it didn't go so well. At least this time I have good moral support and a shoulder to cry on," he said, laughing.

"Anything to help, Little Brother, but I can't stay too long, or I'll turn into a pumpkin. I promised Sharon I'd be back by midnight. I figure if she can have Girls' Night Out once a week, I can have Brothers' Night Out once in a blue moon, right?"

"Sounds good to me," Noah agreed, clanking his Heineken to his brother's.

They opened a door marked *Diamond Rodeo Club*, and country music flowed out. Just about everybody in the room was out on the dance floor, line dancing. By the looks on their faces, they must have been really enjoying themselves. Since neither Noah nor Scott knew how to line dance, they exited the room, crossing over to the other side of the building. Heavy metal blasted out as they opened a door marked *Rock House Club*. A live band was playing up on stage while people stood in front watching like zombies. They covered their ears and left the room, walking upstairs to the hip-hop room. Rap music poured out the door as they opened it and stepped inside. Squeezing in between the sweaty people, struggling to make headway across the dark room, they came to another door and headed out. Back downstairs they went, settling at the main bar, where disco music was much more their style.

"I don't think you're going to find your soul mate in a place like this," Scott admitted. "But besides that, I don't get why no one would dance with you last time."

"Who knows? Maybe they saw the real me — the man deprived of a life, living a lie."

"What in the world are you talking about? You've got a life — a great life. You have everything you could possibly need. Believe me, there's not a guy out there who wouldn't trade places with you in a heartbeat," Scott said, looking around the room at the men.

"It's funny you say that, because I'd do just about anything to trade places with *them*. Look at them, Scott," Noah said, gesturing with his head. "Don't you see they're different from us? They get to live *their* lives. Wouldn't it be great to be like them, with no strings attached, free to make choices and free to make mistakes, free to love and free to lose? I want to be like everybody else out there in the real world; I want to be *alive*."

"WOW... check out that vivacious redhead on the dance floor. Talk about *alive*..."

Noah turned his head toward the dance floor and was captivated by a beautiful woman, her hands up in the air and a silver cross bouncing around her neck as she danced with another girl. She had long red hair, freckles, and a natural, girl-next-door kind of beauty. Totally carefree and immersed in the moment, she appeared to be full of life as she mouthed the words to the song, clearly enjoying every beat.

"I suddenly found myself alone in the room with the red-haired beauty. Call it what you want; but I call it... love at first sight."

Scott looked at his gold Rolex and downed the last sip of beer. "And if I want to *stay* alive, I better get going," he said, standing up and placing the bottle on the bar. "Come on, let's get out of here. We can finish this conversation at lunch on Monday."

"What did you say?" Noah asked, mesmerized by the vision on the dance floor.

"I said," Scott yelled over the music, "we should get going."

28

"Yeah okay... I'll see you on Monday," Noah replied, standing up and walking toward the dance floor in a trance, leaving his bewildered brother behind. Noah was forced to stop and wait for the traffic jam of people to clear before he could continue on. By the time he reached the dance floor, the song had changed, and the women were no longer there. Looking around for them, he didn't see them anywhere, so he immediately started searching, eventually spotting them off to the side, near the line of women waiting for the bathroom.

Two men — one tall, one short — were standing nearby, checking them out. They seemed to be arguing over something or someone. Seeing Noah zeroing in, the tall one stepped in front of the redheaded woman just as Noah arrived. He was young, with blonde hair and the face of a Calvin Klein model, and the body to match. The young stud smiled confidently at her, taking her hand and gesturing to the dance floor with his eyes. The woman looked at him, then glanced at Noah standing back with a disappointed look on his face. She pulled her hand away from Model Man and shook her head.

"You're kidding me, right?" he said incredulously, backing up into Noah before grabbing his friend and stalking off.

The woman looked at Noah standing in front of her like a little boy. "I was just wondering, uh..." Noah began nervously. "What it is I'd like to ask you, is uh... what do you think, would you like to —"

She smiled and took his hand, leading him out to the middle of the dance floor.

"So, I take it you *would* like to dance..." Noah confirmed.

As they introduced themselves and started dancing, Robin's friend, Julie, squeezed through the crowd to join them. She was pretty too, about Robin's age, short, Italian, with shoulder-length black hair. Noah soon found himself to be a human sandwich, dancing with Robin close in front and Julie close behind. *Now what could be better than this?* he thought while the three of them danced the rest of the night without leaving the floor.

It was one o'clock, and the crowd had thinned out considerably. The last song, **I Will Be Here** by Steven Curtis Chapman, started playing, and Julie walked off. As Noah and Robin looked deep into each other's eyes, Robin gasped, and time seemed to be standing still. The connection went far beyond simple attraction; it was a meeting of souls. As if awakened from a stupor and feeling truly alive, Noah was living in the moment, a moment of truth and clarity.

His arms glided around her neck as they started to slow dance. He put his head up against hers and could feel her ear brushing up against his. He turned his head slightly and discreetly inhaled the luscious scent of her hair, which smelled sweet, like strawberries. He pressed his lips against her neck and could taste her skin.

The song was coming to an end, and Noah put his face directly in front of Robin's, their lips so close they were practically touching. He gently placed his hand on her face and moistened his lips. With their hearts beating fast and their eyes fixated on each other, there was no one else on earth.

"Can you picture the way she was looking at me?" I say excitedly, sitting up in my hospital bed. "No one else ever looked at me that way before — or after for that matter. The connection in our eyes, the window to our souls, couldn't possibly be any stronger. Yeah, I had found my soul mate all right, and my life would never be the same."

"Well, at least you found her," Josh says, happy for me. "Some people go their whole lives without ever finding that one true love. Consider yourself lucky."

I take a sip from my cup. "Yeah... I guess you're right. I was pretty lucky, wasn't I?" I say, staring off, my mind filled with visions of the sand dollar exploding in my hand. "But there were times when I didn't always feel that way."

"You finished with that?" Josh asks, pointing at my empty plate.

"Here you go," I say, handing him the tray. As he lowers it beneath his cart, I see a little bit of wine left in the cup and motion for him to bring it back. He holds the tray as I take the last sip. It's good — really good.

"If I had only known then what I know now, I would have done things so differently. If ever there was a moment to go back to, this was it... our first kiss..."

Noah's hand was caressing her soft face as his lips were suspended tenderly against her lips. They were leaning up against the side of Robin's silver Honda Civic, the side-view mirror held on with duct tape. Julie was sitting in the passenger seat waiting for them to come up for air so they could go home to sleep.

As his lips pulled slowly away hers, Noah's eyes opened. But something was wrong. Tears were flowing down her white, freckled cheeks as she turned her head away.

"What's the matter?"

Robin looked back into his eyes, hesitating. "I don't know how to tell you this..."

"What is it?"

"I have a boyfriend," she confessed reluctantly. "Been seeing him a couple of months now." Noah's smile vanished. "But he's leaving next month, in the military. Besides, I don't want to be with him; I want to be with you," she said, her eyes looking deep into his, searching for comfort.

"Don't worry," he said, gently kissing one tearful eye and then the other. "Everything's going to be alright."

Robin smiled at the tenderness of his gesture. "Here's my number," she said, handing him a cocktail napkin with writing on it. "Tomorrow's my day off from the homeless shelter. Call me if you'd like to get together."

She gave him a quick kiss good-bye and jumped into the car. The loud noise emanating from the broken muffler tore the peaceful silence of the slumbering street as she waved out the window and turned the corner, her taillights disappearing into the night.

The next morning, Rosa, wearing a white housekeeper's uniform, pulled opened the drapes, allowing bright light to burst into the bedroom, where it fell upon Noah's face. He opened one eye. "Good morning Rosa," he muttered, half asleep. She picked up the clothes scattered around the floor and left the room, whereupon Noah covered his face with his soft down pillow and fell back to sleep, even as she vacuumed nearby.

An hour later, Noah ambled into the shower, his eyes half shut. Steam filled the room as hot water massaged his achy muscles. "Bye, Noah. See you next week," Rosa shouted as she passed by the bathroom. "I washed your pants," she yelled, walking down the large, curved staircase and out the door.

Noah's eyes suddenly opened wide. "SHIT !" he exclaimed, quickly shutting off the water and grabbing a towel as he ran out of the bathroom, soaking wet. He went straight to the laundry room and grabbed a pair of tan pants hanging on a clothes rack with freshly ironed clothes. He put his hand in the pockets — nothing. "Shit !" he repeated, rifling through the other pairs of pants hanging on the rack. He opened the dryer door and found another pair of tan pants. Quickly searching the pockets, relief washed over his face as he pulled out a shredded yet intact paper cocktail napkin. Anxiously placing the pieces on the ironing board, he arranged them back together with cautious precision. The face of victory, however, soon turned to defeat: the telephone number was illegible.

Butterflies

With a Kmart shopping bag in each of her hands, a woman wearing a black leather coat and gray wool hat crossed the busy Weybosset Street intersection in downtown Providence. The sign on top of the concrete building she entered read *Emergency Family Services of Rhode Island.* Standing behind the front desk wearing a white uniform and talking on the phone, Robin smiled at her and motioned with her hand to wait just one second. A young woman with greasy blonde hair and a torn coat waited anxiously beside the desk. Her two young children stared with blank faces at the TV across the lobby. The four-year-old, a cute little girl with curly, brown hair, spotted a penny on the floor, and without calling attention to it, she picked it up, examined it, and placed it in a large glass collection box containing only a handful of spare change.

"So you don't have any beds open either, huh?" Robin said disappointedly into the phone. "Well, call me as soon as one opens up, okay? We're filled to capacity over here too, and I'm running out of options for these people. Okay, thanks, Cheryl. Bye," she said, hanging up with a frustrated sigh.

"Here you go," said the woman in the black leather coat, handing Robin her white plastic bags.

"Wow, thanks," Robin said, looking at packages of men and women's underwear inside one of the bags. "I know a lot of people who could use these."

"I'm just glad I could help," the woman said, depositing a dollar into the collection box as she left, crossing the street in front of a red convertible Ferrari that was just pulling up.

Out of the car jumped Noah, who walked rapidly over to a homeless man leaning up against the side of a building, questioning him. The man pointed toward the shelter. Noah walked over to the window, cupped his hands around his eyes, and peered in. There she was, behind the counter — Robin. He had been searching for her for a month, unsuccessfully, but today was different — he'd found her. Looking to his left, he noticed a woman walking out of the building next door with a bouquet of flowers. It was Clarke Flower Shoppe.

Robin's coworker, Theresa, walked up to the young family and said, "I'm sorry to tell you this, ma'am, but there are still no beds available. I even double-checked just to make sure. Why don't you try back again tomorrow? I'm sorry."

"Wait a second," Robin called out to the disheartened family walking away. "What are you talking about?" she whispered to Theresa. "We can't just throw this family out into the street; it's cold outside."

"Well, what can we do about it? Have them sleep in the utility closet? We just don't have enough beds."

Robin looked over at the utility closet, trying to think of a solution. "Come on, let's go," the dejected woman instructed her kids, walking to the door with her children lagging behind.

"Where we gonna go now, Mommy? I'm hungry," the little girl said sadly. Robin stared at her as her mother bent down and zipped up her coat. The door opened in back of them, and Noah, holding a bouquet of red roses, politely held it open for them to leave.

"STOP RIGHT THERE," Robin commanded the family. "Come back; I've got a room for you."

The family stopped in the doorway and looked back at Robin as she unlocked the door behind her, walking into the closet-sized room.

"What are you doing?" Theresa complained, watching as Robin pushed a two-drawer filing cabinet on wheels out of the small room. "They can't sleep in there... that's your office."

"No?" Robin shot back. "Then just watch me," she said stubbornly, marching right back in.

Noah watched as Robin tried to push a heavy, wooden desk stuck to the floor. "Here, let me help you with that," he said, grabbing one end of the desk.

"Why didn't you ever call me?" she said, angry, violently shaking the desk, loosening it from the grips of the heavily waxed floor.

"You're not exactly easy to find, you know," he responded as the two of them raised the desk together and walked it out of the room.

"Well, don't think those roses are going to get you anywhere. I waited all month for you to call," she added, dropping her end of the desk onto the hallway floor.

"It's not that I didn't want to call," he said, setting down his end of the desk gently. "Turns out they don't make paper napkins like they used to."

Robin looked at him curiously as she reached for one of the shopping bags and emptied the contents onto the desk, all except for one. "Hold that thought," she said, walking across the lobby to a man sitting on the worn-out sofa, watching TV. He was African American, with gray hair and a scraggly beard.

"Happy birthday, Harry," she said, handing him the plastic bag.

"Wow, thanks," he exclaimed, removing a package of Hanes briefs. "But today's not my birthday," he said, jumping up from the sofa and scampering off with his gift. Removing the cushions from the sofa where Harry had been sitting, she carried them into her office and arranged them on the floor, along with some blankets.

"This should hold you over until something opens up in a day or so," Robin said to the homeless woman, grabbing a few pillows for her.

"Thanks, you're a life saver," she said, giving Robin a hug.

"I'm Robin."

"Hi, Robin, I'm Gail, and this is Peter and Ashley," she said, pointing at her children.

"Hey guys," Robin said to the kids, kneeling down. "You know what?" The kids shook their heads. "I'm really glad you're here," she said with a sweet smile, handing them brightly colored lollipops — the kind you see at the bank. "You know, Ashley, I've got a little girl just your age. Her name's Brittany. Would you like to meet her sometime?"

Ashley nodded, her face beaming.

"That was really admirable," Noah said to Robin as she stepped outside the room to talk to him.

"It was nothing... really. I'm sure you'd do the same thing," she said, glancing at the flowers in his hand. "Saving those for somebody?"

"Oh..." he said, holding them out to her. "Forgiven?" he asked.

"Forgiven," she confirmed, accepting the flowers and smelling them. "But only because they're so beautiful," she said, smiling and placing them in a vase in her former office. Robin grabbed her pocketbook and a small bag. "I'll be right back. Don't go anywhere."

Noah was staring curiously at the sign on top of the glass collection box when Robin came back wearing jeans and a sweater, carrying packages of peanut butter crackers. She handed them out to the young family, patting Ashley on the head as she ate one. Noah took Robin's hand and headed for the door, glancing at the collection box as they walked past it. The faded, torn sign on top read *Help us raise $250,000 to expand our facility and open 50 more beds.* A drawing of a shaded thermometer illustrated that only $153 had been raised so far.

"Such a gentleman," she remarked as he opened the passenger door of his car for her. "I'm not used to being treated so good. Careful you don't spoil me," she warned as she got in.

As they drove away, Noah glanced over at Robin sitting beside him. She was staring at him intensely with a look of vulnerability in her eyes. "Why do you keep looking at me like that?" he asked.

"Because you give me butterflies."

"I know what you mean. When I look at you looking back at me like that... I get them too."

A little while later, Noah and Robin were holding hands across a table in the outdoor courtyard at Venda Ravioli on Federal Hill. The butterflies in their stomachs made it impossible to eat — so they didn't. When the waiter came over to see how they were doing, he seemed disappointed that their plates were still full. Clearing the table, the waiter asked nervously, "So... care for dessert?" They shook their heads and smiled.

After dinner, Noah and Robin watched **When A Man Loves A Woman**, with Andy Garcia and Meg Ryan, playing at the Cable Car Cinema. Cuddled up in each other's arms, each time Andy kissed Meg on the big screen, so too did Noah kiss Robin.

It was late when Noah pulled up in front of the shelter. "Thanks, I had a wonderful time," Robin said, looking deep into Noah's eyes.

"Me too," Noah replied, unbuckling his seatbelt.

"I really like you," she admitted, their eye connection broken only by the passionate kiss they now shared.

Noah got out of the car and opened her door. As she walked to her car, Noah called out, "Hey... when am I going to get to see you again?"

Robin smiled at him. "Anytime you want, Noah."

"How about tomorrow?"

"I can't wait," she said, walking backwards slowly, unwilling to take her eyes off of him. "Sweet dreams, Noah."

The next day, Noah was standing outside a three-story tenement house in Central Falls. An old, rusty Chevy with different colored doors was up on blocks in the driveway. Laundry was hanging on a clothesline out of a window on the third floor, and the building next door was boarded up. The front door opened and a cute little girl with strawberry blonde hair stood in the doorway looking up at him.

"Hey, Noah, come on in," Julie said, appearing in the doorway behind the girl. "Robin will be right out."

He walked into the apartment and looked around. The furniture didn't match, the wall-to-wall shag rug was worn and musty, and the windows were bare — no curtains. A top-loading VHS player sat on a bookshelf constructed of cinderblocks and plywood next to a twenty-year-old television with a bent wire hanger for an antenna. Cinderella was playing on the TV.

The little girl stood staring at Noah. He knelt down to her level and asked sweetly, "What's your name?"

"Brittany. Who are you?" the little girl shot back.

Noah laughed. "I'm Noah," he said, extending his hand to greet her. "It's a pleasure to make your acquaintance, Miss Brittany."

Brittany smiled. Instead of shaking his hand, she grabbed it and pulled him over to sit him down at a small plastic table and chair set in front of the television. She put a plastic cup and saucer in front of him and plopped a wooden Pinocchio puppet on the chair next to him. "Would you like some tea, Mr. Noah?" she asked politely, pretending to pour him some. Noah nodded.

On television, the clock struck twelve, and Brittany's attention shifted to it. Noah looked down at Pinocchio slumped over in the chair beside him. He picked up the puppet bar and maneuvered Pinocchio's arms toward the saucer. Her eyes glued to the television set, Brittany was mesmerized as Cinderella hurried down the red-carpeted granite steps of the castle, losing her glass slipper as the clock sounded off deeply.

"Cinderella, right?" Noah announced proudly, setting Pinocchio back down on the chair, releasing its strings.

"Yeah, it's my favorite movie," she said, not taking her eyes off of it as the last stroke of midnight was about to sound, and the beautiful Cinderella jumped into the white stagecoach, making her escape into the night.

A minute later, Robin came out of her bedroom looking absolutely beautiful, her silky, red hair rustling, her eyes smiling, her lips red and moist, and her skin soft and white. She stopped abruptly and started laughing. Noah was sitting in a tiny plastic chair wearing a bonnet and boa while Brittany took pink lipstick from her plastic pocketbook and placed it up against his lips.

The day played out like a montage in a romantic comedy as Noah, Robin, and Brittany explored Roger Williams Park Zoo in Providence. They rode the carousel and took a ride on a miniature train that toured around the park. Standing in front of the giraffe pavilion, Robin and Noah shared a cup of Dels frozen lemonade while Brittany sat on Noah's shoulders eating an ice cream cone. As Robin readied to take their picture, a woman offered to take it of all three of them. Robin handed the woman the camera as they posed in front of the giraffe walking towards them. The volunteer photographer stepped back to get them all in the frame. As she took the picture, the giraffe stretched his head down and snatched Brittany's ice cream right out of her hand, and Brittany screamed. Robin and Noah tried not to laugh as they walked away in search of another ice cream vendor.

A baby monkey clung to its mother as it swung through a tree behind a mesh enclosure. Brittany gestured for her mother to crouch down so that she could whisper something in her ear. Robin couldn't quite make it out, so she crouched even lower. Brittany wrapped her arms around her mother's neck and hung on like a monkey, looking up and giggling as her mother smiled down at her and gave her a kiss.

A bit later, Brittany was petting an old, funny-looking goat in the petting area of the zoo. "Say cheese," Robin said, taking out her camera. Brittany looked at her hands, making sure she had no food before smiling for the camera. Screaming as the picture was taken, Brittany tried to pull away as the goat started chewing on her jacket. Noah quickly snatched her up and comforted her. "Thanks for saving my life," she said tearfully, nestling her head into his shoulder as she wrapped her arms around him.

Next, they headed for the butterfly building, which seemed like a safer bet for kids. The humid interior featured a running stream, exotic flowers, and hundreds of colorful butterflies flittering about.

"Don't you just love them?" Robin said, spinning around with her arms extended.

Noah ducked as a couple of butterflies circled his head. "Uh... do they bite?" he asked as a spotted yellow butterfly landed on his nose. Noah jostled his head from side to side, hoping to jar it off.

"Aw, it's just a harmless little butterfly," Robin soothed, touching her index finger to the tip of his nose. The butterfly flitted onto her finger, and she held it in front of her eyes. "You ever wonder what it would be like to be a butterfly? So beautiful... so carefree." Very carefully, she touched the tip of her finger to Brittany's, and the butterfly journeyed across.

Standing next to a sign that read *WARNING: FEEDING THE GEESE IS AT YOUR OWN RISK*, Robin ripped bread into small pieces and tossed it to a few of the one hundred Canadian Geese congregated in a clearing next to the lake. They paddled on the lake in a large swan-boat, and afterwards, they rolled out a blanket under an old willow tree to have a picnic. Jumping to their feet, they grabbed their things and ran as the crowd of uninvited Canadian geese arrived for dinner.

As they passed through the large, black iron gates on their way out, Brittany held both of their hands and swung off the ground between them. On the way home, Noah adjusted the rear-view mirror to see Brittany sleeping soundly in the back seat of the car, clutching her new stuffed giraffe.

"I think she likes me," he announced proudly.

"No... I think she *loves* you."

Great Expectations

With a fresh coat of polish, Noah's immaculate 1966 Ferrari pulled into Hartman Enterprises behind a beat-up, blue Mustang convertible, also a 1966 model. Noah followed the Mustang to the back corner of the lot and parked next to it. The driver, wearing a navy maintenance uniform, got out of the car and opened the trunk.

"Hey, Mike, I didn't know you drove a classic," Noah said, shutting his door.

"Hey, Noah," the man replied, closing his trunk and putting a tool belt around his waist. "Yeah, that's because I almost never drive it. I only take it out a couple times a year, just to air it out."

"Sweet ride," Noah said, peeking inside the Mustang. "I like the Pony seats."

"The chassis is kind of beat up — not refurbished like yours."

"What are you talking about? She's a beaut," Noah exclaimed, walking around the car, checking it out. "Besides, I don't look at the outside so much as I do the inside. That's where the real beauty is," he said, stopping at the front of the car. "Do you mind?" he said, pointing at the hood.

"Of course not," Mike said, popping it open.

"Impressive engine. Two-eighty-nine V8 with original four-barrel carb. Sweet. It's a sixty-six, right?"

"Yeah, how'd you know?"

"First year they introduced an automatic tranny. You got power steering and disc brakes too?"

"Yup, first year for that too."

"I know. It's a great car you've got here. You should drive it more often. Talk to you later, Mike," he said, grabbing his briefcase and walking toward the mirrored building.

"Hey, Noah..."

Noah stopped and turned around.

"I'll see ya around," Mike said with a proud smile. Noah returned the smile as Mike closed the hood to his beat-up treasure.

"Hey, Stan," Noah called as he walked past Security and stepped into an elevator. When he stepped off on the top floor, he walked up to a glass door and put his hand on the brass handle, waiting for it to unlock. "Good afternoon, Leslie," he said to the white-haired secretary buzzing him in.

Walking down the hallway, Noah stopped in front of a large, vacant office and glanced in. He admired the oak desk and plush office chair, and then headed down the hallway, stopping at a door that read *Jerry Hartman, President*. Noah pushed open the door, revealing an expansive office with panoramic views of the meandering Pawtuxet River. It was decorated with antique furniture, French Impressionist paintings, and a silk Persian rug. Noah sat down in the brown leather sofa and waited his turn. Spotlighted on the wall in back of him was an original Claude Monet oil painting. An executive in a gray pinstriped suit was standing in front of a large mahogany desk where Jerry sat, signing a document. Jerry was a good-looking sixty-two-year-old man, with manicured silver hair and a presence that commanded respect. The executive took the signed document and put it into his briefcase, thanking Jerry and nodding at Noah on his way out.

"Hey, Dad, want to go for lunch with Scott and me?" Noah asked.

"I wish I could, but I have an important meeting at one with Terry."

"Terry?"

"You know — the president of the bank."

Noah nodded.

"So what's up?" Jerry asked, his hand set impatiently on the phone.

"You probably don't know this, but today's my fifteen-year anniversary working for the company."

"Congratulations."

"I was just wondering..." Noah said, taking a deep breath, "you know the vacant office down the aisle? Well — "

As soon as the phone in Jerry's hand started to ring, he answered it and started talking. Noah looked at his watch and bit his nails. It was 12:22 p.m. He looked around the room, his eyes settling on a framed photograph on the wall of his father shaking hands with Ronald Reagan. His eyes shifted to a table with an intricate model under glass of Jerry's new pride and joy — Hartman Place — a fifty-acre upscale mixed-use development complex with shopping, dining, condos, office space, and more. Noah took a deep breath and waited patiently.

Looking at his watch, it was now 12:34 p.m., and Jerry was still on the phone talking business. Noah stood up and headed for the door.

"Hold on, Noah. Hey, Tom, let me call you back after the meeting... okay, great... bye," he said, hanging up. "Sorry about that. What were you saying again?"

"Well, I was just wondering if it would be okay if I could have an office in this building... in your aisle?" he asked nervously, sitting back down.

"Absolutely not," Jerry said bluntly.

"Why not?"

"I can't have someone visiting you at your level accidently overhearing what's going on at my level."

"Well then, how about promoting me out of my level? My projects are the most profitable in the company, my occupancy rates are off the charts, and I'm ready to take on more responsibility. I work harder than anyone else here, working nights, weekends, whatever it takes."

"That's just it. Your organizational skills are terrible, and you're always scrambling to meet your deadlines. If you could get your work done in the same timely fashion as the other project managers, you wouldn't have to stay late. How would it look if I promoted the person who, our contractors complain, constantly gives them insufficient lead times? Look, if you're ever going to run this company someday, you've got to become more organized. Besides, since you're not the most qualified person for the job, our stockholders would think it's nepotism."

"Then forget the promotion. Just let me work as your apprentice," Noah pleaded, trying to turn the tide. "You could teach me what you know about finances, bring me to important meetings, and introduce me to important people. Why not take me under your wing and groom me?"

"And what are you going to do all day, just sit around and watch me? Look, you've always known it's your company too, right? And being that it's your company too, you should want to do what's in the company's best interest. Noah, the company needs you as a project manager. *I* need you as a project manager."

Noah sat there, his hopes dead in the water, the air taken out of his sails. He had pleaded his case before the judge and was overruled. It was time to retreat to safer ground. "Okay," he said, standing up, defeated.

Jerry got up from behind the desk and walked over to Noah, putting a hand on his back. "Look, your occupancy rates are terrific; keep up the good work," he said, trying to be encouraging. "And congratulations on the fifteen years."

Jerry watched as Noah walked toward the door, head down, shoulders slumped. "Wait a minute," Jerry called out in an upbeat voice.

Noah turned around with the beginning of a smile.

"Don't feel bad... I wouldn't let your brother have an office in the executive building either," Jerry said reassuringly.

Noah's eyes shifted to the large painting hanging in back of his father's desk. It was a family portrait, with Noah and Scott wearing white tennis sweaters standing in front of Jerry and Miriam, painted when Noah was just six years old. His smile faded as he thought back to the expectations placed on him and his brother ever since they were little.

Six-year-old Noah, eight-year-old Scott, and Miriam sat around the long, antique dining table in their formal dining room. Noah and Scott looked like twins, dressed in matching Harvard t-shirts as Jerry entered the room wearing a raincoat and hat.

"Hi, honey. Sorry I'm late," he said, kissing Miriam. "Worst flooding in twenty years. Had to take the back roads to get home," he explained, taking off his hat and coat, and joining them at the table.

"Maria, you can bring dinner in now," Miriam called out.

The kitchen door swung open and Maria walked in wearing a white uniform and carrying a tray of food. She placed a bowl of matzah ball soup in front of each person at the table, along with a shiny sterling silver spoon.

"How was work today, honey?" Miriam asked, taking a sip of soup. Jerry nodded his head while sipping his soup. "Someday, all three of you will be coming home from work together," she announced, looking over at her two young boys. "Won't that be great? You and Scott helping Daddy run Hartman Enterprises? That's what you want, right, Noah?" she asked in a wheedling tone.

"Okay, Mommy," Noah replied, sipping his soup.

"Right, Scott?"

"Yes, of course, Mom," Scott answered immediately.

43

"Great. Then it's all settled. When you boys are old enough, you'll help Daddy run the company," she said, relieved, smiling victoriously at Jerry, who continued to sip his soup silently.

"Noah... Noah..."

Noah snapped out of his daydream, turning his head toward the woman in the gray pinstriped Armani skirt suit with salt and pepper hair who was standing next to him, calling his name.

"Oh, hi, Aunt Harriet. How are you?" Noah said politely.

"I'm fine, thanks. Noah, do you mind leaving so I can talk with your father? It's very important."

"Oh? What's it about?"

"Sorry, it's official company business, on a need-to-know basis. You understand."

While Aunt Harriet held the door open for him, Noah glanced over at his father, who did not object.

"Of course... I understand," Noah said sadly.

The door to my hospital room opens and in comes Scott, looking pretty good for eighty-two. "Hey, it's Scott," I announce to Josh, happy to see him.

"I came as soon as I heard," Scott says apologetically, approaching me.

"I'm the baby in the family, can't you tell?" I say, looking at Josh. "Scott's two years older. Hey, Scott, I want you to meet my new friend, Josh," I announce proudly.

"*New* friend? Heck, I'm an *old* friend," Josh jokes.

"Hey, you're not *that* old, you're younger than I am, you know, ha."

Josh and I share a good laugh while Scott remains focused on me, ignoring our antics with a somber look.

"Seriously, thanks for coming, Big Brother," I say, curtailing my smile.

"How you doing, Little Brother?" he asks softly, tears in his eyes.

"Not too bad under the circumstances," I say, winking at Josh.

"I don't think I ever told you this before..." Scott says, taking my hand.

"Go on..." I say nervously, shooting an awkward glance at Josh.

"But I love you, Noah," Scott says, wiping a tear.

"Thanks, that's really sweet of you. And I love you too, Scott. But no worries; I never told you either."

"Now don't that figure?" Josh says, shaking his head, bewildered. "Why do we always hold back what's really in our hearts on a day-to-day basis, only to go and blurt it all out someday when it maybe too late? I never understood that."

"Well, at least we're saying it now, huh, Scott? Anyway, like I was saying, Scott and I used to eat lunch together every day in the cafeteria at work. On this one particular day, Cindy and the other secretaries were sitting just two tables away, checking out my big brother." I smile at Scott because we both know that's not exactly how it happened.

Noah was standing in line next to Scott at the buffet counter in the company cafeteria. "So how's your class coming along?" Noah asked.

"It's going really well. I'm learning a lot about screenwriting, and I'm almost finished writing my first screenplay."

"Wow, that's great. I'm really proud of you," he said, paying for both lunches and sitting down at a table with Scott.

Scott turned his head and noticed a table full of pretty, young secretaries talking to each other while smiling at Noah. "I think Cindy over there has the hots for you."

Noah stopped eating and glanced over at Cindy, who was ogling him with wide eyes and a seductive smile. "Me? Nah, it's *you* she wants," Noah insisted, taking a bite of food.

Scott turned to look at Cindy again. "You might be right..." he said, dubiously, "but I don't think so. You're the hot bachelor, not me. I've got a wife and two kids at home. Too bad Dad won't let you fraternize with the help."

"Yeah, God forbid I actually befriend any of the ten thousand employees who work for him," Noah said sarcastically, taking a bite of food, shaking his head. "It might be nice to have a friend or two, don't you think?"

"You've got me as your friend," Scott said reassuringly. "So tell me, Noah, what was as all that nonsense the other night about not feeling alive? Should I be concerned?"

Noah glanced at him, not sure if he should go there or not. "Are you happy here? I mean, if Mom and Dad hadn't chosen this career for us, would you still want to do this?"

"HELL, NO !" Scott said emphatically, looking directly into his brother's eyes. "I don't know why I even bother to speak sometimes, with Dad and Aunt Harriet never listening to any of my great ideas on how to modernize and grow the business. Why do you think I'm taking that night class? If I could write screenplays for a living, I'd be out of here in a second. But I can't just quit without having a job already lined up. Sharon would kill me if we ever had to give up the nanny or sell the house. How about you? Are you happy here?"

"Well, it's not exactly what I expected. But what else can I do for a living? Ever since we were little kids, this is all I've ever known," Noah said, glancing over at Cindy, who was still smiling at him. "Who are we trying to fool, anyway? Mom and Dad would never let us leave. Not to mention our golden handcuffs. Say good-bye to the company car, the boat, the house, and God knows what else. With our salaries being as high as they are, there's no way we could afford that kind of lifestyle working anywhere else. If either of us leaves, we both know what happens next... the money runs dry. Yeah, I know they're only material things, and I'm sure I could live without them, but every time I get up the courage to leave, Mom and Dad persuade me that I could never make it out there on my own — you know, in the *real world*, where ordinary people live. I guess I'm just scared."

"You need to have a plan — like me. Take a class or do something else on the side until you find something that works. Do it the smart way. Then you can leave."

Noah thought about what his brother just said. It made perfect sense. "Don't you ever wonder what it would be like to feel alive, like the life you're living is actually your own, not someone else's? To live by your own decisions, and just imagine... when the wind and rain hits your face, you actually feel it. Don't you ever wonder what that's like, Scott?"

Scott stopped in mid-motion as he brought the fork up to his mouth, looking at Noah with crinkled eyebrows just as Jerry and Aunt Harriet approached the table. Noah looked up at them and put on a smile as they sat down to join them.

Total Surrender

$\mathcal{N}$oah's hair was riffled by the wind as he tacked his sixty-foot sailboat, her boom swinging across mid-ship as her sails filled with air. Majestic orange and red cliffs reflecting the setting sun welcomed her as she entered the mouth of Narragansett Bay into Newport Harbor. Gliding through the glistening water, seagulls squawked as they flew across her bow. The name on her transom read *Freedom; Jamestown, RI.*

As she lay on the teak bow, Robin looked back at Noah and smiled as they sailed by the abandoned lighthouse on the small private island, her red hair trailing in the breeze. Noah took a deep breath of the fresh air surrounding Freedom and smiled with contentment. He was living in the moment.

"Some people find it up on a roof, gazing at a billion stars on a crystal clear night. Some people find it on top of a mountain, with beautiful vistas of peaceful valleys below. Some people find it on a secluded pond, or a secret hiding spot, or maybe even in a special chair, one with special memories."

"But for me, I find it out on the water, sailing on a boat. It's where I find peace and tranquility. Where everything makes perfect sense, and all my troubles disappear. My soul surrenders to it. To put it simply, it's where I find my God. Oh, I'm not talking about religion; I'm talking about spirit... something deep inside."

"Out on the water, the gentle breeze caressing my face, the warmth of the sun kisses my skin, and my eyes are enchanted by thousands of sparkling diamonds, dancing on top of the water's surface. Out on the water, the air is fresh and the sounds of the sea sing out loud. When I want to feel alive... when I want to feel free... I know exactly where to go to find it."

An antique red Ferrari drove over the train tracks, past the abandoned station, and into a vacant lot. With blueprints under his arm, Noah stepped out of his car and walked past the sign — *Coming soon, HARTMAN RIVER-LOFTS, featuring 200 luxury condominiums & deluxe fitness studio.* Behind it was a large brick building with a tower at each end, one with a bell, one with a clock. Situated on the Pawtuxet River, the textile mill was once used to spin cotton. But like all other New England mills of its day, it was abandoned a half-century earlier when all the textile jobs moved south.

Noah fumbled with a bunch of keys as he opened the padlock on the temporary plywood door and entered the building. He looked around the dusty, gutted edifice, and then looked up at the sky through the open ceiling. He put down his blueprints on a table saw and grabbed a tool belt, buckling it around his jeans. He removed the hammer from his belt and smacked a nail into the jack stud alongside the door, hanging up his Ralph Lauren sport shirt. Tossing a yellow helmet onto his head, he wiped the sawdust off of his white tank-top undershirt as he ascended a ladder.

Taking several ladders to reach the roof, Noah gawked at the open ceiling joists stretching between him and the tower, fifty feet away. He took a deep breath and moved his right foot slowly along the edge of a joist. With his arms out, wobbling slightly, he moved his left foot along the edge of a parallel joist, sixteen inches apart. "It's just a walk in the park," he reassured himself as he walked gingerly along the edges of the two boards. "Our guys do this all the time, no problem." Stopping halfway across, he looked down in between his feet at the ground floor, sixty feet below, and nearly lost his balance. "On second thought, all the parks I know seem to be located on the ground..." Moving a little faster as he reached the end, he let out a sigh of relief and opened the door to the tower, stepping inside.

A silver Honda Civic pulled up to the building, and Robin got out holding a picnic basket and bottle of wine. "Noah?" she called as she entered the building, looking at the shirt hanging by the door. "Surprise... it's me," she said, looking around, drawn toward the two large wooden barn doors dead ahead. She put down her basket and lifted up the wooden latch in the center of the two doors. "Wow," she exclaimed as the doors swung open, staring at an old water wheel spinning alongside a waterfall.

Noah climbed up the wooden ladder built into the wall of the tower, startled by the abrupt departure of a bunch of pigeons as he reached the top. He looked at the large bell sitting on the floor, unattached, and began measuring it. Wiping the sweat from his forehead, he glanced out the arched opening and suddenly noticed Robin standing at the edge of the river in her underwear.

"Hey," he yelled as she jumped into the water, carefree, the noise from the waterfall drowning him out.

A few minutes later, Noah was standing at the water's edge. He looked around, but the only sign of her were her clothes sprawled out on a boulder. He looked down into the dark water.

"Hey, good-lookin'," she said, emerging from the other side of the waterfall. "Care to join me?" she said with a seductive smile, her body wet, her white underwear see-through.

"What, are you crazy? I'm not going in there."

"See, that's your problem, Noah. You're afraid to live. You'd be surprised at how much fun it is. Come join me; I dare you."

Noah just stood there.

"Don't you want me?" she asked, lowering the straps to her bra.

"Of course I do, but that's not the point."

"The point?" she echoed, removing her bra.

Noah gulped.

"If you really want me..." she said with a mischievous smile, "then come and get me."

Noah looked around and didn't see anyone. Hesitating, he took off his L.L. Bean work boots and dropped his jeans to the ground, folding them neatly and placing them on the rock along with his folded undershirt.

Taking in his thin waist, washboard abs, muscular chest, and undulating arms, Robin's eyes bulged.

"But it's cold," he complained, standing in his boxers and dipping his foot in.

Robin frowned.

"Alright, I can do this," he said, sliding into the cold water, smiling when he reached her.

Robin turned around and disappeared through the waterfall. Noah followed cautiously, stopping just short of it. He could barely make out her image through the gushing water. The power of the water smashed down on his hand as he reached in, and he was suddenly pulled through to the other side.

As Robin backed away from him, he couldn't take his eyes off of her. Droplets of water rolled down her curvy body as she gazed at him with intense desire. Noah walked up to her, his lips inching closer to hers, his chest quivering from the slightest touch of her supple breasts. He put his hand on her face as he kissed her tenderly, then passionately.

She jumped up and wrapped herself around him. "Do you surrender?" she breathed in his ear.

"Surrender?" he questioned, breathing heavily. "What do you mean?"

As he continued to kiss her, he backed into the waterfall. With water crashing down upon them, she put her feet down on the ground and moved her hands down his back to the dimples of his firm buttocks. Knocked to the ground by the pressure of the raging water, his boxers were no longer there. She felt around and realized that her thong had suffered the same fate. Clutching each other, they plunged back into the river.

As they stared at each other, the tension between them was intense, their bodies aching for one another. "Do you surrender?" she asked suggestively, moving closer.

"What was that?" Noah interrupted, glancing toward the building. "I think I heard something."

"No you didn't. You didn't hear anything," she insisted.

"*Uh, yeah... I did,*" he said, looking around, listening.

On the other side of the building, a white truck beeped its horn a second time. "Shit, I totally forgot," Noah said, rushing out of the water and grabbing his pants. "I'm supposed to meet up with Russ at one."

Robin let out an exasperated breath as she fell back into the water.

The rain slapped the windshield as Noah waited in his car outside of her apartment. Robin made a mad dash against the wind and rain. He opened the door and in she jumped, looking more beautiful than ever, her hair soaking wet and wind-blown. She couldn't stop staring at him as he drove off, swerving around fallen tree branches in the street. He looked over at her, smiled, and took her hand.

A little while later, they were sitting on the same side of a booth in a silver, retro-style diner. "What's the matter? You don't like your breakfast?" Noah inquired, looking down at Robin's plate full of food.

Robin smiled and shrugged. "Sorry, it's those darn butterflies again. I guess I just don't have an appetite," she said, glancing down at Noah's plate full of food. "So, what's your excuse?"

Noah smiled and shrugged. "Butterflies... It does make it hard to eat, doesn't it?"

She nodded in agreement. "By the way, I told my parents all about you, and they can't wait to meet you," Robin said.

"Oh...? Good or bad?"

"What do *you* think?" she said with a smirk. "I told them you're amazing. Not only do you have the most amazing blue eyes — the color of the sea — but you've got these amazing full lips — great for kissing, by the way."

"No, really... what did you tell them?"

"What...? You don't believe I told them that? But it's *true*," she said coyly. "Alright, I told them you're the nicest guy I've ever met; how's that?"

"Not bad... go on..."

"I said, 'Noah puts me so high up on a pedestal that my feet don't even touch the ground.'"

"You said that? Why?"

"Because it's true. I don't want to be woken up from this dream, Noah. I keep thinking you're too good for me. And when you figure that out, I'm afraid you won't be sticking around anymore."

"That's ridiculous."

"Is it? For the life of me, I don't know what I did to deserve you. You could have any woman you want — someone from *your* world, with your background, your education, your religion, your status... your dollars. I'm not any of that. So why me?"

"First of all, money has nothing to do with anything — certainly not love. Second of all, I can't have any woman I want. I —"

"Yes you can !"

"I don't know — maybe — but that's not the point. The point is... I don't want just *any* woman; I want *you*. I don't care about any of that other stuff. None of that's important to me. What's important is how I feel when I'm with you. And when I'm with you, I feel something I've never felt before, like I'm becoming alive inside. It's both scary and exciting at the same time. All you have to do is look into my eyes, and I melt. Do you realize the effect you have over me? 'Cause it's like some unseen force is drawing me toward you."

"I feel drawn in too. There's no denying it."

"Maybe it's destiny, who knows?"

"Or maybe I'm just really lucky."

"*I'm* the lucky one," Noah retorted.

"So, what did you tell your parents about me?" she asked, smiling.

Noah exhaled and looked away.

"What...? They don't like me?"

"How could they not like you? They haven't met you."

"Then what's the problem?"

"It's just that... I haven't told them yet." Robin frowned. "You don't understand what they're like; they're very powerful people. And they think they know what's best for me, but they really don't have a clue. Only *I* know what's best for me... and that's you. I'm planning on telling everybody tomorrow night at dinner. So don't worry, once they see how happy I am, they'll be thrilled. I promise," he said, kissing her forehead.

Noah tossed some money on top of the bill and stood up. "Come on, let's get out of here," he said, grabbing her hand and leading her out.

The ocean was turbulent from the brewing tempest, the water white and sudsy as large waves pounded the beach. It was a rare sight, seen only in hurricanes and extremely powerful storms. Up on the hill at a safe distance from the tumultuous ocean sat Noah's majestic house. Through a large arched window, Noah and Robin were watching the ocean's dramatic spectacle.

Reaching gently toward her, Noah slowly started unbuttoning Robin's shirt while Robin unbuckled his belt. Their clothes fell to the floor, and they lay down on the bed. The tempestuous ocean outside was matched only by the heated passion that was building inside. As they made love for the very first time, their eyes told each other how much they wanted one another, not only in this moment, but for all eternity.

"Like a drug that we just couldn't get enough of, once we got a taste of each other, we couldn't stop wanting more and more. As our two bodies merged to one, so did our souls. The connection couldn't be more intense. No matter how close we got to each other, we just had to get even closer. We were completely and utterly in love. It was total surrender: Mind. Body. Soul."

Meet The Parents

A valet driver opened the door to Noah's Ferrari convertible as it pulled up in front of Capriccio restaurant in downtown Providence. Inside the elegant Italian restaurant, the ambiance was warm and charming, with a cobblestoned floor, columns with decorative moldings, and tables glowing under candlelight. The pianist at the baby grand was playing **The Way You Look Tonight** by Frank Sinatra as Noah, holding a small gift bag, walked over to the alcove where Scott, Sharon, Miriam, and Jerry were sitting.

"Happy birthday, Mom," Noah said, kissing his mother's cheek.

"Come here for a second," she said, motioning for him to duck down.

Noah grimaced, lowering his head as Miriam proceeded to lick her hand and pat his hair down. As a tuxedoed waiter approached, Noah pulled away and sat down at the empty seat beside his brother. As the waiter made his way around the table with a bottle of Dom Pérignon, he poured Champagne into everyone's glasses.

"I can't wait for all of you to meet her," Noah announced. "She's amazing. I'm so in love. I'm telling you, she's *the one*. I'm going to marry her someday."

"Congratulations, Little Brother. I'm really happy for you," Scott said, patting Noah on the back.

"This is exciting news," Sharon, Noah's sister-in-law, said. "I can't wait to meet her."

"You guys will get along great. And she's got the cutest little girl, Brittany."

"Is she Jewish?" Miriam asked, getting right to the crux of the matter.

Noah shook his head.

"Where did she go to college?" Miriam asked, frowning.

"She didn't go to college; she was in the Army."

Miriam and Jerry locked eyes, eyebrows raised.

"Where does she work?" Jerry inquired.

"Downtown, at Emergency Family Services."

"What's that?" Miriam asked.

"A homeless shelter."

"*Oy*," said Miriam, looking over at Jerry with deep concern.

Noah could see that his answers were not scoring any points with his parents. Translation — uneducated, no money, and definitely not Jewish. Based on the facts, she obviously was not good enough for their son.

"Hey, Noah, why don't you bring her down to Mom and Dad's summer house this weekend so we can all meet her," Sharon suggested enthusiastically, ignoring her in-laws' interrogation tactics. "We're going to be there for the Fourth of July fireworks. The kids can swim in the pool together, and I can get to know my future sister-in-law."

"Sure, we'd love to come," Noah replied, relieved.

While everyone else laughed and chatted, Miriam and Jerry continued to exchange glances as the waiter began to clear the plates.

"Would anyone care to take home the leftovers?" the waiter inquired politely.

Everyone shook their heads. "We only eat fresh food in this family," the matriarch explained to the waiter as he removed her plate. Several more waiters appeared holding a lit birthday cake and singing **Happy Birthday** in Italian. As they set the cake before Miriam, she frowned at Noah and shook her head, making her wish and blowing out the candles.

"Happy birthday, Mom," Noah said, getting up to give her a kiss, and handing her a floral gift bag. "It's from all of us, including Dad."

"*Oy*. You shouldn't have spent your money on me," she said, accepting it reluctantly.

"I picked it out myself. Thought you might like it," Noah said with a warm smile. "It took me quite some time to find it," he added.

As she opened the gift, Noah, Scott, and Sharon exchanged looks. "Wow, it's gorgeous," Miriam announced delightedly. "Thank you so much," she said, blowing a kiss to everyone around the table, holding up an exquisite butterfly broach. She passed it around the table so everyone could get a closer look. When it made its way to Noah, he smiled as he took it out of the box and held it close to the candle, mesmerized by how it sparkled under the light. The butterfly broach was set in eighteen-karat gold with emerald wings and two one-karat diamonds for eyes. Noah's smile turned to sadness as his thoughts returned to his childhood.

Six-year-old Noah ran into his bedroom, grabbed his piggy bank, stuffed it in his backpack, and ran back out. Pedaling his bike down the street, he turned into the fairground beneath a large arched iron gate with a banner that read *Butler On The Green*.

It was warm and sunny, with a hundred people strolling about on the green, enjoying the day. Noah walked his bike past Frenchy's ice cream truck, past a cluster of vendors selling flowers, pocket books, scarves, and women's accessories, stopping at a table filled with costume jewelry. A rhinestone butterfly broach caught his eye. He picked it up, admiring how it sparkled in the sunlight.

"I think you just found the best one," said the salesman on the other side of the table.

Noah nodded in agreement.

"Something as special as that must be for someone pretty special, huh?"

"Yeah, it's for my mommy. Today's her birthday."

"Well, in that case, your mommy is going to be one lucky lady to receive such a thoughtful gift from such a wonderful son."

Noah nodded again. "How much is it?"

"For you? Fifty cents."

Noah put down his backpack and pulled out his piggy bank, emptying the contents, about forty pennies, onto the table. "Is that enough?" he asked nervously.

The man smiled, scooping up most of the coins. While Noah deposited the remaining pennies back into his piggy bank, the man wrapped the gift in manila paper. Waving good-bye, Noah pedaled off, gripping the precious package securely in his hand.

Noah couldn't wait to give the present to his mom. "Happy birthday, Mommy," he called, running upstairs to her bedroom, his face beaming as he handed her the gift.

"Oh, Noah, you shouldn't have spent your money on

me," Miriam said, reluctantly opening the package. "Now isn't that pretty?" she said absently as she glanced at the cheap butterfly broach. "Thank you, sweetie," she said, giving Noah a kiss on the head, and setting the broach down on the dresser without removing it from its wrapper. She picked up a black gown off the bed and left the room, calling out for Maria, the maid.

Later that evening, Noah caught his parents dressed up and about to go out. As they were putting on their coats, he ran over to his mother to see if she was wearing her new broach. "Mommy, why aren't you wearing the butterfly pin I got you for your birthday?"

"That was very sweet of you, Noah," she said, glancing down at him. "But you might as well learn this lesson at an early age. I believe in always telling the truth, don't you?" Noah nodded. "Well, the truth is I don't wear costume jewelry. So I am not going to *pretend* to wear this thing every time I go out, not tonight, not ever."

Noah looked like he was about to cry. "You know Mommy loves you, right?" Miriam said. Noah nodded, trying to hold back the tears. Miriam looked at him and smiled. "Here," she said, taking the rhinestone broach out of her pocketbook and handing it to him. "Someday, sweetie, when you're old enough to afford to buy me real jewelry, with real gold and real diamonds, then you can buy me jewelry for my birthday, okay?" she said, patting him on the head as she turned and left the house with Jerry.

With tears rolling down his face, Noah stood in the doorway watching as his parents drove away in his dad's beige Bentley convertible.

It was another hectic day at the office — no different than any other day. Noah was sitting at his desk holding a construction-cost datasheet while Russ, the construction manager for the Hartman Towers development project in Boston, sat on the other side, waiting for an answer. Blueprints littered his desk and walls, cluttering the office. Diane was on the phone trying to track down a shipment of Better Header beams that was holding up the framers at the Hartman Promenade construction site in downtown Providence, already two months behind schedule.

Larry popped his head in, and Russ turned his head to see who it was. "You almost ready for me yet?"

"Give me a few more minutes," Noah replied.

"Okay then, I'll be outside in the lobby," Larry said looking at his watch as Noah's phone started ringing.

"I'll call you right back," Diane said, quickly hanging up her phone and answering Noah's. "Noah Hartman's office... No, he's not. He's in a meeting. May I take a message?"

"Excuse me, Noah? Got your profit projections done yet?" asked Bob, the accounting manager, sticking his head in the doorway and giving Russ a friendly nod. "You're the last one, and your father needs his budgets by tomorrow."

"I'll make sure I'll leave it on your desk before I leave tonight — whatever time that is."

"Appreciate it," Bob said, changing places with Aunt Harriet in the doorway.

"Noah, I want you to go to Hartman Resort and Spa in Newport and meet with the building inspector tomorrow," Aunt Harriet said, waving to Russ. "I had his parents over the house the other night for dinner, and they told me that he recently became a new father. So I want you to give him this for me," she said, stepping over to Noah's desk and handing him a package.

"Boy or girl?"

"Boy. Also, I'm still waiting for your C.A.M. analysis that was due last week, and your dad's still waiting for his budgets."

"I know. I'll have them both done before I leave tonight."

"Good. Have you been to the Wasserstein's new waterfront condo and recreation club in Portsmouth yet? Got to know your competition."

Noah shook his head.

"Well... what are you waiting for? Get over there already," she said with a wink and a smile as she left the office.

Noah's phone rang again, and Diane answered it. "Noah, Max wants to know if you're going to the New York convention on Friday or Saturday?"

"Saturday."

Linda, the Human Resources director, walked in quietly and handed Noah some forms. As she turned to leave, Noah looked at the medical forms and called out, "Hey, Linda, what's this all about?"

"Sorry to interrupt your meeting, Noah," she said, pausing to smile at Russ. "We're switching over to Blue Cross next week, and all the paperwork needs to be filled out again. Oh... I almost forgot... here's an organ donor card," she added, holding it out to him.

"Sorry, that's where I draw the line," Noah said sharply, holding up his hand.

"Noah Hartman... big humanitarian," Diane called in sarcastically, overhearing the conversation. "What do you care what happens to your body after you're dead, anyway?"

"It's just not my style, that's all."

"Not your style?" Diane mocked. "Imagine there's some helpless guy out there at the mercy of a long waiting list for a new liver, wondering if he'll ever live long enough to get to the top of that list. Then one day, he gets a phone call telling him to hurry up and get over to the hospital before it's too late. Over all the other people on the list, he's just been selected to be the lucky recipient of a new liver, courtesy of Noah Hartman, who has just saved his life. A day later, and he would have died. Wouldn't that make you feel great about yourself, Noah?"

"No, not really. I think I'd be feeling pretty dead by that point," he said sarcastically.

Undaunted, Diane continued. "Okay, Noah, how about this? Now imagine that there is no liver available. And that desperate, scared guy out there doesn't know if today's going to be the last day of his life, or the first day of the rest of his life. Are you picturing this yet, Noah?"

"Yeah... got it."

"Okay, good. Now imagine that guy is Noah Hartman. Well? Kind of changes everything, doesn't it?"

Noah didn't reply.

"Noah, you know I love you," Diane continued, "but stop being so self-centered and start thinking about others for a change. You'd be surprised at how good it makes you feel."

"Well, tell you what. I'll just leave it here on the desk just in case you change your mind," Linda said, setting the card down on the desk and leaving.

Max, a senior shopping center development manager, entered the doorway. "Just in case you haven't seen the operating statements that just came out, you

58

were number one again this month. Not too shabby, kid," Max said jovially, looking over at Russ, acknowledging him.

"That's because I learned from the best," Noah said, winking at his mentor as he left the room.

Noah's phone rang again. "Noah Hartman's office," Diane said. "No, I'm sorry, he's in a meeting. May I take a message? Oh... I'm sorry, Mr. Hartman, I didn't recognize your voice," she said nervously. "Here he is, hold on," she said, transferring the call to Noah's phone.

"Hi, Dad," Noah said cheerfully. He paused. "But I've got Russ sitting right here, and a commercial realtor out in the lobby who's been waiting for over an hour," he added. "All right, I'll be right there," he said, hanging up the phone.

Noah shrugged at Russ apologetically and stood up.

Jerry was sitting behind his large, mahogany desk when there was a soft knock at the door. "Come on in," he called out.

"You wanted to see me, Dad?" Noah said, peeking his head in the doorway.

"Come on in and have a seat."

Noah walked into the office and sat down on the brown leather sofa.

"Shut the door."

Noah stood back up, shut the door, and returned to his seat, biting his nails.

"Your mother and I are very concerned about this Robin person. You said you want to marry her? How long have you been dating her for?"

"Three months."

"Don't you think it's very irresponsible of you to be making those kind of statements?"

Noah shrugged.

"Look, I'm going to be straight with you," Jerry said in a firm voice. "We don't want you to be with a person like that. She's uneducated, has no money, a lousy job, a child you'll end up having to support, and who knows what other problems. She's not the type of person we'd expect you to be with. You have nothing in common with her, and frankly, it doesn't make any sense."

"I can't believe you ordered me in here just to tell me whom I can and cannot date. Don't you think you're being a little prejudiced considering the fact that you haven't even met her yet? And besides, it's not your decision anyway. *God...* I hate it when you and mom try to control my life !"

59

"There's no reason to get all defensive; I'm only trying to help. Look, I know you're not stupid; you went to my alma mater. I know if you think this through carefully, you'll realize that you can do a lot better, which brings me to my next point. Have you had sex with her yet?"

"That's none of your business," Noah shot back, surprised by his frankness.

"I'm your father; so *your* business is *my* business. Whatever you do, make sure to wear protection. I don't trust her type. There are a lot of unscrupulous women out there who'd intentionally try to trick a guy like you into getting them pregnant, just so they can collect Child Support. I'm sure Robin sees you as her meal ticket out, so try to avoid sleeping with her, if you can."

Noah took a deep breath, trying to maintain composure. "Robin is not like that. And besides, I'm planning on spending the rest of my life with her, remember?"

"And what if she gets pregnant?" his father added. " Have you thought about that?"

"What about it?"

"Will she convert? What about the children? Do you think she'll object to bringing them up Jewish?"

"I don't know. We haven't talked about that yet."

"I thought so. Well I sure hope we raised you well enough to appreciate how important it is to marry someone within our own faith. You've heard the same sermons I've heard: the Jewish population is shrinking, year after year, and it's up to you and every generation to come to keep it going strong. Otherwise, someday it could become extinct. All I'm asking is for you to think about it. I'm sure you could just as easily fall in love with a nice Jewish girl."

"Look, Dad, you can't tell me who to love. It's my life — not yours."

"Noah, you don't understand, your mother and I love you very much, and we only want what's best for you. I think it would be prudent of you to end this right now before it goes any further, for your sake, not mine."

With Jerry staring at him waiting for a response, Noah paused, summoning his wits. "Dad, if you could only see the way she gazes into my eyes, you'd understand why I love her so much. All she has to do is just look at me that way, and my heart starts melting. That's what it is, Dad. I feel the way I do about her simply because of the way she looks at me."

"Well, I'm sure there are lots of women out there that could make you feel that way, by whatever you just said... looking at you."

"That's where you're wrong, Dad. She's the only one. She's genuine — not fake like all the others. It's my soul she cares about — not my money."

"You mean *my* money."

"And she's so filled with life," Noah continued, ignoring his father's remark. "When she laughs and smiles, I just want to latch onto it and go for the ride, because when I'm with her, for the first time in my life I feel alive."

"You look alive to me, Noah," Jerry answered dryly.

"Oh, really?" Noah said sarcastically. "Look, all I can do right now is follow my heart, and whether you like it or not, there's only one person in this world right now holding the key. I have no choice, I'm helpless... helplessly in love."

"That's absolute nonsense," Jerry said, throwing up his hands. "You can have any girl you want, and you know it. How about that Schwartz girl whom Mom likes? She's seems nice... cute, too."

"Sarah Schwartz?" Noah asked incredulously. "Isn't she, like, in fifth grade?"

"You haven't seen her lately. She's all grown up, going to Brown Med School in the fall. I'm playing golf with her father on Sunday at Spring Valley. Want me to fix you up?"

"No... no, I don't," Noah said, annoyed, standing up. "Is there any thing else, Dad? Russ is waiting patiently for me in my office."

"Yeah, one more thing... You know you're always welcome to visit us anytime you want at the summer house, right? But just not with this Robin character, okay? I don't mind so much, but you know your mother. She's very upset about this, and that would only add fuel to the fire. She can't help the way she feels, so she'd appreciate it if you'd respect her wishes. I'm sure you understand."

Noah nodded curtly. As he reached the door, his father called, "Hey, don't worry about it. Eventually your mother will come around; she always does. Just give her time. She may have a funny way of showing it, but she really does have a huge heart, and she loves you very much. She'd do anything for you."

"As angry as I was at their misguided attempts at controlling my life, I clung to the conviction that my parents loved me as best they could — albeit with conditions attached. And whether I liked what they had to say or not, they'd always be my parents, and I loved them... no matter what."

Brushing by Noah as if he were invisible, Aunt Harriet entered the office and began talking to Jerry, something about a major anchor tenant going bankrupt at several of the Hartman properties. Noah listened to them for a moment, then quietly headed back to his office with a heavy heart.

The Real World

*H*igh on a cliff overlooking a sandy beach, Zeke was giving Noah a huge bear hug in front of an old trailer at the trailer park. Zeke was big and burly, nearly double Noah's size, with a thick beard.

"Sorry, we're big huggers in our family," Zeke admitted, releasing him. "Me and Mary are so glad to finally meet you. Robin has told us so much about you. And anyone who treats our little girl with love and respect is always welcome here."

"Thanks, that's really nice of you to say," Noah said, recovering from the hug.

Mary was short, with long, salt and pepper hair. "Hi, Noah, I'm Mary," she said, kissing his cheek and making him blush. "You sure are easy on the eyes."

"Thanks, Mrs. Jaworski."

"Mrs. Jaworski? Who's that? Call me Mary. Who knows, maybe someday you'll even call me Mom."

"Sure thing... *MOM*."

Brittany set her plastic tea set all around the wooden picnic table for everyone to enjoy, and started drinking tea with her pal, Pinocchio. While Zeke threw hot dogs and burgers on the fire, Noah talked with him about the Red Sox's declining chances that summer. Robin and Mary sat in plastic lounge chairs drinking beer, chatting and laughing while faint music from a distant festival resonated in the background.

"Do you love him?" Mary asked, taking a sip of beer from a red plastic cup.

"*MOM !*" she objected loudly, looking over at Noah talking to Zeke by the fire pit. Noah turned his head to look at her, smiled, and continued talking.

"Well... do you love him?"

Robin took a sip of beer and lowered her cup, revealing a big grin.

"Hot damn !" Mary exclaimed, clapping her hands. "Mother's intuition. I just knew it. I could tell by the way you look at him. And he looks at you the same way."

"Yeah, I love him," she admitted, smiling, looking over at him fondly. "He's the sweetest guy, Mom. Never met anyone like him before. All the guys I've dated have all treated me like trash... but not Noah. He treats me like I'm some goddamn princess in a fairy tale. And he can't be convinced otherwise — I already tried. You know, despite his silver spoon upbringing, he somehow managed to stay down-to-earth. And I love that about him."

"Well, you want to know what your mother thinks?" she said with a stern face.

Robin looked concerned, afraid of what she might say.

"I love him, too !" she cried out, standing up to give her daughter a hug.

"Hey, keep your hands off him. He's all mine," Robin said jokingly. "Besides, you've got Zeke," she added, taking a sip.

"Yeah, Zeke's a keeper, alright," Mary said, looking at him. "So tell me... this prince of yours... is he real, like the rest of us... or is he just part of a fairy tale?"

"I don't know," Robin answered, looking over at him, locking eyes with him. "I just don't know."

Brittany watched as a flame engulfed a marshmallow at the end of her tree branch. Walking over to blow out the black inferno at the end of the stick, her mother kissed her on the head and said, "Britt, you be good for Grammy and Grandpa, okay?"

Brittany nodded, smiling when Zeke handed her a lit sparkler.

"Thanks for watching Britt for us," Robin said, kissing and hugging both of her parents. "We'll pick her up in the morning."

"It was a pleasure meeting you," Noah said, kissing Mary's cheek and shaking Zeke's hand.

"Likewise," Zeke said, reeling him in for another bear hug.

"So, where are you guys off to?" Mary asked.

"Meeting Julie and her new boyfriend, Jake, down at the beach. The whole gang's having a bonfire."

"Hey, that sounds like a lot fun. Mind if a couple of old geezers tag along?" Zeke kidded.

"*Yeah, sure,*" Robin replied, laughing. "Britt will just put herself to bed."

"You guys have fun now," Mary said, waving to them as they walked off, holding hands.

"Don't do anything we'd do," Zeke yelled, pinching Mary on the butt.

Noah felt like a fish out of water walking through the trailer park in his Ralph Lauren seersucker dress shirt, Tommy Bahama silk pleated pants, Sperry Top-Sider loafers, and yellow cashmere cable-knit sweater draped around his neck. The residents, in their ribbed undershirts, oversized t-shirts, and bathing suits, stopped setting off their firecrackers to stare at him.

As Noah and Robin crossed through a carnival that had vendors selling doughboys, pretzels, cotton candy, and kettle corn, they stopped at an outdoor stage to slow dance to a local band playing **Look Heart, No Hands**. When the song was over, Robin took Noah's hand and led him over a dune to the beach, where they watched the first of many fireworks exploding just offshore.

"Happy Independence Day," Noah said with a smile, launching a passionate kiss.

"As the fireworks started going off above my head, so too were they going off inside my heart. And so I felt compelled to let her know."

Noah whispered in her ear, but she couldn't hear him over the explosions.

"WHAT?" she yelled.

He repeated it in her ear, a little louder this time.

"I can't hear you," she yelled back at him, shaking her head and pointing up to the sky.

"I LOVE YOU !" he yelled.

Hearing him loud and clear this time, she looked deep into his blue eyes and smiled as she leaned forward to kiss him. "I love you too," she whispered in his ear.

Crossing over the dunes, they headed down the beach toward the far end, where about twenty people had gathered around a blazing bonfire. As they approached, they heard music and laughter. Everybody was wearing tank tops, t-shirts, hooded sweatshirts, and bathing suits. "Am I too conservative?" Noah asked, looking down at his preppy wardrobe.

"If you're talking about your outfit, don't worry, you look fine."

"Hey guys !" said Julie, Robin's roommate, handing them Budweisers. "I want you to meet Jake."

"Hi, Jake. I'm Noah," he said, shaking his hand.

"And I'm Robin," she said with a smile.

"Nice to meet you," Jake responded, returning the smile.

"Me and Robin have been best friends since like second grade, huh, Robin?" Julie said, giving Robin a friendly squeeze. "Jake, why don't you go introduce Noah to the guys while I talk to Robin," she said, clutching Robin's arm as she stepped aside with her.

"Sure thing," Jake said, patting Noah on the back as he led him away. "So what do you do?"

"Me? I uh... I... work for my dad," Noah said humbly, eager to change the subject. "How about you?"

"Fireman," Jake replied as they walked toward the people standing around the bonfire.

"But what about...?"

"Oh, right... the fire. What do you think? Should I put it out?"

Noah shook his head.

"Good idea. I'll just leave it then," he said, laughing with him.

Jake put his hand to his mouth and whistled loudly, getting everyone's attention as the music was turned down. "Everybody, this is Noah. Noah, this is everybody," he announced as the friendly, down-to-earth group of people started introducing themselves to Noah, making him feel welcome.

"Can I get you another beer?" Jake asked, walking off toward the cooler.

"No, I'm all set; but thanks," Noah replied, sitting down on a log and looking around at the friendly crowd. They were drinking, laughing, singing, and dancing around the fire. Yearning to be a part of their world, Noah suddenly envied what they had. *This is what's missing*, he thought to himself. They were not only enjoying a simple moment of friendship, they were celebrating life. And no one seemed to celebrate life better than Robin, smiling and laughing as she talked.

"As I watched Robin standing there interacting with her friends, I realized why I was so drawn to her. She was filled with the one thing that I could never have... LIFE."

Robin noticed Noah looking lovingly at her, and she smiled at him. With fireworks exploding in the distant background, she took his hand and began to dance.

The North Star

"It was great sailing weather that summer, and I got to spend time with my two loves — Robin and Freedom. Now what could better than that?"

As long as you had a boat, there was always plenty to do on Narragansett Bay during the summer months in the Ocean State. Noah's sailboat was one of a thousand boats anchored off the Quonset Point Air Force Base for the annual air show. Brittany was wearing a purple life preserver, trying to follow the dazzling display of aeronautics through a pair of oversized binoculars. Noah took a picture of Robin blowing a kiss to him just as The Blue Angels flew by with a thunderous roar.

A month later, Jimmy Buffet was singing **Cheeseburger In Paradise** at the Newport Folk Festival to a packed audience on the lawn at Fort Adams. Among a hundred other boats anchored just offshore, Noah's boat was rafted up to Scott's fifty-foot Sea Ray Sedan Bridge. Scott and Sharon never condoned their parents' prejudice against Robin. On the contrary, they welcomed her into the family with open arms. Robin, Sharon, and Julie were cuddled in the arms of their men, enjoying the music, dinking wine coolers, and snacking on cheese, crackers, and grapes as the sun dipped down behind the Newport Bridge.

Labor Day — the official end to summer — had arrived all too soon. With thousands of boats sailing out on the bay, Robin stood behind the helm steering Freedom with Noah standing directly behind her, kissing her neck. Their destination — the small island with the old, abandoned lighthouse. A jet ski whisked by them as they dropped anchor, the boat slowly drifting back as one hundred feet of chain clanked through the windlass.

"I love it out here. It's so much fun," Robin declared, her feet dangling in the water as she sat on the teak swim platform with a margarita glass in her hand.

"Too bad it's not for sale," Noah said, taking a sip from his glass, gazing at the lighthouse. "Wouldn't it be cool to convert that old thing into a beautiful bed-and-breakfast? It would even be a great location for our wedding, don't you think? We could run the inn together, you and I. I could shuttle the guests over by boat, and you could make the beds and vacuum the floors," he declared, sparking a playful splashing war.

"I think it's a great idea," she replied, slurping the last sip, "provided *you* do all the dirty work. Yeah, I can picture it now... Robin Hartman, the hostess with the mostest. It's got a catchy ring to it, don't you think? Too bad your dream's not for sale, Noah."

A million stars sparkled in the sky that night as the full moon illuminated a path on the flat water to Noah's sailboat, still anchored by the lighthouse. All alone, with no other boats in sight, they jumped off the stern holding hands. As they hit the water, hundreds of tiny effervescent bubbles glowed fluorescent green all around their naked bodies, skinny-dipping. They kissed as they treaded water and then climbed back up the ladder onto the swim platform, Robin first. Noah took the transom hose and slowly rinsed her off, bathing her body with warm, flowing water as they shared a sultry kiss. Without removing her lips from his, she took the hose away from his hand. Warm water cascaded down his chiseled chest onto her supple breasts as she lowered the showerhead.

"Do you surrender?" she asked tantalizingly.

"Yes... I surrender," he breathed.

As Noah and Robin headed home on what would be their last ride of the season, the GPS monitor at the helm flickered for a moment and then went off. Noah tapped it, hoping to get it started again.

"Without navigation, how are we going to get home?" Robin asked, sounding worried. "Everything looks so black, and I can't make out where the water ends and the land starts."

"There's nothing to be afraid of; trust me. Must be a loose wire. It's no big deal; I'll fix it tomorrow. Besides, there's always navigation. You just don't see it," Noah said as he gently took her hand. "See the Big Dipper up there?" he said, raising her hand up to the heavens, pointing her index finger at the constellation.

She looked up her arm and nodded. "See the two stars on the bowl furthest from the handle? Now draw a line connecting them and extend it out..." he said, moving her finger across the sky, "to over there," pointing her finger at the North Star. "You see that bright star, the first one in the handle of the Little Dipper? That's Polaris, the North Star. Its direction always points true north. It sits in the sky directly above the Earth's axis of rotation above the North Pole. As the Earth rotates, it's the only star in the sky that doesn't move. As the night goes on, all the other stars seem to rotate around it. So when I need a beacon to guide me home, all I have to do is look up at the sky, at Polaris, and it points me back to you."

"And what do you do if it's cloudy out, big shot?"

"Oh, good question. Well then, I simply follow my heart, which I know will always lead me back to you," he said, leaning in for a kiss, gently stroking the nape of her neck.

"That's why I love you so much — you're so romantic," she said, hugging him.

Noah looked back up at Polaris. "You know, a thousand years from now, as the Earth slowly wobbles, some other star in the sky will become the North Star, instead of Polaris. And you know what we'll do then... when Polaris no longer brings me home to you?"

"A thousand years from now? But we'll be in heaven," she said, confused, looking at him, waiting for an explanation.

"I'll build ourselves a boat. And on that day, you and I will simply sail away..."

Robin gazed at him with a sweet smile. "Alright then, it's a promise," she said, leaning in to him, while high above, the North Star guided them home.

The Marriage Proposal

My seventy-seven-year-old sister-in-law enters my hospital room and walks over to my brother standing beside my bed. "Hi, honey," she says, kissing him. "Hi, Noah," she says softly, looking down at me.

"Hi, Sharon. Thanks for coming," I say, happy to see her. "I'd like you to meet my new friend Josh over here. I was just telling him the story about Robin and me."

She looks into my eyes, smiles, and kisses my head, making me blush.

"You know, Noah, you're a man after my own heart," Josh admits. "I had no idea you were such a romantic. 'And on that day you and I will simply sail away into heaven together' — now that's good stuff. Did you think of that all by yourself? Anyway, go on, go on; I love a good love story."

They were all looking at me with pleasant eyes that encouraged me to continue. "So, like I was saying... it was a wonderful summer that I'll never forget. But all good things must eventually come to an end. The air was getting colder and the leaves were starting to fall. And like the song says, 'Seasons were made for change', and there was nothing I could do to stop it. Nothing could have prepared me for what would happen next..."

Orange and brown leaves were falling as Noah and Brittany sat at a picnic table beside a heap of leaves, painting funny faces on pumpkins with acrylic paint while Jake cooked burgers on the gas grill. It was fairly cold — cold enough for sweaters and jackets. Inside the apartment, Julie and Robin were drinking Gallo Chablis, discussing the upcoming big event.

"Does Noah know yet?" Julie asked.

"I'm a little worried about Joe being there," Robin admitted. "Even though we broke up ages ago, I'm afraid of how I might feel seeing him again. No, I haven't told Noah, and I'm not going to, either."

"Robin, you have to tell him. He deserves to know."

"I don't think I can," she said, shaking her head subtly. "I'm too afraid of losing him. I love him too much. Noah's not like any guy I've ever dated before — he's nice. And he couldn't care less that we come from two different worlds, because when I'm with him, no one else in the world matters... You ever get butterflies?"

"Butterflies?"

"Yeah, I get them every time I look into his beautiful blue eyes."

"Then don't go to Cathy's wedding in North Carolina. Stay home with Noah. You don't know what's going to happen when you see Joe again. You know how your brain works."

"Come on... just because I was dating Joe for a couple of months before I met Noah, doesn't mean I'm going to go running back to him the second I see him again. I do have *some* self control, you know."

"I hope you know what you're doing. Just don't blow it with Noah, okay? I really like that guy. He's charming."

Robin took a sip of wine as she looked out the window at Noah chasing after Brittany, tackling her in a pile of leaves and lifting her up in the air above him as she laughed hysterically. "Yeah, even my shrink calls him that. Except he calls him *Prince* Charming."

Noah pulled up to Green Airport with Robin and Brittany. He took their luggage out of the trunk and carried it over to the Southwest curbside counter. He gave Robin a hug and patted Brittany on the head.

"Well, I better get going," Noah said, watching closely as a police officer stood in back of a car, writing a ticket. "I love you," he said, giving Robin a quick kiss good-bye, watching the cop put the ticket under the wiper blade and head toward their car.

"I love you too," she responded. "Noah, wait !" she said urgently, grabbing his jacket as he pulled away.

"I can't; I have to go," he called out, running to the car, reaching it at the same time as the officer. "Sorry about that, officer. I'm leaving right now," he said, opening the door.

"But there's something I need to tell you," Robin yelled.

Noah looked over at her, waiting for her to speak. Instead, she just stood there, frozen.

"Well? You gonna move this thing, or what?" questioned the police officer.

"Hold on a sec," Noah said, holding out his hand. "What do you need to tell me?" he yelled back to her.

Shaking his head, the officer raised his pad and walked to the back of the car to take down the license plate number.

"I'll see you in three days," she yelled.

Noah nodded and quickly drove away, avoiding the ticket.

Robin was writing on butterfly-themed stationery as she sat on the plane next to Brittany, who was coloring in a Cinderella coloring book with Pinocchio by her side. Even though Robin's letter was addressed to Noah, it was really her way of reassuring herself that nothing was going to happen with Joe — at least that's what she kept telling herself, anyway.

Meanwhile, Noah walked into Ross Simons jewelry store in Warwick for his appointment with Steve. He followed him back to his office and sat down in a comfortable leather chair. Steve closed the door behind them and opened his private safe, removing a 3.75-carat round solitaire diamond engagement ring with platinum setting. He handed it to Noah, who admired its brilliance as it sparkled under the bright lamp.

The next day, Robin and Brittany sat down at a round banquet table in a modest restaurant for the rehearsal dinner. Robin glanced across the table at the handsome man with the baby face, military-cut hair, and full dress Air Force uniform. Joe looked back at Robin and smiled.

Meanwhile, Noah had a welder's mask covering his face as tiny sparks flew out in front of him, engraving a brick.

The following day, a bride and groom kissed each other at the altar, a twelve-foot high statue of Jesus nailed to the cross in the background. Robin was sitting in the tenth row, with Brittany on one side of her and Joe on the other. Joe reached over to hold Robin's hand, but she quickly pulled away, glaring at him. She looked over at Brittany to see if she'd seen anything. She had not. The audience inside the

72

church stood, applauding loudly as the bride and groom walked back down the aisle. As everyone emptied out of their seats, Joe tried reaching for Robin's hand once again, this time capturing it.

Meanwhile, Noah opened his mailbox and shuffled through the mail until he came to an envelope with butterfly illustrations, postmarked from North Carolina. He opened it immediately.

Dear Noah,

I wish you could have come with me to my friend's wedding. I'm sorry you weren't invited. I can't stop thinking about you. I think I miss your full lips and warm blue eyes the most. Before we know it, I'll be back home and we'll be together once again, this time forever. I promise I'll never leave you again, not for one minute. I can't wait to spend the rest of my life with you. You truly are my soul mate, and I'm so lucky to have you in my life. The plane is about to land, so I better get going. I'm counting the days until we're back in each other's arms for good.

Loving you forever,
Robin

Later that evening, Robin was slow dancing with Joe at the reception while Brittany's head rested on the dinner table, sleeping. Joe moved his lips close to Robin's. She quickly turned her head. Joe slowly turned her face back toward him and noticed a tear rolling down her cheek.

Meanwhile, Noah was aggressively pushing and pulling on a crowbar in the dark, trying to pluck a brick from the sidewalk in front of Robin's apartment. The outside light turned on in front of the apartment, and the front door opened just as the brick popped out. Noah dropped the engraved brick in its place, grabbed the crowbar and the old brick, and took off running down the street, just as Julie stepped out the front door. As she walked past the new brick that was sticking up slightly above the other bricks, she looked around suspiciously, not certain if she had seen anything or not.

Back at the wedding reception, Joe was kissing Robin on the lips. As she moved her arms around his neck, she suddenly remembered how much she cared for Joe.

Robin was staring out the passenger window as Noah drove them home from the airport.

"So, how was the wedding?" Noah asked, breaking the awkward silence.

"Good," she replied without elaborating.

"Good," he said tersely, glancing over at her, then back at the road. "So, was she a beautiful bride?"

Robin didn't answer.

Noah waited a few seconds, then asked gently, "Is there something you want to tell me?"

"No..." she said, turning her head to look at Brittany in the back seat. "Not right now."

"I knew something was wrong right away. No one was talking, and the tension was so thick you could practically cut it with a knife."

Noah pulled up in front of her apartment and carried the luggage inside. As he came back out, Robin said to Brittany, "Go on inside, honey. I need to talk to Noah." Brittany obediently walked in the door.

"Come on over here, I want to show you something," Noah said, taking Robin by the hand and leading her over to the section of sidewalk where he had placed the engraved brick. He took the engagement ring out of his pocket and concealed it in his hand, glancing down nervously at the brick. He looked at her and smiled. Her breathing was labored as she looked away, not noticing the brick.

"What's the matter?" he asked, his smile fading.

"Remember that guy I was dating for a couple of months up until we met?"

"Yeah... so what? I don't care about him," Noah said, his face frozen.

"Well, he was there... at the wedding."

"Oh? And...?"

"Apparently, he never had any closure," she said, her words striking Noah hard. "I promise you, nothing happened; Britt was right there beside me the whole time. But you should have seen how happy she was to see him. Brittany loves him, and he loves her."

"Yeah, and what about me? I love Brittany too, you know."

"Anyway, we decided to get back together and give *us* another chance. I'm sorry, Noah... it's over," she said, walking back to the apartment and slamming the door behind her without a backwards glance.

Noah glared down at the engagement ring in his hand and just stood there in disbelief. Even after night had fallen, Noah was still standing there, cold and shivering in the dark.

The Company He Keeps

The phone was ringing off the hook as Noah lay motionless on the bed. Rosa walked into the bedroom and answered the phone on the nightstand. "Hello. Oh, hi, Mr. Hartman. Yes, Noah's here, but he no want to talk right now. He knows it's been two weeks since he's been to work. He knows the budgets are past due. Okay, I tell him. Bye, Mr. Hartman." No sooner had she hung up the phone than it rang again. "Hello. Oh, hi, Mrs. Hartman. No, Noah no want to come for dinner tonight. He still no feel good. Okay, I tell him. Bye, Mrs. Hartman," she said, hanging up and leaving the room. The phone rang again, and Rosa could be heard speaking down the hall. "Hello. Oh, hi, Scott. No, Noah no want to talk right now. Okay, I tell him..."

"My life was not the same without Robin in it. I was depressed, and nothing could make me happy — nothing except for Robin, that is."

His fake gold Rolex and thick gold chain around his neck contrasted against a dark tan. Although he wore no wedding ring, the tan line on Tony's left ring finger suggested otherwise. "Go on..." he nudged, sitting back in his chair and staring at her.

"I don't understand what happened," Robin told her psychiatrist. "I swear it didn't matter that Joe was there, because I kept telling myself how much I loved Noah, over and over again. I tried to hang onto that for as long as I could, I really did — "

"Robin, stop torturing yourself. We go through this every time this happens. I keep explaining to you that it's not your fault; you can't help it. Your brain is just wired that way, that's all." She nodded. "If you want, I can put you on different medication."

"I don't know," she said, clenching her teeth. "None of the meds so far have made any difference. If anything, they only seem to make things worse."

"It's your call. So, what else is happening in your life?"

"I got a letter today in the mail," she said, handing over an envelope. He removed the letter and started reading it. "Apparently, my biological father died a couple of months back from a heart attack. It says there he died alone, with no immediate family to speak of. As it turns out, I'm his sole heir. The lawyers had a tough time finding me. Since he didn't have a will, I guess *his* money is now *my* money."

"Wow, Robin, that's a substantial amount," he exclaimed, handing her back the letter. "What are you going to do with all that money? Buy a small house somewhere?"

"Not exactly... I'm going to burn it."

"Robin, you're not going to burn it. Think about Brittany's future."

"Well... maybe not," Robin acquiesced, looking away. "But, that son of a bitch abandoned my mom and I when I was just a baby. And for the last twenty-five years, I didn't even know he was still alive. That bastard's not my dad — Zeke is. He can keep his goddamn money and burn in hell as far as I'm concerned."

"Come on, Robin, let it go. It's not healthy for you. The only person this negative energy is hurting is yourself."

Robin nodded. "Alright... I'll give it a try."

"I'm sure you'll figure out what to do with that money," he said reassuringly.

Sporting a scraggly beard and a gray hooded coat, Noah sat staring off into space in the waiting area in the executive building outside a door that read *Harriet Hartman, Executive Vice President.* He had lost the love of his life, and he was struggling to come to grips with how unhappy he was working for the company. Not only was it a job that he didn't choose for himself, but it was a job that he knew he could never leave. He felt trapped.

"You okay, Noah? You don't look so good," said the project manager sitting next to him, waiting his turn to go in.

The door opened and Max walked out, visibly agitated.

"Hey, Max, how'd your review go?" asked the nervous project manager.

"Great... Just terrific," Max replied sarcastically, shaking his head in disbelief. "Thirty-two years of dedication and loyalty. Thirty-two years of starting Jerry's shopping center division from scratch and turning it into a multi-billion-dollar division. And how do they thank me? They fire me because we lose a couple of major anchors all in the same year. I got to go pack up my stuff and get the hell out of here... Oh, hi, Noah. I didn't recognize you with that beard. I feel bad for you, kid, I really do."

Aunt Harriet opened the door and popped her head out. "Noah, you're up next."

Noah glanced at Max and trudged into the office, lowering himself into a big leather armchair across from his father.

"Hi, Noah," Jerry said with a pleasant smile.

"So, let's get started," Aunt Harriet announced, shutting the door. "Looking at your final numbers for the year, Noah, you had another outstanding year. In fact, you're one of our brightest stars. Out of the twenty-two project managers we have working for us at the company, you and Carol are the only ones to actually show a profit increase over last year. Not only did you have an astounding twenty percent increase in occupancy rates, but you also had a twenty-seven percent increase in profit."

Noah sat numbly, unresponsive.

"Great job, Noah. Based on your exceptional numbers, your dad and I feel you've earned another $25,000 bonus this year, same as last year. Congratulations." Aunt Harriet and Jerry stood up to shake his hand.

"Thanks," Noah said without emotion, standing and extended his hand reluctantly. "Is that it? Can I go now?"

Aunt Harriet nodded, and Noah dragged himself toward the door. "Oh, Noah, wait a second," she exclaimed. Noah stopped. "Your father and I have been talking. He mentioned to me that you're looking to take on more responsibility. So how'd you like to add our shopping center portfolio to your current responsibilities?"

Noah stood there for a moment. "How could you fire Max after all these years?" he said, not turning to face them.

"Noah, your father and I agonized over this one. You know very well that ever since the last recession, our occupancy rates and rental income have consistently dropped, year after year. The only way to survive is to cut back on expenses wherever we can and do more with less. We're not in business to lose money, and we just couldn't afford Max's lofty salary anymore. If we didn't let him go, then two other project managers would have to be let go in his place. We had no choice. I admit, Max is a great guy, but business is business. He'll be all right; we gave him a great severance package. So what do you say, star? You wanted more responsibility, now you've got it."

"Not like this," he said, walking through the door.

Noah was eating lunch all by himself in the cafeteria when Cindy invited herself to join him. Although she was young and pretty, Noah didn't pay much attention to her and the fact that she may have had one too many buttons opened on her shirt that day.

"Hey, Noah. I like the new look — the beard," she said, taking her lunch out of a brown paper bag.

Noah continued to eat his lunch without acknowledging her.

"I heard you broke up with your girlfriend. I'm sorry to hear that. If you ever need a friend to talk to — or a shoulder to lean on — I'm your gal."

"Hi, Noah," Diane said, walking briskly over to them. "Cindy, I don't think you know what you're doin' over here. Come sit down with the rest of us at our table."

"Yeah, okay... be there in a few," Cindy replied placatingly while smiling at Noah and opening her yogurt.

"Noah, tell Cindy she needs to get up now," Diane insisted, glancing over at Stan, the security guard who was sitting across the cafeteria, eating his lunch and glaring at them. "They're watching you, Noah," she warned in a low voice. Noah didn't respond. He just kept on eating. "It's your funeral," she said to Cindy, walking back to sit with the other secretaries.

Noah had managed to make it through a long, cold winter. The tulips were in bloom in front of Hartman Enterprises as Noah's convertible pulled into the company parking lot with the top down. Cindy rode in the passenger seat wearing sunglasses, her hair windblown. Noah didn't pull into his usual reserved parking space, like he always does. Instead, he drove to the back corner of the lot. Glancing around and not seeing anyone, he kissed Cindy before getting out of the car.

As they walked into the building separately, not acknowledging each other, a surveillance camera zoomed in on Cindy. Inside the company's security office, Stan rewound the tape, viewing the segment again as he picked up the phone.

"Hello, Jerry? It's Stan here in security..."

Later that day, Noah was sitting in his office talking to Russ when Diane came storming in. She grabbed Russ' leasing brochure out of his hand and threw it at Noah, just missing his head.

"What the hell?" Noah exclaimed.

"Noah, you asshole. They just canned Cindy."

"Shit," he said, burying his head in his hands. "I'm so sorry."

Destiny

*L*ight gusts of wind blew brown leaves in swirling patterns as Noah, rid of his beard, sat at his desk staring out the window, surprised to see a red robin sitting on the sill, waiting patiently for her mate to arrive with another twig. Like clockwork, the other red robin flew in, placed the twig in the nest, and flew away to go find another twig.

Diane sat at her desk watching him. "Noah, you okay? You gotta snap out of it and finish the profit projections that were due yesterday. Noah... Noah?"

"I can't stop thinking about her. It just doesn't make any sense."

"Who? Cindy?"

"No... Robin. She was *the one*. I don't understand what happened," he said morosely. "Robin, I don't understand," he said softly to himself.

"Destiny's funny that way. If it was meant to be, Robin will come back to you. If she doesn't, then it was never meant to be. It's like that saying, *If you love something, set it free...*"

Noah leaped up, grabbed his briefcase, and strode toward the door.

"Hey, where you going? What about the projections?"

Noah stopped and looked at her. "To pay a visit to destiny," he said, dropping the completed budgets on her desk and disappearing down the hallway.

Noah stood in front of Robin's apartment door, holding the diamond ring in one hand and a folded letter in the other. The door opened.

"Hi, Noah," she greeted him with a pleasant smile.

"Hey," he said, surprised that Robin actually seemed happy to see him. "How've you been?"

"Good... You?"

"Not bad... How's Brittany doing?"

"She's doing great, thanks for asking."

"Tell her I said hello, okay?"

"I will."

There was an uncomfortable silence as Noah stood there, clenching the diamond ring. "Well, this is for you," he said, handing her the letter, his eyes taking her in one last time. "Call me if you want to talk," he conceded as he turned and walked back to his car. *The timing just isn't right*, he thought to himself as he stared at the diamond in his hand, tossing it into the glove box and speeding away.

As Robin stepped back into her apartment, she unfolded the letter and began to read it.

The Beautiful Red Bird

Once upon a time, there was a beautiful red bird. One day, the beautiful red bird decided to fly right through my window and into my life. Never had I seen a more beautiful creature. My life would never be the same, because never did I love anything more.

I remember the moment I first laid eyes on the beautiful red bird. She was so full of life as she smiled and danced with her hands up in the air. There was no one else in the room.

I remember our first kiss. I kissed away the tears from her sad but beautiful eyes. My heart skipped a beat.

I remember the butterflies. We couldn't even eat.

I remember the tumultuous ocean on the day our bodies and souls first truly connected.

I remember Polaris, the star that always leads me back to her.

But most of all, I remember the way she used to gaze deep into my eyes, and through her eyes, I fell deeply and madly in love with her beautiful soul.

These things I will always remember until the day I die.

And so I wonder, What does the beautiful red bird remember? Because on one sad day, for some inexplicable reason, the beautiful red bird decided to just get up and fly right back out that window.

Oh, how I miss the beautiful red bird. I just want to tell her that the window is still open, just in case she ever wants to fly back in again. As long as I'm alive, that window will always be left open.

Robin, I love you, and I always will, until the end of time.

Noah

The wind was howling that cold Friday night in October when Noah returned to Mardi Gras. He was wearing a long, puffy down coat, the fur hood pulled up over his head.

"This was it... the place I first met Robin. Maybe if I were lucky she'd be there again, I thought. Who knows, maybe I'd get to see her smile... talk to her for awhile... dance with her even..."

Noah checked his coat and started searching the crowd for Robin's face. He thought back to that fateful night, the night he first laid eyes on her, dancing with her hands up in the air, so happy, so full of life. He bought a Captain and Coke, then another, and another, all the while hoping she'd somehow magically appear.

Suddenly, there she was — a woman with long, red hair just like Robin's. As she turned, his heart raced. The side of her face looked just like Robin's. He hurried over to her and put his hand on her shoulder. The woman turned and smiled at him, but he was heartbroken to see she wasn't Robin. Although she did look a lot like her, a copy would never be quite the same as the original. "Sorry," he said as his face fell, walking away.

Noah left the nightclub and got into his car, which rolled slowly into a telephone pole. A police officer on detail at the club ran over to the car and opened the driver's door. Inside the slightly damaged vehicle, Noah was out like a light, unharmed and fast asleep.

Noah ended up spending the night in jail, sleeping it off. Appearing before a judge the next morning, he released him on his own recognizance. Ben, a litigant on the payroll of Hartman Enterprises, told Noah not to worry about the D.U.I. charge, the judge being his brother-in-law.

The next night, Julie and Robin got dressed up for a night out on the town. As they left their apartment, they headed down the dimly lit sidewalk, and Robin tripped, breaking the glass heel off of one of her transparent Benjamin Walk shoes.

"Damn it, these were my favorite shoes," she exclaimed, taking off the broken shoe and examining it.

Julie looked down and noticed an engraved brick sticking up through the leaves. She bent down and brushed it off, using her lighter to read it.

"Holy shit, Robin, did you see this?"

"Oh my God..." Robin breathed as she bent down and read the words on the brick — *Robin, Will you marry me? LOVE always, Noah.* "He never said anything to me."

"You're shitting me, right? He carves a frickin' marriage proposal in stone in front of our apartment, and he never mentions this to you?"

"Yeah, I know, right? I mean, who does that?"

"When do you think he did it?"

"I don't know... last year, maybe."

"What are you going to do?"

"What *can* I do? We live in two different worlds, remember? And you can't mix 'em together."

"I guess you're right... Come on, let's go get drunk."

A half-hour later, Robin and Julie arrived at Mardi Gras, while Noah arrived at the Art Bar across town, driving a rental car. He searched the crowd aimlessly for Robin, then sat at the bar by himself for the rest of the night, drinking only water.

The Art Bar was closing, so Noah left a tip, fetched his puffy down coat from the coat-check, and headed home, disappointed. As he parked the car in his driveway and headed toward his house with his fur hood pulled up over his head, he heard a car driving down the street.

"All I could think about that night was Robin. What was the chance that while I was looking for her, she'd be looking for me? No way could that car coming down the street so late at night be her..."

"This is a really dumb idea. Just turn the car around, and let's go home," Julie said to Robin as Robin's silver car zipped down Noah's street.

"He's never going to know I was ever here. It's one-thirty in the morning, and if I know him, he was out like a light by ten."

"And what if you're wrong, and he sees you?"

"Trust me, he's not going to see me."

"Just let the poor guy move on with his life, and let's get the hell out of here. Besides, with your history, you can't even promise that you won't do it to him again, can you?"

As the car sped by, Noah looked over his shoulder, but he couldn't make out the car over the bright headlights.

"SHIT ! Who the hell was that?" Robin exclaimed.

"Some fat old lady. I didn't recognize the car."

Noah walked back to his rental car and pretended to put the key into the passenger door, waiting for the car to return, hoping it would somehow be Robin. The Honda came to a screeching halt at the end of the dead end street. Backing up and quickly turning around, the car raced back up the street. Noah ran out into the middle of the road just as it passed him, his hood falling down from his face. It was Robin's license plate.

"That ain't no fat old lady..." Robin screeched, looking in her rear-view mirror. "That's Noah !"

Noah jumped in the rental car and gave chase, catching up to her at a red light and pulling up beside her on the wrong side of the road. He beeped his horn to get her attention, but she wouldn't look. The light changed, and she was off to the races again. But Noah was in close pursuit. He pulled in front of her and started slowing down. She lost him by making an abrupt turn to the right, fleeing down a small dirt road. Noah looked in his rear-view mirror, slammed on the brakes, and quickly started backing up. Slamming on her brakes, Robin stopped on a boat ramp just short of the water as Noah pulled up behind her, blocking her in.

They jumped out of their cars and walked quickly toward each other. While Noah was ecstatic to see her, it quickly became apparent that Robin did not share the same sentiment. She stormed toward him with the broken transparent shoe in her hand, throwing it at him and missing his head as he ducked. Noah grabbed hold of her as she pounded on his chest.

"Stop, I surrender," he pleaded, struggling unsuccessfully to contain her blows.

Suddenly memories of loving Noah started coming back, precipitated by the fact that his lips were now pressing against hers. As if a switch inside her brain was magically triggered, she stopped hitting him, and stared.

"It's me... Noah," he said, releasing her.

"I know," she said with a loving smile, gazing at him. "I remember now."

Robin's lips rushed to meet his again, kissing him as if he'd been away at sea for years on end. Just then, a police car pulled up and shined a high beam light onto them. Not paying any attention, they kept right on kissing. The officer shined the light onto Julie sitting in the passenger seat. She turned around and waved at the officer, calling out, "Don't worry, everything's fine !"

As the police radio crackled, "0500 burglary in progress..." the police car sped off into the night with its lights flashing and siren sounding. And while Robin and Noah continued kissing without interruption, the constellations above them shined bright and clear.

"And so that night... destiny paid a visit to me."

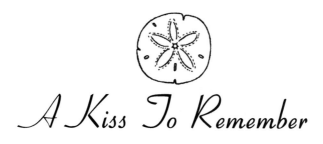

A Kiss To Remember

As Noah loaded a cardboard box into the back of a small U-haul truck, Robin, wearing her new diamond engagement ring, hugged Julie in front of her apartment.

"I'm going to miss you," Julie said to Robin. "One piece of advice... keep him this time, okay?"

"Oh, believe me, I will. I love him, and nothing could ever change my mind about that."

"Well, maybe you should write yourself a letter... just in case."

Robin laughed as she kissed Julie good-bye and headed for the truck.

Forty-five minutes later, the U-haul truck pulled into Noah's cobblestone driveway in Jamestown. While Noah grabbed a carton from the back of the truck, Robin stood on the threshold fumbling with an orange foam keychain with her daughter standing beside her, clutching onto Pinocchio and anxious to go in. As soon as the door opened, Brittany ran up the stairs to find her new room, her smile fading as she entered. The walls were brown, the curtains brown, the comforter brown, and the dresser was black.

"Mommy," she called out. "MOMMY !" she screamed nervously, not getting an immediate response.

"What is it, honey?" Robin asked, appearing next to her in the doorway.

"I'm scared !" she said, pointing at her masculine bedroom.

"Don't be scared, sweetheart. The room just needs mommy's touch, that's all, and some good old-fashioned lovin'. Before you know it, it'll feel just like home. I promise," she said, kissing Brittany on the head. "Come over here; I want to show you something. Look, you've got your own balcony," she said, opening the French doors. "You can even have tea out here with Pinocchio if you want. And I have a pretty good idea he's going to really like the view."

Brittany's mouth dropped as she stepped out onto the deck overlooking the mouth of the bay. "Okay, Mommy... I'll take it," she said, nodding sweetly.

Noah was sleeping like a baby when the alarm went off at six a.m. As usual, he slept through the buzzing sound that was getting louder by the second. Robin rolled over him, reached up, and yanked the clock out of the wall, dropping it to the floor.

"Honey, aren't you getting up for work?"

"I don't feel so good," Noah groaned. "Must have been the food you made last night."

Robin frowned, felt his forehead, and went downstairs to make coffee. An hour later, she was dressed in her white uniform, kissing him on the head as he continued to sleep. The moment the front door slammed shut, Noah's eyes popped open. He pushed the curtain aside and watched Robin wave good-bye to Brittany as she hopped onto the school bus. He continued watching until she had driven down the street on her way to work. Noah opened the front door and put his hand to his mouth, whistling loudly, and two white vans marked *Hartman Enterprises* pulled right up. Two men wearing white overalls jumped out of one van, while Mike, the maintenance guy, jumped out of the other.

Mike and Noah made a good team, building a bunk bed in the shape of an opulent castle, while the other two men primed the walls and then painted them pink. Noah and Mike hung Princess curtains on the windows and rolled out a Princess rug on the floor, while the painters painted a large mural of Cinderella on a wall. A delivery truck from Cardi's Furniture pulled up in front of the house, and two men brought up a white dresser, vanity, mattress, and an oversized purple shaggy beanbag chair. They took the old furniture with them as they left. As the *pièce de résistance*, Noah hung a framed limited edition Disney animation cel of Pinocchio on the wall. Looking at his watch, it was now 2:05 p.m. They had finished just in time.

"Hey, Denise. How are you?" Robin said, walking up to the teller at Old Stone Bank.

"ROBIN !" she exclaimed. "Thank you so much for getting little Joey for me last week."

"No problem, he's a doll. How's your mom doing?"

"She's doing much better now that they have her on antibiotics. I don't know how I would have gotten her to the hospital if it wasn't for you picking up Joey from daycare and watching him all night for me."

"It was no big deal, really. I'm sure you'd do the same for me."

"So, how are things with you? What's goin' on?"

"You're never going to believe this, but I got this check in the mail," Robin said, embarrassed as she handed it to her.

"Oh my God, Robin, that's amazing. What, did you win the lottery or something?"

"Not exactly, my biological father died."

"Zeke died?" she said, raising her voice, concerned.

"No... no, Zeke's fine. Anyway, I'd like you to make out a bank check for me."

"Sure, how much?"

"All of it. Here's who I want it to go to," Robin said, handing her a note.

Denise read the name on the note and looked up. "Are you sure you want to do this?" she asked cautiously, looking at her.

"Yes, I'm sure."

"Okay," Denise said, smiling. "Let me just go get the bank manager's signature, and I'll be right back."

She left and came back to her station a few minutes later, handing Robin a red envelope. Robin opened the envelope and looked at the bank check inside made out for $257,000. She inserted a note written on butterfly-themed stationery into the red envelope and sealed it.

"Anything else?" Denise asked.

"Yeah, how about some more sweets for the kids?"

"Of course," she laughed, handing her a bag full of brightly colored lollipops.

Brittany stepped off the school bus and ran into her mother's outstretched arms, skipping into the house arm-in-arm. Robin headed into the kitchen to put away the groceries while Brittany scampered upstairs. A moment later Robin heard a scream, and she ran upstairs to find Brittany jumping up and down in her room, laughing with joy. In disbelief, Robin took in the transformation of the room, which now resembled Cinderella's enchanted castle.

The moment Noah walked through the door into the foyer, Robin surprised him by grabbing hold of him and giving him a passionate kiss that seemed to last a lifetime. She looked deep into his eyes, thanking him without words for his thoughtfulness.

"Can you picture the way she kissed me? No one ever kissed me like that before — or after, for that matter. You can't imagine how wonderful that made me feel. This is why I loved her so much. Of all the kisses I ever received my entire life, I would never forget this particular one. No words were ever spoken. No words were needed. I knew from that kiss that Robin missed me all day long and couldn't wait to see me. I knew from that kiss that I was loved."

Robin handed Noah a red envelope.

"What's this?" he asked, examining the sealed envelope.

"I need you to hold onto this for me for safekeeping. It's important, so don't lose it. Promise me you'll never open it."

"Okay, I promise," he said, curious about the contents of the envelope. He read the words on the front of the envelope — *Deliver to Robin when the time is right.*

"But how will I know when the time is right?"

"That's something I hope you never have to find out," she said, exiting the foyer with a mischievous smile.

Noah continued to have a puzzled look on his face as he stared at the mysterious envelope in his hand.

The holidays were a time of joy. Brittany was running around the house with Scott and Sharon's two kids. Sam was five, the same age as Brittany, and David was seven. Julie was there, pregnant, with her fiancé Jake. Scott and Sharon talked to Zeke and Mary while Robin opened the front door, embracing Jerry and Miriam, who stiffly returned the gesture. Robin walked over to join Noah sitting on the side of the sofa. More than words, she expressed her love by wrapping her arms around him and kissing his head. Noah rested his hands on top of hers and smiled.

A little while later, everyone sat down at the dinner table for the feast. Noah rose to say the blessing. "We're thankful for all the people in our lives whom we love. May they always share a special place in our hearts, our homes, and our lives. And thanks for the simple things in life," he said, looking at Robin. "It's always the simple things that we cherish the most and never forget." He looked around the room at everybody and raised his glass. "Happy Thanksgiving, everyone."

Noah was fast asleep at five o'clock in the morning, spooning Robin, when Brittany ran into their bedroom and started jumping on the bed. Brittany pulled them out of bed and down the stairs, excited to open the presents beneath the Christmas tree. The glass of milk left for Santa sitting on the granite island in the kitchen was mostly empty, the cookies on the tray mostly eaten. Brittany spotted a trail of what looked like hoof marks going across the kitchen floor, leading back to the fireplace in the living room. Noah looked up the fireplace flue and was surprised to pull out a large, black boot covered in soot. "It must have fallen off of Santa's foot as he was leaving," Noah told Brittany, her mouth open in amazement. Robin laughed, shoving Noah. Noah put the boot aside and lit the fireplace, and while Brittany excitedly unwrapped her presents, they kissed in front of it.

A Shack In The Woods

Forty-nine-year-old Brittany walks into my hospital room and joins Scott, Sharon, and Josh around my bed.

"Thanks for coming, Britt," I say appreciatively.

"*This* is little Brittany?" Josh exclaims, surprised. "Wow, she sure turned into a beautiful woman, didn't she?"

Brittany places her hand gently on my face and looks deep into my eyes with her warm, loving eyes. I return the sentiment.

"How's your mom doing?" Scott asks her.

"I just left her room," she says, looking over at Scott. "Olivia's still there with her now. When she and Noah arrived in the ambulance, she was hysterical. The doctor had to sedate her twice just to calm her down."

"Is Robin okay? What happened?" I ask, concerned.

"She's okay now," Brittany says, moving my hair away from my eyes and mouthing the words *I love you* to me. "She's resting comfortably. Besides, she's much better off not knowing what's about to happen to Noah," she says, looking back at Scott.

"Britt, what are you talking about? What's about to happen to me? Can't I just go home?"

"Honey... I think I smell something burning," Noah said nervously, watching a thin plume of white smoke float in between Brittany and him as they sat at the kitchen table waiting for dinner. Brittany looked up and screamed, running upstairs to her bedroom and slamming the door behind her.

Robin was standing in the kitchen reading some papers while food on the stove burned in front of her. "What the hell is this?" she demanded, marching over to Noah and holding up the papers.

"Oh, I see you found the prenup..." he said matter-of-factly.

"And when were you planning on telling me about this? Or were you hoping I'd just discover it sitting here on the kitchen counter?"

"Well, I've been meaning to talk to you about that. I, uh... can't get married without one."

"*Oh, great* !" she remarked sarcastically. "So what choice do I have? If I don't sign it, we don't get married?" Noah shrugged. "What ever happened to the old-fashioned, romantic idea of planning to grow old together? You know... because we love each other?"

"Look, you don't understand. I've already been through one nasty divorce, and I need to be better prepared this time."

"So your first marriage to Rachel ends in disaster, and I get to pay the price. I guess all you care about is keeping your stuff, huh? What about the people in your life? Don't they mean anything to you? Or does money mean more to you than me?" Noah sat there silently. "This should be the happiest time of our lives. We haven't even gotten married yet, and all you can think of is an exit strategy... just in case. That's a hell of a way to enter into a union that's supposed to last a lifetime, don't you think? Or are you planning on screwing up?"

"I don't have a choice in the matter. If I don't have a prenup, I can't get married."

"That's ridiculous. You always have a choice."

"You don't understand, if I don't have a prenup, my parents will disown me."

"Well, guess what? If your parents actually disowned you, that would be the best thing that could ever happen to you."

"I didn't make the rules — I just play by them."

"I'm not marrying your goddamn parents, Noah, I'm marrying *you*. For God's sake, when are you going to stand up to your parents and start making your own decisions for a change?"

"But I have to protect the company stock."

"Bullshit ! The only thing you're interested in protecting is your stuff. What about me, Noah? Don't you care about me?"

"Of course I care about you."

"Then tell me I don't need to sign this thing."

He looked at her and exhaled, shaking his head.

"Screw your parents, and for that matter, screw you. I wish you didn't have any money," she said, throwing the papers at him and storming out of the room, going upstairs to check on her daughter.

Noah picked up the prenup, turned off the burners on the stove, and opened the windows to dissipate some of the smoke still permeating the room.

Later that night, Noah shut the TV off in the den and went upstairs. He turned the handle to the bedroom door, but it was locked.

"Robin..." he called out, knocking. "Robin?"

There was no answer. He opened the guestroom door and turned the light on, staring at the empty bed in the corner that he'd soon call *home*.

The sign on the door read *The Law Offices of Brown & Sons*. Inside the large conference room, Noah and Robin sat on opposite sides of a long conference table, their lawyers beside them.

"Well, quite frankly," her lawyer said, "I've seen a lot of prenups in my day, and this one's about as lopsided as they get."

"Well, this is just the starting point, Steve," Ben, Noah's lawyer, explained. "That's why we're here: to work out the kinks. Our clients are in love, and we want to make this as painless as possible for them. Tell us what you want, and let's start the negotiation process."

"NEGOTIATION PROCESS?" Robin said angrily. "Is that what this is? Noah goes to his corner, and I go to mine? Is this a glimpse of what our marriage is going to be like?" she asked Noah. "You make all the decisions, and who cares what I want? What are we going to do when we disagree? Call our lawyers to start another negotiation process?"

"No, n-n-not at all," Noah stuttered. "This is all just a formality. Once we get through this minor sticking point, then it's smooth sailing."

"Oh, really? You mean as long as I'm a good little wife, keeping my mouth shut and going along with whatever you say, then everything will be just fine and dandy. Is that the way it's going to be? Because if it is, I don't want to sign up for this. Whatever happened to us being a team? — You know, equal partners on an equal playing field."

"Look, Robin, none of us wants the two of you to end up in divorce," Ben said in a placating tone. "But if for some horrible, inexplicable reason it ever happens, then we feel it's only fair that what belongs to Noah before the marriage, including any and all Hartman Enterprises stock, should stay with Noah, and what belongs to you, should stay with you. Now what's wrong with that line of thinking? And just to show Noah's appreciation, if you do end up getting divorced, he'll give you thirty thousand dollars for every year the two of you were married — prorated, of course. That's three hundred thousand dollars if you stay married for ten years, which I may point out, is three hundred thousand dollars more than what you have now. It's nothing to sneeze at, and it would definitely be more than enough for a down payment on a new house."

"I understand what you're saying, Ben," Steve kicked in, "but what Robin is concerned about here, is that her house will not feel like her *home*."

"That's because it's not her home — it's *Noah's* home," Ben rebuked.

"That's exactly Robin's point. Someday down the road, Noah could get tired of her. Maybe he wants a newer, prettier model — who knows? He could abandon her and throw her and any children they might have together out on the street, and Noah's life goes on uninterrupted, as if nothing ever happened. He comes out smelling like a rose — no harm, no foul. Can you imagine what it would be like for Robin in that situation? Always wondering when or if her own husband is going to wake up someday and say, 'Oh, by the way, I'm getting kind of tired of you, Robin, it's time for you to pack your bags and leave *my* house'."

"Well, in that case, Noah will be happy to put Robin's name on the deed as long as she pays him for half the equity up front."

"Ha, that's a laugh," Robin called out. "You know I can't even afford my own gas. How do you expect me to come up with money to buy half a house?"

"There's no need to get upset," Ben said calmly. "We're all here to help. The wedding is only two months away, and we have to get this settled so the two of you can start enjoying a long, happy life together. So what's it going to take to get you to sign this thing? A new BMW? A Lexus? How about a Range Rover?"

As Robin shot a scornful look across the table, Noah lowered his head in shame. He knew the prenuptial agreement was a necessary evil; he just wished there were an easier way. Ben opened his briefcase and removed catalogs from Mercedes, BMW, Lexus, Land Rover, and others. Robin looked at Noah, shook her head, and tossed the catalogs aside, storming from the room.

Karen, Larry's pretty, new assistant, was sitting in Noah's office next to her boss, taking notes. She was young and slim, with shoulder-length blonde hair and a dainty Southern accent.

"Impressive brochure," Noah commented, picking up the Hartman Towers leasing brochure and turning it over, revealing the words *Wentworth Leasing and Sales*. "And you did a great job for me on our Portsmouth waterfront project. However, I need Wentworth to take a ten percent cut in commission on this one. Ever since my parents had dinner at Al Forno with Sol Cohen from Commercial Properties, my dad's been stopping by my office every day to review their proposal. I've been negotiating with them and got them to sharpen their pencils considerably. They'd do anything to eat your lunch. But don't worry, I told my dad that all things remaining equal, we've got to stick with the vendor of record — you guys."

"I appreciate that. Anything else?" Larry inquired.

"Yeah, I need a fifteen percent increase in co-op advertising."

"Gee, I'm so glad I asked," Larry said sarcastically. "Tell you what, I'll find out and get back to you by Friday. How's that?"

"Fair enough, Larry."

As Karen bent over his desk to pick up the stack of brochures, she looked up at Noah and smiled. Like a gentleman, Noah quickly looked away, trying to avoid the view down her beige silk blouse.

Noah stood up and shook Larry's hand and then Karen's. "It was a pleasure meeting you... Karen, is it?" he said to her as the two real estate agents left the office.

"Hey, Little Brother," Scott said, popping his head in the doorway. "Ready for lunch? You can fill me in on the wedding plans."

Just then Karen came dashing back into the office. "I forgot to give you this," she said, handing Noah her business card. "Just in case you need to get a hold of me," she said with a suggestive smile, running back out.

Noah turned the card over and read the message on the back.

The man in the cafeteria line in front of Scott and Noah kept looking back at them, accidentally knocking over his cup of soda. As the man attempted to clean up the spill with a couple of small paper napkins, Noah ran in back of the counter and grabbed a dishtowel, getting down on his hands and knees to wipe it up.

"Wow," the man said, amazed. "I can't believe the owner's son would actually do that for me. Thanks."

Noah stood up and handed the wet towel to the server behind the counter. "It's nothing, really," he said, pouring another soda from the fountain machine and handing it to him. "Careful with this one," he said jokingly.

Scott paid for both his and Noah's meal, sitting down at an empty table next to a group of white-haired women.

"The wedding is only a month away," Noah confided in his brother, "and I'm not even looking forward to it. All we do is argue, and we haven't even had sex in three months, ever since I handed her that frickin' prenup, which, by the way, still isn't signed yet."

"Shhh... keep it down," Scott warned, looking over his shoulder at the elderly secretaries, who by their sudden silence were likely eavesdropping.

"And if she doesn't sign it, then what?" Noah asked.

"Then you don't get married," Scott insisted.

"*PERFECT.* Then we won't have anything to argue about then, will we?"

"What are you arguing about?"

"She argues about the prenup, and I argue about the sex."

"Sex?"

"Yeah, sex. I HAVE TO HAVE SEX, SCOTT; I HAVE TO HAVE IT !" Noah exclaimed loudly, grabbing hold of Scott's shirt. Glancing over at the old ladies, who were gawking at him with their mouths open, he smiled awkwardly and let go of Scott's shirt.

"To tell you the truth," Noah said quietly, "it seems like we're arguing about every little thing these days. Isn't the arguing supposed to start *after* you get married?"

"Look, Noah, if you're having second thoughts, if there's any doubt whatsoever in your mind, then you've got to postpone the wedding. You don't have to cancel it, just give yourself more time to work things out."

"I can't do that to her. She'd be devastated. And over what? The prenup?"

"In case you haven't noticed, we don't live in a utopian society. Stop being so idealistic and start being practical. You've got to postpone the wedding."

"How do I do that? The invitations have already gone out, and Dad has pretty much paid for everything already."

"Forget the money; it's water under the bridge. Stop worrying about other people and start thinking about yourself. Believe me, you don't want the foundation of your marriage to be based on this."

"You know, despite all the problems we've been having lately, deep down beneath all the arguing, I'm still just as madly in love with her as the day we first met. If I postpone the wedding now, she'll probably never marry me. And for the rest of my life I'll be looking back, wondering if I made a terrible mistake, regretting it. No... I have to go through with this. I have to find out for myself," Noah said, glancing at the white-haired ladies, who turned quickly back to their bag lunches.

"I don't give a damn about your house, your boat, your precious toys," Robin sobbed as Noah packed a suit into a suitcase on their bed. "You should know that about me by now. You think I'm with you because of your money? Is that it?" Noah kept on packing without looking at her. "Well it's not it. I love *you*, not your goddamn money. It's not about how many dollars you have or what you own; it's about who you love. And I love *people*, Noah, not things. I guess you really don't know me that well after all. No..." she said, shaking her head, "*I* don't want your money... but I do know who does. Just think of all the desperate people you could feed or shelter simply by selling your boat or living in a smaller house. Wouldn't that make you feel great about yourself? Helping complete strangers in need?"

She looked at him packing his suitcase absently, and she let out a scream of frustration. "I wish you didn't have any money. I wish you were poor, just like me." Noah stopped packing and looked at her. "That's right. You heard me. I wish you poverty. POVERTY. So every morning when you open your eyes and see me lying next to you, you'd know... you'd know that the only reason why I love you so damn much is because of one thing and one thing only: your beautiful soul," she said, her voice softening. "It's your soul I'm in love with, Noah, not your money."

Noah continued to pack. "You can keep your precious things," she continued, shaking her head. "I don't want them. But please... please don't make me sign that horrible paper. It doesn't make me feel safe in this house. Don't you see how important that is to me? I need to feel safe here."

"I'll be back from Las Vegas on Monday," he said, zipping up his suitcase. "We can continue our talk then," he said, taking his suitcase and leaving without kissing her good-bye.

Posters of shopping centers on large, lit-up displays framed the spacious Hartman Enterprises booth at the Las Vegas Convention Center, featuring the large mixed-use development model from Jerry's office. With spotlights shining down on it, the replica of Hartman Place included one million square feet of upscale open-air shopping and dining, a water fountain with a synchronized light and music show, a movie theater, and two 30-story mirrored buildings, one for office space and one for luxury condos. Larry and his entourage spotted Noah standing under the *Hartman Enterprises* banner and headed toward him.

"This is my boss, Charlie Wentworth, VP of Sales and Leasing," Larry said, introducing him to Noah. "And you've met my assistant, Karen."

"Very impressive," Charlie praised, glancing at the model as he shook Noah's hand. "We look forward to representing you on this," he said, handing him a business card.

"It was Max's baby," Noah said, staring blankly at the model.

"A bunch of us are going to Top Of The World for dinner tonight — top floor of the Stratosphere Hotel. Care to join us?" Larry asked.

"Sure, why not?" he said as Karen put on a smile. "I've never eaten there before."

"The reservation's for seven," Larry added.

"Okay, thanks. See you tonight," Noah said, waving to them as they left the booth.

Noah took out his brown business card binder and put Charlie's card in the next available slot, one slot below Karen's business card. He took out her card and read the back: *My cell 563-2213. Call me day or <u>NIGHT!</u> Karen* ♥

The waiter brought over a couple of bottles of wine and started filling everyone's glasses as Larry, Charlie, Noah, Karen, and two other agents sat at the table, 800 feet above the Las Vegas Strip.

"Oh, look…" Karen exclaimed, pointing toward the window and leaning into Noah, placing her hand on his thigh. "Isn't it breathtaking?"

Noah took in the beautiful vista of the Las Vegas skyline, and took a sip of wine. She removed her hand and picked up the bottle of wine, refilling his glass.

"Where are you staying?" Larry asked Noah, opening the door to the taxi for him after dinner.

"The Four Seasons. How about you?" Noah said, getting in.

"We are too."

"Great; hop in. We'll share," Noah said, sliding over as Karen got in next, her leg rubbing up against his as the cab pulled away.

Noah opened the door to his hotel room and looked at the phone on the nightstand — no messages. He took off his suit jacket and tie, and sat down on the bed, removing his shoes and rubbing his feet. As he picked up the phone and started dialing home, there was a knock at the door. He put the phone down and walked sluggishly to the door.

"Will you please open this for me?" Karen asked, handing him a bottle of Taittinger Champagne as she barged into the room. "A lady should never have to open Champagne all by herself."

Noah looked at the bottle and then looked at her, hesitating as he shut the door behind him. "I think I should inform you, Karen, I'm kind of wiped out..."

She put on a fake pout, and Noah laughed. "Oh, boy... what am I getting myself into?" he said, peeling the gold foil off of the bottle, shaking his head.

The cork popped loudly as it flew off the bottle, with bubbly pouring all over the carpet. They laughed as Noah ran with the overflowing bottle into the bathroom, coming back out with a white hand towel draped around the neck of the bottle. His mouth dropped open.

Karen was standing there in a black lace teddy, her little black dress nestled around her feet. He smiled nervously as she stepped out of her dress and sauntered toward him seductively. Her perfectly toned body and tantalizing smile mesmerized him as she put her arms around his neck. Noah physically longed for her — what man wouldn't? Especially not a man in his prime who hadn't had sex in three months.

As she moved in for the kiss, the phone started ringing, breaking him out of his trance. Noah stood there, frozen, staring at the phone as it continued ringing. A moment later there was silence, and the red message light came on.

"I couldn't go through with it. Despite the problems we were having, I was still deeply in love with Robin."

Noah removed her arms from around his neck and walked toward the door. "Perhaps this isn't such a good idea after all," he said, picking her dress up off the floor and holding it out to her.

"Maybe Noah's just a little tense," she suggested, a fake pout on her face as she did a catwalk over to him and knelt down in front of him. "Let me help with that," she insisted, unzipping his pants.

Noah grabbed her hands and pulled her to her feet, zipping up his pants.

"I'm sorry, Karen, but I just can't go through with it. After all, I'm still engaged to be married. You understand, don't you?"

Karen let out an exasperated breath as she stepped back into her dress. Noah held the door open for her as she stormed out of the room. "Asshole," she called over her shoulder as he shut the door.

"Hello," Robin answered the phone, relieved to hear Noah's voice on the other end as she lay on the bed in her terrycloth robe, tissues in hand, eyes swollen from crying.

It was Monday evening when the plane landed back in Providence. Soon after, Noah walked through the front door of his house, his briefcase in one hand and his suitcase in the other. He set the briefcase down and walked over to Brittany sitting on the sofa in the living room, watching her favorite animated Disney classic on TV.

"Hi, sweetie," he said, kissing the top of her head. "Where's Mommy?"

"Upstairs lying down."

Noah walked upstairs with his suitcase and glanced into Brittany's room as he passed by it. He stopped and walked back into her room. Robin was staring at the mural on the wall, holding the photograph from the zoo in one hand, some folded papers in the other hand.

"Hey, I'm back," he said, standing in the doorway.

"Let's get out of here, Noah," she pleaded, setting the frame on the dresser, looking at him. "Sell the house, the boat, whatever you have to do, and let's get the hell out of here. I hate Rhode Island, and I don't want to live here anymore."

"You know I can't do that; I have responsibilities. Where else can I make six figures, large bonuses, a company car... We have everything we need right here to live a very comfortable life together."

"Who do you think you're fooling? You hate your job, and you know it. Your parents bribe you to keep you exactly where they want you, and you subscribe to it."

"My parents are very generous people. They only want what's best for me."

"Maybe so, but they treat you like a six-year-old child on strings. And who the hell wants to live like a puppet, anyway?"

Noah walked over to her, the Pinocchio poster hanging in the background. "Okay, you're right... I hate my job. And it really sucks that my parents treat me like a child, trying to make all my decisions for me. But all that goes away the moment I step through the door, coming home to you and Britt here in our little castle by the sea."

"You just don't see it, do you? For God's sake, Noah, you only go around once in this world, and you're blowing your only chance at it. Do you really want to be eighty years old, dying in some bed somewhere someday, and wondering where all the years went? Feeling bad for yourself, and blaming your parents, ironically, for robbing you of the one life that they gave you? Regretting that you never made a change when you could have? Now imagine that some angel hears all your senseless bickering about how you squandered your life away, and decides to send you back some forty years or so for a do-over, making you think that it was all just some kind of weird dream."

"WAKE UP, NOAH ! No one gets a do-over in this lifetime. Every day you waste is one less day to change your fate. It's time to cut the cord with your parents, and time to start living. It's *your* life, Noah — not theirs."

"Robin, I'd love to be able to do that... but I can't. The price is just too great."

"Oh, really? And what exactly is the price of freedom these days? The writing's on the wall, literally, written in large letters on the back of your boat. It's a cry for help, and you know it. Well, guess what? Here I am to help. Why? Because I love you. Think of me as that angel forty years from now coming to you in that strange dream of yours. And all of a sudden you wake up, right here, right now, in this time and space. Well, congratulations, Noah, you're not eighty years old anymore, and you still have your whole life ahead of you. So what are you going to do now that you have a second chance at life? You can't blame the same people twice, you know. The decision to either live your own life here in the present or allow someone else to live it for you is ultimately yours to make. So what's it going to be?"

Noah was about to speak, but stopped himself.

"Just what exactly are you afraid of? Living? Admit it: you're afraid to live."

Noah didn't know what to say. Agreeing with her was one thing; having the courage to live in the real world was quite another. He knew that if he ever quit his job with the company, his parents would no longer reward him financially, and he'd be forced to give up all the finer things in life that he'd grown so accustomed to.

"Can't you see how this place is smothering us? Let's get a fresh start someplace new, away from the influence of your parents, away from all this stuff that binds you. You don't have to allow your parents' money to enslave you anymore if you don't want it to. The secret to unlock your golden handcuffs is something your parents don't ever want you to know about. Aren't you at all curious to know what that is?"

Noah waited for the answer.

"The secret is... there's no key, Noah. The only place they're locked is in your head. And all you have to do to free yourself is just take them off."

Noah walked over to the bookcase built into the side of the castle-bed and picked up a book, staring at it blankly.

"It's time for the prince to finally break free, take his maiden by his side, and get the hell out of the kingdom that reigns over him," Robin said, looking at the Cinderella mural on the wall. "He can always start a new kingdom somewhere else in some distant land, where the prince can be king, and the maiden, queen."

"Robin, I love you, and what you're saying has a lot of merit... but what you're asking me to do: just pack up and rid myself of all my worldly possessions, everything that I've worked hard for in the last sixteen years... Well, I just can't do that. Where would we go? What would I do for a job? Where would the money come from?"

"I don't care about the money; I care about *you*. Just think, for once in your life you can set your life's compass on true north, true to who you really are. You can finally do whatever it is you've always dreamed of doing — whatever makes you happy. I'll even work two jobs if that's what it takes. Don't you get it, Noah? No matter where we live, we'd still be in our little castle. Heck, I'd live in a shack in the woods if I had to, and I'd be happy. You know why?"

Noah shook his head.

"Because I'd be with *you*."

Noah stood there staring at the *PINOCCHIO* book in his hand. Robin looked at him and shook her head.

"I guess what *you* say goes, huh?" she conceded, having no more energy left to fight. "What *I* want means nothing?"

He put the book back on the shelf and shrugged.

"Just forget I ever mentioned it, okay?" she said with tears in her eyes, shoving the papers into his gut as she left the room.

Noah unfolded the papers in his hands and stared at it. It was the prenuptial agreement, with smudges from water droplets... smudges from where her tears must have landed. He turned to the last page and looked at it. Robin had signed it.

A loud rumbling noise announced her arrival as Robin's silver car pulled up to the curb in front of Emergency Family Services in downtown Providence, the muffler dragging along the ground.

Theresa ran up to Robin as soon as she entered the building. "You're never going to believe this ! Some anonymous donor just mailed us a check for $257,000 !" she said excitedly, handing Robin the note that accompanied the check, written on butterfly-themed stationery.

"WOW, that's amazing," Robin said as she glanced at the note.

"We can finally build the addition and add all the beds we need. No more turning people away into the street. Isn't that great?"

"Yeah... that's really great," Robin replied with a subdued smile.

Smooth Sailing

*J*une 10th, 1996 turned out to be a beautiful day for sailing, with hardly a cloud in the sky. A sleek, black helicopter was flying just above the Newport Bridge with its door wide open. Inside the helicopter, a videographer motioned for the pilot to fly lower so he could get a different angle on the sailboat he was filming, which was sailing briskly toward the expansive structure. The name on the transom read *Rockin' Robin*.

Noah was at the helm with Robin tucked underneath his arm. She was wearing a white wedding gown and a big smile. Her long red hair was flowing freely in the breeze. Noah, Scott, Jerry, Zeke, Jake, and two other men were wearing black tuxedos. Julie, Sharon, and two other young women were wearing long lavender bridesmaids dresses. Miriam and Mary were also onboard, wearing elegant floral dresses. Brittany wore a pretty pink dress covered by a purple life preserver. Scott and Sharon's two boys, David and Sam, were wearing orange life preservers as they sat on the port side hanging onto the railing, their feet dangling off the side. Unlike the others onboard who were smiling and enjoying the moment, Jerry and Miriam seemed to be just along for the ride.

"Isn't it bad luck to change the name of the boat?" Robin asked worriedly. "Doesn't that mean the boat's going to sink or something?"

"Nah, that's just a silly superstition," Noah replied. "The boat's never going to sink... not as long as I'm captain, anyway," he said, giving Robin a reassuring kiss.

They dropped anchor next to Rose Island in Newport Harbor, and everybody moved forward to the bow. With the bride and groom leaning against the pulpit rail, the ceremony commenced.

"I now pronounce you husband and wife," the Justice of the Peace concluded fifteen minutes later. "You may kiss the bride."

Bending backwards like that famous picture of a nurse being kissed in Times Square by a sailor, Robin succumbed to Noah's passionate kiss. Transmitted wirelessly from the helicopter above, the longwinded kiss was broadcast on a large video monitor on the middle deck of the 180-foot blue-hulled ship anchored beside them. With a burst of applause from the hundred wedding guests aboard the *Hartman E*, waiters popped Champagne corks over a pyramid of Champagne glasses while the band jumped right into playing Reggae music. The guests were dressed casually in Hawaiian shirts, shorts, and floral sundresses. Many had drinks in their hands as they watched the ceremony unfold on the large video monitor, while others watched directly through binoculars.

As the bride and groom came back to life from their kiss, the wedding party started ripping off their clothes, revealing bathing suits underneath. Screaming in jubilation as they jumped off the teak swim platform into the cool water, the guests onboard the ship broke out laughing.

"May I help you... Mr. Hartman?" Robin asked with a titillating look as Noah swam up to his bikini-clad bride.

"That's very nice of you to offer — Mrs. Hartman — but I think I'll just help myself, thank you," he said before diving down, removing her white garter from around her thigh with his teeth. Climbing swiftly back up onto the sailboat, he flung the garter out over the water, where three single groomsmen were waiting for it. Jake was the lucky one to catch it on the fly.

Brittany handed Robin the bouquet as she climbed back onto the sailboat, throwing it over her shoulder at the three single bridesmaids who were treading water. Julie swam vigorously to retrieve it before it sank. Swimming over to her with a sly smile, Jake dove down and slipped the garter onto Julie's leg as she screamed with laughter.

As the black helicopter landed on the helipad on the upper deck, a small transport boat delivered everyone from Noah's sailboat over to the ship. The band started playing **I Will Be Here,** and everyone was called into the main salon. Noah walked over to the middle of the dance floor, turned around, and held his hand out toward his new bride, who was walking toward him.

"Here I am... Mr. Hartman," she said upon arrival.

"Here I am... Mrs. Hartman," he responded as he took her in his arms to slow dance.

As the slow song came to an end, the band jumped right into playing the fast-paced **Hora.** Everyone rushed to the center of the dance floor, holding hands as they formed a circle around the newlyweds, dancing festively in a circular motion around them. The groomsmen pulled two chairs into the middle of the circle and

106

seated the bride and groom, raising them up into the air while they remained connected by holding onto opposite ends of a beige cloth.

Later on, the wedding cake was brought out, and Robin cut the first piece. Smushing it all over his face, she managed to miss Noah's mouth entirely. With cake dropping off of his face, and seeking sweet revenge, Noah took a large chunk of cake and held it up in the air for all to see. With the audience cheering him on, he lovingly shoved it *all* into her mouth, every last bit, except for the morsel that didn't quite fit, which he graciously placed on the tip of her nose. They ate what was left off of their faces, followed by a long, messy kiss.

The warm glow from the setting sun silhouetted the ship as music and laughter echoed throughout the harbor.

The Curse Of Jean Pierre

A small island-hopper plane took off from the Saint Maarten airport. It offered one seat on each side of the aisle, a cabin not tall enough to stand up in, and no flight attendant. A white Igloo cooler filled with soft drinks was secured in the cabin for those thirsty enough to dare unbuckle in flight.

As the plane approached the neighboring island, it began its descent. Without a cockpit door, Noah and Robin held onto each other tightly as they watched the pilots fly the small aircraft downward at a steep 45-degree angle just above the treetops of the mountainous terrain. Noah wondered where the horizon had gone as the runway — growing ever so large by the second — filled the entire forward view through the front windshield. At the last possible moment, the plane leveled off and touched down. As the plane raced down the short runway, the brakes were applied, and the plane started slowing down, coming to a stop at the very end, where two topless women walked in front of the plane on a white sand beach.

"*Bienvenue à Saint-Barth,*" the pilot announced proudly as the plane veered right, heading toward the small terminal. "Welcome to Saint Barts !"

Perched on top of a huge rock at the end of Saint Jean Beach, Hotel Eden Rock jutted out into the bay. Surrounded entirely by ocean, every room was waterfront, each with its own theme. Noah and Robin entered the spacious Howard Hughes Suite, their eyes drawn to the turquoise ocean surrounding their room. Rose petals covered the bed, and Dom Pérignon sat on ice. As the cork flew off the bottle, their clothes fell to the floor around their ankles, and they lay down on the bed.

"I love you, Mrs. Hartman," Noah said as he carefully poured a drop of cold Champagne onto her body.

"I love you, too... Mr. Hartman," she responded with a flinch and a giggle as he slowly sipped it off.

The next day, Robin was sitting in the passenger seat of a red Jeep Wrangler as Noah hugged a cliff that traced the contours of the shoreline. With her hand clutching the safety handle tightly and her teeth clenched, they drove along the narrow road with no guardrails and down the steep incline to the secluded beach below.

Noah removed his shirt and started chasing after her down the vacant beach. Robin screamed as she took off running, removing her shirt and throwing it back at him in an attempt to evade her eager pursuer. She stopped, turned around, and motioned for timeout. She removed her shorts and threw them at him, bolting off again, attempting a daring escape into the open sea. She screamed, laughing as he caught up to her in the waist-deep turquoise water. As he kissed the side of her neck, she removed her bra and threw it back onto the sandy beach. After all, Saint Barts was a French island, and when in Rome...

Back at the beach that bordered the hotel, they ordered two frozen fruity drinks from the grass tiki hut, while kite surfers flew over waves and into the air in the background. Strolling by the pool in their bathing suits, Robin asked to taste Noah's drink.

"Mmmm," she said, savoring the sweet, tropical taste. "It's delectable," she continued, her hips moving fast and hard to the side, bumping Noah into the pool. She lay down on her lounge chair and took a sip from both drinks, smiling victoriously.

"Hey," Noah complained, swimming over to the side of the pool, "that's *my* drink."

Robin shrugged as Noah splashed water in her direction, sharing a laugh.

Later in the day, they held hands as they meandered in and out of the small shops that lined the sidewalks selling Caribbean apparel. "I want to buy you a souvenir every day that we're here, so you'll always remember this place," Noah announced, purchasing her a sexy, backless dress.

Further down the road, they ate ice cream as they strolled along the main road into town, admiring the numerous 200-foot+ mega-yachts docked there.

Soothing music was playing softly in a candlelit room as they lay next to each other on padded tables, lying on their stomachs with plush, white towels spread across their butts. Warm, smooth rocks were rubbed all over their oily bodies as they relaxed. "Mmmm," Robin moaned with pleasure. "Does this feeling ever have to end?"

On the terrace outside their room, a private dinner was served to them as the setting sun colored the ocean-background red and purple. They drank wine and reminisced about their memorable day. After an indulgent dessert, Noah brought the bottle of wine inside the room and put a CD into the boombox. As **I Will Be Here** started playing, Noah took Robin in his arms and danced her over to the bed, unzipping her sexy, backless dress.

The next day, Noah, Robin, and three other couples were sailing on a large catamaran on a temperate afternoon. Lying on what looked like a large mesh trampoline making up the mid-section of the bow, they looked down through the porous fabric at the billowing water beneath the swift boat, laughing hysterically when an occasional spray of water splashed up at them.

The catamaran dropped its anchor in a secluded horseshoe-shaped cove. The water was flat in the lee, and a steep cliff rose up from the nearby white sand beach. The captain of the boat was French and gorgeous. Tan and in great shape, he had long blonde wavy hair and a chiseled face. He was wearing a Hawaiian shirt — open, of course — along with beige shorts and Caribbean sandals.

"My name is Jean Pierre," said the captain with a French accent. "Before you *départ*, I must tell you one thing, *s'il vous plaît*. Whatever you do, don't touch nothing in ze sea, okay? It's bad luck. I cannot say to you of ze last person who disturbed something, but I tell you this. It was, how you say... *catastrophe*. So don't do it, *d'accord*? Now go... go and enjoy your big adventure."

"Ooh la la," Noah teased softly in Robin's ear with an exaggerated French accent, "Beware of zee curse of zee capitaine Jean Pierre." Robin laughed, hitting him on the head lightly with a fin.

As the passengers donned fins, snorkels, and masks, they stepped down the fiberglass steps that were molded into the stern and floated off into the balmy water. While the others snorkeled close to the boat, Robin and Noah swam to the nearby beach. Lying at the water's edge, they kissed as the water rolled gently over them. With the catamaran and snorkelers in the distance, they went for a short walk down the beach holding hands.

Back in the warm, crystal clear turquoise water, they floated effortlessly with their arms and legs outstretched. Robin took out a disposable underwater camera and started taking pictures of the vibrant, colorful fish swimming all around them. Suddenly Noah spotted a lone sand dollar sitting undisturbed on the ocean floor below. He tapped Robin on the shoulder and motioned toward it. Diving down, he picked up the sand dollar and resurfaced, proudly holding out his prize as

Robin took an underwater picture of him. He handed it over to her, and after a brief underwater examination, she handed it back to him.

What happened next would prove to be a defining moment in Noah's life. Seemingly safe and secure in his hand, the sand dollar suddenly exploded into a thousand tiny grains of sand, disappearing through his fingers into the vast sea around him. They looked at each other, worried. *What now of the curse of Jean Pierre?* they wondered.

"Our amazing week together in Saint Barts was suddenly shrouded in mystery. We had been warned that it was bad luck to disturb anything in the sea, but that was just a silly superstition... right? At any rate, it was time to leave paradise behind and head for home. The honeymoon was over."

The Problem With Memories

$\mathcal{J}$ony had a kind of arrogance about him, gawking at Robin as she reclined in the chair in his office and straightened her blouse.

"So how was your honeymoon?" he asked, laying a picture frame on his desk face down.

"Perfect... like a fairy tale," she replied. "Which reminds me, did you ever see **Pretty Woman**, the movie?"

Before he could answer, she continued, "Julia Roberts wanted the fairy tale, remember?"

Tony nodded.

"Well, that's what I got — the fairy tale. The only problem is... it's a frickin' fairy tale. I mean... that stuff only happens in the movies, right?"

Tony opened his mouth, but Robin spoke first. "I keep thinking any minute the clock's gonna strike twelve, and I'm gonna get tossed aside, sent back to where I came from, while Prince Charming over here rides off into the sunset with someone else on the back of his fancy white horse. I hate feeling insecure like this. It's a terrible feeling..." she said, shaking her head, "expecting that someday everything is going to be taken away from me, ya know what I mean? And where does that leave me, huh?" she said, looking at Tony, waiting for an answer.

He paused to observe her body language, and figuring it was safe to speak, he started to talk.

"ABANDONED, that's where !" she shouted. "I don't know, what do you think? Is it really too good to be true?" she asked desperately.

Tony sat there wordlessly.

"WELL?" she prodded. "Aren't you going to say anything?"

Tony got up from behind his desk, stood in front of her, and looked into her eyes.

"Robin, you trust me, right?"

She nodded.

"As your psychiatrist, I'm trained to give you expert advice to help *you*, not me. Even though advice may sometimes be hard to swallow, it wouldn't be fair to you if I held anything back; don't you agree?"

She nodded again.

Tony walked slowly behind her, putting his hands into her long, silky hair, lightly stroking it to the ends. He lowered his head so his face was next to hers. "I hate to tell you this, Robin," he said softly into her ear, "but if you think it's too good to be true... then it is," he said, looking down her blouse at her shapely cleavage.

Robin sat there frozen.

"Here's a script for a new medication that will help open up your mind to new possibilities," he said, sticking the slip of paper into her hand, and leaving his hand on top of hers momentarily.

"Now tell me again about your childhood," he commanded, walking back behind his desk, sitting down and gawking at her.

Robin took a pill and poured herself a glass of wine, her hands shaking as she went outside to smoke a cigarette. Upstairs, Noah was reading the last page of *PINOCCHIO* to Brittany, who was cuddled up under his arm on the purple, castle-shaped bunk bed.

"'Who worked all this magic, father?' Pinocchio asked. 'You,' Geppetto answered. 'I wonder where the old Pinocchio has gone?' Pinocchio asked. 'Look over there,' Geppetto replied, pointing to a large wooden puppet slumped against a chair. Its head was nodding to one side, its arms dangling uselessly. Pinocchio stared at his former self for a long while. 'How funny it was to be made of wood,' he said to himself at last, 'and how splendid it is to be alive !' THE. END," Noah said, kissing Brittany on the forehead and crawling out. "Sweet dreams," he said as he put the book away and turned off the light.

"Just one more story, please..."

"But Britt, I've still got work to do. My Six Month Plan was due six months ago."

"Can't you just do it six months from now?" He exhaled. "Oh, please, Noah, please. You're getting a lot better at reading, and who knows, I might even fall asleep this time," she said encouragingly, pretending to yawn. "I think one more story might just do it."

"Okay, Brit," he said, laughing, "You win. But I'm leaving the lights off," he said, lying back down on the bed, recounting his slightly twisted version of *THE THREE BEARS* off the top of his head.

"And the daddy bear says," then switching to a deep, low voice, "someone's been sleeping in my bed, hmmmmmmmmmmmm." Speaking normally again, "And the mommy bear says," then switching to a sweet, feminine voice, "Oh d-d-d-d-dear, someone's been sleeping in my bed, and I have no idea whom it possibly could have been. Hmmmmmmm, let me think for a second... Nope, not a clue." Speaking normally again, "And the baby bear says," then switching to a high, squeaky voice, "Um, excuse me, excuse me, hello, hello... someone's been sleeping in my bed, and um, well you see, that someone... that someone... IS STILL THERE !"

Noah looked down at Brittany, who was finally fast asleep. He pulled his arm out slowly from underneath her head and inched his way off of the bed so as not to wake her. He pulled the covers up over her, kissed her head lightly, and tiptoed out of the room. Brittany opened her eyes and smiled as she rolled over, adjusting her pillow.

Meanwhile, Robin was pacing outside on the deck. She took a puff of her cigarette and looked down at the glass of wine shaking in her hand. As she stared at the glass, she began to remember a disturbing memory from her childhood that had long since been forgotten.

Just three years old, Robin was standing next to her mother in the shadowy foyer. The glass in the sidelight window suddenly exploded, the pieces shattering to the floor as a gun in a man's hand smashed through.

The wine glass in Robin's hand suddenly exploded, the pieces shattering to the deck.

Robin and Mary watched in horror as the man's hand inched through the broken window and slowly reached for the doorknob. Mary snatched up her little girl and ran quietly down the hall. Holding the gun out in front of him, he opened the door and stepped slowly into the gloomy foyer, looking around and listening for sound.

With Robin sitting quietly in the passenger seat of the man's dilapidated station wagon, her mother put her finger to her lips and started yanking wires out from beneath the dash. With her hand full of wires, she began touching each one to what looked in the dark to be the red wire. Upon contact with the yellow wire, the starter began spinning the flywheel around uselessly, making a whining sound. Mary glanced up at the rearview mirror and saw the gunman dashing out of the house. As Mary rifled through the last few wires, Robin screamed. Holding the last wire in her hand, she looked over her shoulder at the man with the toothless grin, who was tapping on the window with his gun.

As the window beside her head exploded, Mary touched the purple wire against the red wire. With ignition and a sparkplug backfire, the tires started burning rubber, and the door opened. Running alongside the car, the man held onto the open door with one hand and grabbed the back of Mary's head with the other. Robin continued screaming as the man slammed her mother's head against the steering wheel.

Suddenly silent, she and her mother glared at each other, the door and man having been blown off the car by the tree it had sideswiped. In the rearview mirror, the man stood up and raised his gun as they turned onto the street, disappearing into the night.

"Are you okay?" Noah asked, walking through the sliding door onto the deck. "What just happened?"

Robin snapped out of her flashback visibly shaken, putting her bleeding hand to her mouth and sucking it.

"No, Noah, I'm not okay."

"Does it hurt?" he asked, taking her hand and examining it.

"What? My hand? No, my hand's fine," she said, pulling her hand away to pick up the pieces.

"Then what's the matter? I don't understand," he said as he helped her pick up the broken glass.

"Of course you don't understand," she said, shaking her head. "You never did, and you never will."

"Robin, I'm your husband. Of course I understand you."

"No, believe me... *you don't*."

"Then enlighten me."

They went back inside and threw the broken pieces of glass into the garbage. Noah opened a drawer and removed an emergency kit, applying a Band-Aid to her hand as she poured herself another glass of wine with her other hand.

"I want to explain it to you, but I don't know how," she said, looking at the bandage on her hand. "I don't know what's wrong with me. It's like I need a new drug or something, you know what I mean?"

"What are you talking about? You don't need a drug. You're fine. You're just having a bad day, that's all."

"Oh, okay, Noah, if you say so," she said sarcastically, giving him an exasperated look as she sat down on the sofa with her drink. She took a sip and set her glass down on the side table. "The problem with memories is... you can't bury them forever. No matter how hard I try, they always come back to haunt me. Every last one of them... except for one."

"What the hell are you talking about?"

"I was just a child."

"What happened to you when you were a child, Robin?"

"I don't know."

"What do you mean, you don't know?"

"I DON'T KNOW, OKAY?" she yelled. "I mean... I just don't remember. I was young, very young. It was horrible... frightening."

"What do you mean, frightening?"

"It had to do with my mom... no... my mom and I."

"What happened, Robin?" he asked softly, sitting down beside her.

"I told you, I don't remember !" she exclaimed, raising her voice. "I don't remember, okay? I just don't remember," she said softly, crying.

Noah put his arms around her, trying unsuccessfully to comfort her.

"I remember thinking, Maybe she was right; maybe there was something about her that I didn't understand. Maybe there was something about her that I'd never understand."

The following morning, Robin pulled up to the trailer park in her new, beige Range Rover, and knocked on the door to her parents' trailer. Mary fixed her a glass of lemonade in the kitchen area while Zeke watched TV in the salon.

"I need to know what happened when I was a kid. It's important, Mom."

"Shhh... I don't want Zeke to hear," her mother said quietly, looking over at him. "Let's go talk outside."

Once outside, Mary took out a pack of cigarettes and offered one to her daughter. They both lit up.

"Ya know, I've always dreaded this day," her mother admitted, shaking her head. "Just let it go. Let the memory rest in peace."

"I can't, Mom. You have to tell me. I deserve to know."

Mary stared at her daughter for a moment. "Okay. Here goes," she said, blowing a smoke ring. "After your dad abandoned us and took off with that skanky waitress, this guy from your dad's shop started comin' round to check up on me, ya know, to make sure I was okay, or so he said. He seemed nice enough, although I always wondered why he didn't have any teeth. Then one day, he knocked on my door, all agitated and everything, so I invited him in for some lemonade. No sooner did I open the door, he rushed in, put a knife to my throat, and dragged me by my hair into the bedroom. He raped me, Robin. He raped me while you played in front of the bed." Robin's mouth hung open in shock. "You had no idea what was happening, you were just a baby. He said if I screamed, or if I ever called the police, he'd hunt me down wherever I was, kill you right in front of me, then kill me and burn the evidence."

"Oh my God, Mom," Robin said, horrified.

"When he finally finished what he came to do, he went over to the fridge and was pissed that there weren't no beer. He grabbed some money out of my purse, said he was goin' to the liquor store. Told me to start dinner, even kissed you good-bye as he was leavin'. Called you Robbie Robin. As soon as he left, I threw you into the car and took off. I left everything behind, everything."

"Where'd you go, Mom? What happened next?"

"Not long after, we were staying with my brother over in Winnetka, when he showed up looking for us, this time with a gun. For the next two years, we went on the run, always looking over our shoulders. That's when I met Zeke, and he moved us out here to Rhode Island to open up Zeke's Diner."

"What's this guy's name? What ever happened to him? Where is he now?"

"Well..." she said, hesitantly, "he did find us again... many years later. You were sixteen, so sweet, so innocent. You really don't remember any of this, do you?"

Robin shook her head.

"Believe me, Robin, there's a reason why the good Lord made you forget all about this... Now that's enough ramblin'," she said impatiently. "I've told you too much already. Leave it be."

"But Mom — "

"BURY IT!" Mary said sternly, dropping her cigarette to the ground and stomping on it, twisting her foot back and forth. "You heard what you needed to hear, now bury it," Mary said, turning and tramping back to the trailer, the screen door slamming behind her.

A Casualty Of Words

Robin and Noah were dining alfresco at Trattoria Simpatico in Jamestown as a jazz trio played instrumental music under an old beech tree in the background. The waiter removed an empty bottle of Pinot Grigio from the table and walked away.

"What's wrong?" Noah asked, watching Robin push the roasted potatoes around her plate. "You barely touched your food."

"Sorry, I just have a lot on my mind."

"Like what?"

"It's no big deal. I was just thinking about what my shrink said to me the other day, that's all," she said, looking away.

"*And...* what did he say?"

"Nothing really. Just talked about fairy tales."

Noah took a sip of wine. "I just don't understand you lately," he said, setting the glass down. "Ever since we got back from our honeymoon, you seem distant for some reason. Did I do something wrong?"

"No, you didn't do anything. I told you, I just have a lot on my mind."

"You used to love going out on the boat, and you haven't gone out on it with me once since we got back. For that matter, you won't even hang out on it with me at the dock."

"You spend too much time on that thing as it is."

"The boat's not a bad thing, you know. You treat it like it's some kind of other woman."

"Look, just because you named your expensive yacht after me doesn't mean I have to like it, okay?"

Noah looked at her, puzzled. "And every time I walk up to you to show you the least bit of affectionate, you walk away. You're never interested in making love anymore. It's not so much about the sex as it is about expressing our love for each

119

other in a way that only intimacy can achieve. So what's bothering you? Is it me? Is there anything I can do to help?"

Robin hesitated, took a deep breath, and spoke. "Yeah, there is something you can do to help..."

Noah leaned in.

"You can quit your job and sell your house so we can get far, far away from this place before it's too late," she said boldly, downing the last bit of wine in her glass.

"Is that what this is all about? We've had this discussion lots of times before, and you know I can't do that."

Robin shook her head and looked away.

"And what do you mean, before it's too late?"

"Excuse me, waiter, could I get a doggie bag, please?" she said as the waiter walked toward the table.

Noah waited patiently for the waiter to finish clearing the table. "Why can't you just open up to me and tell me what's really bothering you? You talk to your shrink every Thursday; what does he have to say about all of this?"

"He doesn't usually say too much. He just sits there staring at me with a funny look on his face while I do all the talking."

Noah frowned, interrupted by the waiter returning with the check and the doggie bag.

"I know the perfect thing to get your mind off of it," Noah said, driving Robin's Range Rover home. "The annual Jimmy Buffet dock party," he said excitedly. "Scott and Sharon will be on their boat making their killer margaritas."

"Nah... I'm kind of tired. Let's just go home."

"Come on, it's right up the street. It's a beautiful night. Let's just hang there for a half an hour or so. We can drink margaritas and cuddle up under the stars. I'll even point out some more constellations."

She shook her head.

"Come on, it'll be good for you."

"STOP THE CAR !" she screamed.

"WHAT?" Noah exclaimed, slamming on the brakes, the car coming to an abrupt stop. "What's the matter?"

She jumped out of the car and ran over to a man sitting on the sidewalk. He was perched up against the side of Village Liquors, drinking from a brown paper bag.

"What the hell are you doing?" Noah yelled, lowering the window. "This is a dangerous neighborhood; get back in here," he instructed her, locking his door and glancing at the scantily-clad woman leaning over the side of a car stopped at the light ahead, propositioning the driver.

"It's Harry," Robin called to Noah. "Come on, help me get him into the car."

"*Excuse me?* Who the hell is Harry, and why does he need to get into our car?"

"So we can bring him back to the shelter."

"Are you crazy? That's a half an hour from here," he said, watching Harry attempting to get up, then falling down and rolling over. "Besides, look at him. He's plastered."

She looked down at Harry, then looked beseechingly at Noah. "But he needs our help."

"What he needs is to sleep it off. Tomorrow's another day. I promise you, he'll be just fine; don't worry. Now please... get back in the car."

Robin looked down at Harry and sighed. She knelt and put her hands underneath his torso, trying unsuccessfully to sit him up.

Meanwhile, the pounding bass of rap music became louder and louder. "I don't believe this," Noah murmured, looking in his rear-view mirror at the black 1970 Chevy Impala lowrider with peeling paint that had just pulled up behind him. Noah honked the horn and gestured to Robin. She looked back at him and frowned as she continued to tug on Harry.

"Whatcha doing there, Little Red?" called the large tattooed man sitting in the passenger seat of the Impala. "How 'bout you and me go riding in the hood?" he said with a grin, two of his teeth missing. "We can even visit grandma," he said, snickering at the sexual innuendo.

"Time to get back in the car... NOW !" Noah shouted to Robin.

"Don't pay no attention to the little dude in the fancy whip," said the man getting out of the car with his two ominous-looking cohorts, who also displayed tattoos covering their necks and arms.

"Just go. I'll be fine," Harry slurred, waving her off, slipping back down as he tried to right himself.

"NO. I'm not leaving without you," Robin insisted as she put her hands under his armpits and started pulling him up.

"Shit," Noah said, jumping out of the car, "Could this night get any worse?" He ran over to Robin and helped her lift Harry, walking him back to the car and assisting him into the back seat.

"Hey, Little Red, where ya goin'?" the tattooed man called to Robin. "What about our happy ending? I promise not to bite... well, maybe just a nibble..." he said, laughing with his friends as the Range Rover peeled away.

Heading up the route 95 on-ramp, Robin turned around and handed Harry her doggie bag.

"Thanks, lady. You're more than kind," he said, taking the bag. "Yup, she's a keeper alright," he advised Noah as he stuck his hand into the bag and pulled out a bun. "Mmmm, lobster salad... my favorite !"

"Oh, come on," Noah protested. "He eats lobster?"

Jennifer, Julie's twenty-three-year-old sister, was reading a book to Brittany on the sofa, when Noah and Robin walked through the front door. "Home already?" she questioned, looking up.

Noah walked over to the mahogany cabinet in the butler's pantry and fixed himself a Captain Morgan and Coke, sitting down in the den to watch the end of the Red Sox game as Robin and Jennifer appeared in the doorway.

"Me and Jen are going to Newport for a drink," Robin informed him. "Don't wait up."

"Excuse me? I go through the trouble of hiring a babysitter so *we* can have Date Night, not so the babysitter can have one."

"Jen's not just *any* babysitter, she's a friend of mine. Besides, you already had your turn; now it's mine. Don't forget to read Britt a story before you put her to bed."

"No way. It's our night to spend time together. So come on, let's go to the marina like I originally suggested," he said, standing up and turning off the TV.

"No," she said defiantly. "I'm going out with Jen."

Noah downed the rest of his drink and stormed out of the house, leaving Robin to stay home with Brittany.

"It was such a stupid argument... over nothing, nothing at all. Why didn't I just let her go out with Jen? If only I had let her go..."

Scott handed Noah a large margarita in the cockpit of his Sea Ray flybridge motorboat that was docked at Conanicut Marina, while Sharon talked to a few of her marina friends. Jimmy Buffet was playing on all of the boats as people wearing Hawaiian shirts and drinking frozen drinks partied up and down the dock. Noah thanked Scott as he stepped off the boat, tripping onto the dock. Scott nervously watched his brother stumble down the dock to his sailboat, where it was a little less noisy.

Noah took a big sip from the oversized glass and set it down. Taking the cell phone out of his pocket, he flipped it open and squinted as he dialed a number.

"Please come to the marina," he begged into the phone, slurring his words. "Everyone is having a great time down here — everyone except for me, that is."

"Are you drunk?" Robin asked on the other end.

"Who me? No way. Just a little intoxicated, that's all. So you coming?"

"Sorry, Britt's already in bed."

"Just put her in the car in her pajamas. We can sleep on the boat."

"No, Noah. We're not coming to the boat."

Noah let out a grunt of frustration. "Listen... I want you to come to the boat. Please come to the boat."

"No."

Noah downed the rest of his margarita, wiping his mouth with the back of his hand. "I mean it, Robin. It's a beautiful night, and I want to enjoy it with you. So please put Britt in the car and come on down."

"NO."

"If you love me, you'll come to the boat," he said desperately.

Robin was silent.

"You know... ever since we came back from our honeymoon, everything is so different. I don't think you love me anymore. It's like you hate the boat, and you hate me too. What did *we* ever do to you?"

There was no response.

"THAT'S IT... I GIVE UP ! First the prenup, now this. If you don't get over here right now, then... then I don't want to be married to you anymore," he said, slurring his words.

There was silence on the phone.

"Still there?" he asked.

"Yeah... I'm here," she said softly.

"So, are you coming to the boat or what?"

"No, Noah. I keep telling you, we're not coming to the boat."

He let out a scream, getting Scott's attention from a hundred feet away. "If you don't say you're coming by the time I count to three... I'm going to take off my wedding ring and throw it into the ocean. You hear me?"

No response.

"Okay, it's off my finger now," he said, removing his gold wedding band. "One... two... Are you coming or not?"

No response.

Noah spoke slowly, emphasizing each word. "Are? You? Coming?"

"NO !" Robin shouted.

"THREE !" he screamed, tossing his wedding band into the water, followed by the phone.

Scott said something to Sharon and headed down the dock toward Noah's boat.

"I was so angry at that moment. And a moment later... I was so afraid. What had I done?"

Noah stumbled around, knocking over his glass as the sea swallowed up the gold band. Noah dove into the water, belly flopping with a big splash. Seconds later, Scott appeared in the water next to him. He put his arms around him and used his feet to push off the sandy bottom, pulling Noah back to the surface.

As he awoke on the deck of his sailboat the following morning, a light drizzle fell on Noah's face, and dense fog blanketed the marina. Wearing the clothes he had on the night before, he sat up and put his hand to his aching head, suddenly noticing that his wedding ring was no longer there. "Shit. What did I do?" he muttered to himself.

"It doesn't matter that I didn't mean the hurtful things I said that night, because it was too late, the damage had already been done. And when I woke up, when the smoke had cleared, the one person I loved most in this world lay wounded before me, a

casualty of my words. I prayed to God that the wounds would heal. But sometimes wounds are just too deep, and sometimes... wounds are fatal."

Cigarette butts littered the deck as Robin paced back and forth, smoking a cigarette. Noah slid open the door and walked over to her, his head down.

"I'm so sorry, Robin. Please forgive me," he said, handing her a bouquet of Stop & Shop roses.

"It's too late, Noah," she informed him, refusing the flowers. "You said the one thing you never should have said to me. It's not something you can't take back, and now I'll never feel safe here... never."

"But when I said I didn't want to be married anymore, I didn't mean it. I said it out of anger... and I was drunk. I love you, and I want to spend the rest of my life with you."

"Well, you should have thought of that before you said it. What do you expect me to do now, live here knowing that the next time you get pissed off again, me and Britt will end up getting tossed out on the street? The hell with that."

"No. It won't be like that, I promise. I'll get help. We can use Tony for marriage counseling. Whatever it takes to stay married, I'll do it. I made a horrible mistake last night, and I realize you may never forgive me for it, but please, Robin, let's find a way to make this work. You've got to give me a second chance to make things right."

She looked at him, then looked down at his left hand. "So where's your wedding ring, Noah?"

Noah gulped, looking at her without answering.

As always, Robin looked very attractive for her appointment with her psychiatrist. Tony tried to rally her as she sat there uncertainly. "I'm so proud of you," he said, smiling. "You've come so far. Now you have to finish it."

"I don't know... maybe I should give him one more chance."

"WHY? So he can hurt you all over again? No way, I won't allow it."

Robin looked away, putting a tissue to her face. Tony walked in front of her, bent down, and held her hand. "Look, I don't want to see you get abandoned. I'm sure you'll do the right thing," he said encouragingly, looking into her eyes.

She nodded and tried to smile.

Noah knocked before opening the door to the master bedroom. "Robin, we've only been married for three months, and the last half we've slept alone," he said, looking at her curled up on the bed in her clothes. "We barely speak to each other anymore. I don't know how much more of this I can take. Please, Robin... find a way to forgive me. Let me come back to our bed and cuddle up to you. I promise I won't do anything. I just need to feel loved again."

"All I'm hearing is what *you* need. What about what *I* need? I'm sorry, Noah, I just can't right now."

He thought about what she just said. "Okay, so when do you think you can?"

"I don't know, Noah... maybe never."

He took a deep breath, shutting the door behind him as he left the room.

The next morning, a red robin flew from the bird feeder to the windowsill. As the window started shaking violently, the timid bird quickly took flight. Wearing a pink terry robe with disheveled hair and puffy eyes, Robin was frantically trying to open the window in the living room.

"Are you okay?" Noah asked as he hurried into the room.

She glared at him and continued to shake the window, trying to open it. Noah walked over and opened it with ease. She sat down on the sofa and started rocking back and forth with her arms around her knees.

"No, I'm not okay. I feel like a prisoner here in your house, Noah. I'm suffocating here... dying here. I need to get out."

"Where would you go?"

"Anywhere. I just can't stay here anymore."

"So that's it? One stupid argument, which I admit was totally my fault, and you're calling it quits; you want a divorce?"

She nodded.

"So forget about using Tony for marriage counseling. Forget about trying to save our marriage. Do not pass Go; go straight to Divorce. Is that it?" He looked at her, waiting for an answer. "For God's sake, Robin, we're still newlyweds," he pleaded, watching her as she rocked back and forth.

"Okay, I get it now: you feel like a prisoner here. So what do you want from me? You want to get the hell out of here? Fine, I'll quit my job and sell my house.

I'm sure I can find another job somewhere else. And hey, it's just a house, right? You want to live in a shack in the woods? I'll buy us a shack in the woods. I'll even put your name on the deed — tenants by the entirety. In fact, you pick out the house, any house at all, and I'll buy it. No more feeling like a stranger in your own home, right? It'll be a sanctuary, not a prison. I promise." Noah thought for a second. "I'll do whatever you want, but can I still keep my boat?" he asked, standing there as she rocked in silence.

"I hated to see her like that. She was deteriorating right before my eyes, and it was all my fault. When I threw away my wedding ring, what I really did was throw away her security. And now she no longer felt safe in her own home. It was like she was dying... and I was the one killing her."

"Robin..." She stopped rocking and looked at him. "I can't live like this anymore: the two of us living under the same roof, without touching each other, holding each other... loving each other. I need you back in my life again, and I need you back now. Either we get busy living, or we get busy dying. Which is it going to be?"

"You really want to know?"

Noah looked at her sitting there shaking. "I hate to see you fall apart like this... Okay, forget what I need, it doesn't matter anymore. I DO NOT want to get divorced; do you understand that? But if that's what you really want, if that's what you really need, then I'll give it to you, Robin. I'll give you a divorce... because I love you. But please think it over carefully. I lost you once, and I don't want to lose you again," he said with tears in his eyes. "I'm so sorry, Robin," he said, opening the door to the deck.

"Noah..."

He turned around and smiled at her hopefully.

"I don't need to think it over... I've already made my decision."

To Tell The Truth

"Why did I have to push her into making a decision? Because I couldn't wait to feel loved again? I should have been more patient — you know, wait out the storm until it blows over. I should have given her all the time in the world, whatever she needed. If only I hadn't given up so easily... If only I had held on, never letting go..."

*L*ooking like a Catholic schoolgirl with her hair in braids, a red plaid skirt, stockings, and a white cardigan, Robin was standing in the witness stand at the Newport County courthouse, her right hand in the air and her left hand on a Bible. Noah looked dazed, wearing a suit and sitting next to his lawyer, Ben.

"Do you swear to tell the truth, the whole truth, and nothing but the truth, so help you God?"

"I do," she replied.

I look around at Scott, Sharon, Brittany, and Josh gathered around my hospital bed. "Can't you just picture her?" I say with a pretentious laugh. "Looking like a sweet, innocent Catholic school girl before the judge."

Josh smirks at the word "judge" as he puts on his reading glasses and looks down at the folded linen robes, searching for mine. "Let's see now... extra-large, extra-large, extra-large," he announces, shuffling through the robes. "What are they, all extra-larges? And of course one size never fits all, because everybody's different and unique, right?"

I ignore Josh's interruption and pick up that old picture of me holding out the sand dollar. In my head, the sand dollar explodes in slow motion all over again. "I didn't want this," I say, laying the photograph back down. "I didn't want to be there. Why was this happening to me?"

"Mr. Hartman? Mr. Hartman?" the judge repeated, trying to get Noah's attention in the witness stand.

"I'm sorry, what was that again?" Noah asked, snapping out of his trance.

"Are you okay, Mr. Hartman?" the judge asked. Noah nodded. "Would you like some water?" Noah shook his head as the judge stared at him.

"I'll repeat the question one more time, Mr. Hartman. Are you here because you want to get divorced, under your own freewill?"

Noah stared at Robin wordlessly.

I pull the white hospital sheet up to my chin. "To tell the truth, Robin... I don't want to get divorced," I say with tears in my eyes, imagining her in the yellow vinyl chair beside my bed.

"NO ! That's NOT what I want !"

"MR. HARTMAN?" the judge called out again. Noah turned his eyes from his wife and looked at the judge. "*I said*, is that what you want? To get divorced?"

"Yeah... that's what I want," Noah said hesitantly, wiping the tears from his eyes as he looked away.

The Perfect Storm

*E*ven the sky was gloomy as Noah sailed by the old, abandoned lighthouse on this cold, raw, November day. He was heavily bundled in a thick wool sweater, down jacket, wool hat, and wool gloves. The cold air added a drab shade of blue to a face reddened by the unforgiving wind. With no other boats out on the white-capped bay, Noah was utterly alone.

"It was as if the life had been sucked out of my body, and there was no happiness in the part of me that was left behind. I thought perhaps I could find God out there on the water, but he was nowhere to be found. I determined he must not exist... because it was just me... all alone."

Scott was carving a turkey as Jerry and Miriam helped themselves to the buffet on the large granite island. Sharon was sitting in the breakfast nook, talking to her parents while they ate. The rest of the extended family, including aunts and uncles, were enjoying the Thanksgiving feast in the dining room. David, Sam, and two other children ran through the living room where Noah was sitting all by himself in front of the fire, slouched in an armchair, depressed and not eating.

A month later, Christmas lights adorned the roof, trees, and bushes next door to Noah's house, with large blow-molded plastic figures of the Nativity spread out across the front lawn. The family inside was celebrating with a Christmas Eve dinner. Next to the roaring fireplace, colored bulbs on the tree flashed on and off, lighting up the numerous presents beneath it. An excited eight-year-old boy ripped the wrapping paper off a box and shouted with joy as his aunt and uncle looked on. Removing a telescope from its box, he pulled his relatives outside to explore a few of the million stars that were out on that clear, mild night.

Next door at Noah's house, all of the lights were off. Outside on the back deck, Noah was lying alone on a lounge chair, staring up at the North Star.

"If you're out there... under the same star... here I am, Robin... right over here."

Also under the North Star, Robin was standing on a flagstone veranda while music and laughter resonated from the other side of the large French doors, where an office party was taking place inside.

"I wanted to give you something special, because *you're* special," said the man with the slick smile, handing Robin a Christmas present.

Robin untied the white ribbon from around the small, blue Tiffany box, and opened it. Inside was a sterling silver heart necklace. She smiled and thanked him with a long, wet kiss.

There'd be no need to discuss this with her psychiatrist, Tony, because after all, he was standing right there... kissing her.

Dick Clark was back on TV again, counting down as the lighted ball dropped in Times Square. "Three, Two, One... Happy New Year !" Noah heard him say, followed by a loud cheer and a large *1997* sign popping on.

Noah turned off the TV and rolled over onto his wedding pictures scattered about the bed, his clothes still on. He could remember Robin lying beside him on the bed, smiling at him. He imagined she was there now, gazing into his eyes as he gazed into hers. "Sweet dreams, Robin," he said to her image, which slowly faded away as he closed his eyes and fell asleep.

"Memories of Robin gazing into my eyes are the strongest memories I have of her and the easiest ones to recall. When I missed her the most, all I had to do was imagine her beautiful face gazing at me with loving eyes, and I'd see her soul beaming back at me once again."

Springtime had arrived, right on schedule. With the top down and the wind blowing through his hair as he drove his car, **I Will Be Here** started playing on the radio. His eyes watered as he looked over at the empty passenger seat, and flashbacks of Robin filled his head. He imagined her sitting there, gazing at him intensely with butterflies in her stomach. Staring into each other's eyes, Noah heard a long, deep horn, and he quickly looked back at the road. He had drifted into the oncoming lane of traffic and was heading straight for a tractor-trailer.

Jerking the wheel to the side and slamming on the brakes, the car went into a tailspin, the horn sounding as his body slammed into the steering column. Narrowly missing the truck, the Ferrari came to an abrupt stop just inches away from a large maple tree, startling a flock of birds into flight. Shaken but uninjured, Noah looked up and was amazed at what he saw. He got out of his car and stared up at the red band of clouds stretching across the sky. What looked like an outstretched hand had formed at one end of the long, red streak.

"From across the heavens, the beautiful hand of an angel seemed to be reaching out to me. But how would I know for sure? I needed a sign..."

Noah looked around and was disappointed when he didn't see anything. Just then, a red robin flew back to the tree and perched on a branch, chirping.

"If you really are there, hear my prayer," he said, looking up at the apparition, putting his hands together and kneeling. "My soul is lost, wandering alone, missing its mate. And it's all my fault. I never realized just how fragile she really was. But I've learned my lesson, and I swear I've changed. And so I'm asking you, I'm begging you, please give me one more chance. I'll spend every waking moment loving her with all of my being. Please send her back. I'll cherish every breath she takes. Send her back. I've never wanted anything else in this world more. I'll be a better person, just send her back... send her back..."

"I had no idea whom I was really talking to that day. An angel? God? Myself? Who knows, maybe all three. All I know is, every so often, you get what you ask for. And every so often, what you ask for... turns out not to be what you really wanted."

Sitting on his sailboat's swim platform, Noah's jaw dropped as he lowered his binoculars, staring in awe at the old, abandoned lighthouse. Painted on a sign on the west side of the island were the words "FOR SALE".

"Yeah, I can picture it now... Robin Hartman, the hostess with the mostest," Robin said as she sat down on the swim platform beside Noah with a drink in her hand, appearing to him in a flashback. "It's got a catchy ring to it, don't you think?"

"I love you, Robin," he said, imagining that he was looking into her eyes.

"I love you, too, Noah," she responded, looking right back at him.

As he reached out his hand to touch her face, a crack of thunder snapped him out of his daydream, and she was no longer there.

Donning an orange life preserver and looking up at the purple clouds racing in from the south, he stepped on the rubber footpad at the bow, hoisting the anchor with the electric winch as swells started slapping the boat broadside. The menacing sky cast a dark shadow on the sailboat as it slowly made headway under motor power. Nearby boats disappeared and then reappeared as his boat rode up and down the large swells.

A flash of lightning hit the water ahead of him, followed by a loud crack of thunder. The heavens opened up, and the blanket of rain was so thick that Noah couldn't see his own bow. He threw his throttles into neutral and started pressing buttons on the radar screen, desperately trying to remove all the rain clutter that was being errantly displayed on the screen, so he could locate where the other boats were around him. As he pressed the buttons, the yellow dots on the screen started disappearing. "Come on, you piece of junk, find those boats," he said, pressing the buttons until the screen was completely clear of yellow dots — no rain, no boats.

There was another flash of lightning and another boom, this time much closer and louder. He looked up at the sky as the rain pummeled him.

"How could you let this happen?" he screamed upward. "I loved her. If you're even up there, show yourself, goddamn it. HEY, I'm talking to you !"

There was another bright flash and a spine-chilling crack of thunder. "You want a piece of me? Go ahead. Take your best shot. I'm nobody, ya hear me, nobody."

Just then, lightning struck the mast, and a small explosion halfway up sent the top half crashing down, landing on top of him and knocking him to the deck. Noah lay motionless in a stupor, pinned underneath the mast as the boat drifted closer to the rocks jutting up out of the water only fifty yards away. As the swells rocked the boat side to side, water began swamping the boat, and a yellow life raft deployed from a white canister midship.

Noah came to, and he struggled to push the heavy mast off of him. Managing to crawl out from beneath it, he took a knife out of his pocket and cut the lines, pushing the heavy mast overboard. He put the boat back in gear, full throttle, and bolted away from the rocks that were about to put a hole in the starboard side.

Ten minutes later, visibility was improving as he turned south toward the patch of sunlight shining on the water's surface. The rain had stopped, and the seas had calmed. With no other boats in sight, he turned on the autopilot and hurried into the cabin to turn on some music. Quickly reemerging, he locked the cabin door and turned to walk away, pulled back by the strap on his life preserver that was caught in the door. He turned the key to unlock it, but the key snapped off in the lock. He pulled on the strap, but it wouldn't budge. With a trickle of blood dripping down the side of his face from a cut on his forehead, he looked up at the sky and began laughing. Set on autopilot, the boat was heading out to sea at ten knots with Noah stuck in the cabin door.

Noah imagined Robin standing there as he recalled a conversation he once had with her. "You're not going to believe this," he mentioned to Robin, laughing, "but uh... it's locked," he said, pointing at the door. "Do you mind helping me get free? I'm kind of stuck here," he explained, yanking on the door handle.

"I've already told you how to free yourself, Noah. Don't you remember?" she urged him.

"What are you talking about?"

"You know... the secret..."

"What secret?"

"The secret that there's no key."

"I don't understand," he said, staring at the broken key in his hand. "How do I unlock it without a key?"

"Because it's not locked, Noah. It never was. And all you have to do to free yourself from your golden handcuffs is just take them off. It's time, Noah. Don't be afraid... take them off."

"She was right — always was. It was time... time to cut the cord with my parents... time to start living my own life."

An epiphany is what it was: a soothing smile, an intimate laugh, and a shake of the head as he stared down at the broken key in his hand. Tossing the key overboard, he unzipped his life preserver and stepped out of it, leaving it stuck in the door as he returned to the helm. He turned off the autopilot, regaining control of his boat.

"I was back in the driver's seat and ready to take control of my life. From that point on, I'd leave land behind and head for the horizon. I had no idea where I was going to end up, but I knew where I was and the direction I was heading. I had faith, and that made all the difference."

Noah continued to drive his boat toward the rainbow that had appeared on the horizon.

"God, I love being out on the water. It's the only place I feel the wind and rain on my face. It's the only place the world feels real... the only place I feel alive."

Jerry was sitting at his desk talking on the phone, when Noah barged in, set the keys to the company Ferrari down in front of him, and headed for the door.

"Something just came up. I'll call you right back," Jerry said quickly into the phone, hanging up abruptly.

"Noah, what's this all about? Why'd you give me your keys?"

Noah turned in the doorway. "I quit."

"You can't quit. Who'll hire you at your salary?"

Noah looked at his father for a long moment, shook his head, and left the office.

"You'll starve out there in the real world," Jerry yelled, standing up. "You'll lose your house, your boat, EVERYTHING."

The Educated Decision

A line of Mercedes, Lexus, Range Rovers, BMWs, and Porsches waited in front of Capriccio restaurant, followed by a black Ford F150 pickup truck. Wearing a sport jacket and tie, Noah got out of his new pickup truck and tossed the keys to the valet. He walked into the dimly lit interior and passed a baby grand, where a man in a tuxedo was playing **That's Life** by Frank Sinatra. He joined Scott, Sharon, Jerry, and Miriam at a candle-lit table.

"What on earth were you thinking?" Miriam exclaimed, angry. "How could you just quit like that? There isn't another company around that will pay you half as much money as your dad's been so generously paying you. And this is how you thank him?"

"I don't care about the money," Noah responded. "I care about being happy."

"Don't be a fool," Jerry added. "You could be happy anywhere. It's your responsibility in life to take whatever job pays you the most amount of money. Everyone else seems to enjoy making money. Besides, how do you plan on paying your bills without it?"

"I guess I'll just have to downsize, that's all... sell the house... whatever it takes. At this point in my life, it's more important to me to have a career that I love."

"And what career would that be?" Miriam asked.

"Well, I've got this new idea I'm working on. You know that lighthouse on an island in the bay across from my house? Well, guess what? It's for sale ! I could buy it, fix it up, and turn it into a charming bed-and-breakfast."

"Cool, a lighthouse bed-and-breakfast," Sharon approved enthusiastically.

"Yeah, isn't that a great idea?" Noah added. "I could shuttle people over to the island by Venetian water taxi, pick them up and drop them off whenever they want. I could have weddings there, events, you name it. I'd just have to fix it up, that's all. It only has four bedrooms, but I did a business plan on it, and I know I can make the numbers work."

"ABSOLUTELY NOT !" Jerry interjected. "What do you know about running a B & B? NOTHING. You'll fall flat on your face, and it'll just be one more failure to add to your growing list of failures. It's a crazy idea, and I won't allow it."

"Dad, first of all, I have faith in myself that I can achieve anything I set my mind to, as long as I give it my all and don't give up. Second of all, even if you and the rest of the world think it's a crazy idea, it still doesn't make it a bad idea. And third of all, if for some reason the lighthouse doesn't work out as a bed-and-breakfast, I could always sell the real estate after I've fixed it up. It could be someone's summer island retreat."

"That's utter nonsense. Who'd buy a summer house that you can't even drive to? You'll lose your entire investment, so you can just forget about it."

"Will you stop telling me what I can and cannot do? I'm almost forty years old. When are you going to stop treating me like a child?"

"You'll always be my child," Jerry responded.

"Well, then, just stop treating me like one."

"I'LL STOP TREATING YOU LIKE ONE WHEN YOU STOP ACTING LIKE ONE."

"Boys, boys..." Miriam interjected, holding her hand up. "Noah, honey, stop being so stubborn and listen to your father for a change. He's right; it does sound like a very risky proposition. Besides, your father is only looking out for your best interest. We love you and don't want to see you make a huge mistake, especially a financial one."

"And what's wrong with making mistakes?" Noah retorted. "My whole life, you always forced me into doing whatever *you* wanted me to do under the guise of preventing me from making mistakes. And my whole life, I subscribed to it, rewarded for doing what I was told. Well, I have news for you: I won't allow you to control my life anymore. I want to make mistakes. You know why? Because then they'd be *my* mistakes. That's how I learn. That's how I grow as a human being. That's how I know I'm living *my* life, not yours. Oh, and one more thing: if I try something that I've never done before, something that's particularly difficult for me, and it doesn't work out, that doesn't make it a failure. The fact that I actually succeeded in finishing it makes it a huge success. Think of all the people that never even try."

"See? You're talking just like a child again," Jerry bellowed. "Listen to me. Money doesn't grow on trees. If it weren't for me, you wouldn't have a dollar, and I'll be damned if I let you throw away money that I gave you on some ill-advised investment scheme. It's too risky, and you're not doing it. You're not buying the lighthouse, and that's final — end of discussion. And just so you know I'm serious about this, if you do buy that lighthouse, I'll disinherit you. You'll get nothing. You hear me? NOTHING."

"GREAT !" Scott blurted out. "Then I'll get it all," he said with a mischievous smile. Jerry shot him a disapproving look. "What?" Scott said, shrugging. "I was just kidding."

On the verge of loosing his temper, Noah looked at his brother and tried to smile. He hated it when his parents resorted to threats to manipulate his decisions. He was just trying to live his life and pursue his dreams — he wasn't hurting anyone. Nothing bothered him more than being preempted from making a decision. Refusing to allow his parents to control him anymore, years of pent-up anger were about to explode.

"Noah, sweetie, please try to put yourself in your father's shoes for a moment," Miriam said placatingly. "Don't you think there were plenty of times when your father wanted to go against his father's wishes? Of course there were, but he never did. You know why?" Noah listened silently. "Because he respected his father, and that's just the way things were back then. And thanks to his father's wisdom, things worked out pretty well for him, don't you think? We know that times have changed; it's a new generation these days. But remember, your father didn't become successful by accident. He's very experienced and smarter than you are. So when your father gives you good advice, you should take it and be grateful."

"The bottom line is: your mother and I love you, and we only want what's best for you," Jerry added.

"So, if you still want to go out and buy that awful lighthouse... go ahead," Miriam conceded.

"WHAT?" Jerry objected.

"Go ahead... buy it just to spite us," Miriam continued. "It's your life, and you can do whatever you want with it. We can't stop you from throwing your life away. We just want you to know how we feel about the inheritance thing ahead of time, that's all, so you know what the consequences of your actions are *before* you do something stupid, not after, when it's too late. See? Now you have all the information you need to make —"

"An educated decision?" Noah blurted.

"Yeah, that's right. How'd you know I was going to say that?"

"Oh, I don't know... maybe I've heard it before..." Noah answered, thinking back to his freshman year at college.

Wearing a Harvard sweatshirt, eighteen-year-old Noah dropped a laundry bag in front of the washing machine at his parents' house on the East Side. As he headed out the front door, he was intercepted by his mother.

"Hey, is the big man on campus even going to kiss his mother hello before rushing out?"

"Sorry, Mom. I didn't know you were home," Noah said, giving her a kiss on the cheek. "So when do you think my laundry will be ready? I have a hot date tonight, and I'd like to wear my favorite shirt."

"Maria should have it done in a couple of hours. So tell me about this hot date of yours. Is she pretty? Is she Jewish?"

"She's wonderful, Mom. Been seeing her ever since Orientation Week. She's not Jewish, though. She's actually half Polish and half Portuguese."

"Do you love this girl?" Miriam asked apprehensively, her face stiffening.

"Yeah, I'm crazy about her. I think I'm going to marry her someday. Isn't that great?"

"No, Noah, it's *not* great," she snapped. "Weren't you listening at all to the rabbi's speech on Yom Kippur? The preservation of the Jewish people depends on all of us. Do you want the religion to become extinct? Listen, I want you to know that if you ever have children with this Gentile, and your kids are not brought up Jewish, then your father and I will have nothing to do with them. Do you understand? We won't *see* your children, we won't *talk to* your children, and we won't *love* your children. I'm only telling you this because I love you, Noah, and you deserve to know how your father and I feel before you go and make some big mistake. If you want to marry that *shicksa* and have children with her, go

139

right ahead. It's your life, and we can't stop you. We just want you to know what the consequences are ahead of time, that's all. So you have all the information you need to make an educated decision."

The Three Reasons

Wearing a navy robe with matching slippers, Noah headed out the front door to fetch the Providence Journal, which was on the front lawn resting up against the *For Sale* sign. Shuffling back inside, he sat down at the patio table with the newspaper folded under his arm and a cup of coffee in his hand. It was a dreamy summer morning. The air was dry, and there was a light breeze shooting off the bay. Seagulls squawked as they fought over a scrap of food on the beach below. Noah's coffee was getting cold as he sat there, staring off in the direction of the old lighthouse in the middle of the bay.

Unfolding the Providence Journal and glancing at the date — *June 10th, 1997,* he tore off the corner with the date printed on it, crumpled it up, and tossed it on the ground before getting up and going inside. Upstairs in his closet, he climbed a wooden stepladder and reached for a box on the top shelf. As he grabbed it, a large manila envelope resting on top of the box fell on his head. Sitting on the bed with the box and the manila envelope, he removed the lid from the box and looked inside. Resting on top was his wedding invitation, the date reading *June 10th, 1996.*

"It would have been our first wedding anniversary. We never even made it a year. God, I missed her."

Lifting his wedding pictures out of the box, he started shuffling through them. He and Robin looked so happy together. He laughed as he pulled the next item out of the box, Robin's white garter from the wedding. The last item to come out of the box was the picture that Robin had taken on their honeymoon, the one with Noah holding the sand dollar underwater, right before it exploded. He stared at the picture for a moment and then placed it up against the lamp on his nightstand, putting everything else back in the box and fitting the lid back on.

141

His attention now turned to the mysterious manila envelope sitting next to him. He picked it up and examined both sides before opening it and removing a bunch of old photographs. They were from Robin's childhood, including one of her when she was a baby, cradled in a man's arms, her mother standing nearby. Noah had never seen a picture of Robin's father before. There were several elementary school portraits of her, what appeared to be her senior prom picture, and a picture of her holding Brittany in the hospital on the day she was born.

The next item removed from the manila envelope was a clear, transparent shoe that was missing its heel. He looked at it curiously and then put it aside on the bed, taking out the final item: a red envelope that read *Deliver to Robin when the time is right*. Noah gaped at it, turning it over to open it, stopping as he read the words — *Noah, you promised never to open this*. As much as he wanted to discover what secret lay inside, he knew he could never go back on a promise, especially not one made to Robin. "No... the only person to open this letter would have to be Robin. But do I know if the time is right?" he muttered, putting the red envelope back into the large manila envelope along with her old photographs. He stared at the broken shoe for a moment and then stuck that in there too. He sealed the envelope and started getting dressed.

With the manila envelope addressed to Robin tucked safely under his arm, Noah stood in line at the main post office. As he reached the front of the line, he opened the manila envelope and took out the clear, heelless shoe. As he stared at it sparkling in his hand, the clerk called out, "Next..." The clerk tapped her fingers on the desk and repeated more loudly, "NEXT IN LINE." Noah looked up at the clerk, who was looking directly at him, and then stepped out of line, leaving the building without mailing it.

The manila envelope and clear, heelless shoe sat on the passenger seat as he pulled up in front of Robin's apartment. He walked up to the door and leaned the manila envelope against it, ringing the doorbell and walking back toward his pickup truck.

"Hey," he heard.

He turned around to see Robin standing in the doorway, smiling at him, the manila envelope in her hand. Strangely enough, she actually seemed happy to see him.

"Nice truck," she said, looking out toward the street. "Where's the Ferrari, being serviced?"

"No," he said, shaking his head. "I don't have it anymore. I gave it back. This is what I drive now. What do you think?"

She had a puzzled smile playing on her face, not sure if he was serious or not. "I love it... so what's this?" she asked, holding up the manila envelope.

"An anniversary gift."

"An anniversary gift? Oh... right," she said, hitting her head with the envelope, laughing. "How stupid of me, today's our anniversary. *Today* is our anniversary. Well... happy anniversary, Noah. But unfortunately I don't have a present for *you*," she said jokingly, looking curiously at the envelope.

"It's a bunch of old pictures. Your prom picture... stuff like that. Thought you might want them back."

"Oh... thanks."

Noah stood there, looking at her. "So how's Brittany?"

"Good. She just left yesterday. She's spending the summer at her dad's in Richmond."

Noah nodded. "Well, I'm sure you're going to miss her. I know she means the world to you, and you'd do just about anything for her."

"Yeah... I miss her already."

"You're a wonderful mom."

"Thanks, I appreciate that."

He nodded and looked at her for a long moment. "Hey, I was wondering... since it is our anniversary and everything... how'd you like to join me for our anniversary dinner?"

She looked hesitant for a moment and then shook her head subtly.

"That's okay, I understand," he said, turning and walking back to his truck, stopping.

"What is it, Noah?"

Turning around to face her, he announced, "I quit my job."

"NO WAY ! Are you shittin' me?"

Noah started to nod yes and then corrected himself, shaking his head no.

"That's great Noah; that's really great. Now you can finally have a job you love going to every day." She looked at the blank look on his face. "You don't have any idea what that is, do you?"

"Not a clue," Noah shot back.

"Well, I'm sure you'll figure it out."

Noah nodded and opened the door to his truck, looking back at her one last time. He waved, and she waved back. As he started up the engine, he sat for a moment, reflecting. The passenger door opened suddenly, and Noah was startled to see Robin hopping in, smiling, in what seemed like slow motion. They shared a laugh as she pulled out the broken shoe from underneath her.

They were having dinner together at Guido's restaurant, a quaint BYOB restaurant on the East Side. The aroma was sweet and garlicky, the candle-lit atmosphere romantic. They ate meatballs covered in a tangy red sauce and drank Andre Champagne to celebrate what would have been their one-year anniversary.

The waitress brought over a piece of ganache-infused flowerless chocolate cake for dessert. Noah picked up a fork and fed some to her, Robin's face displaying ecstasy. She reciprocated by feeding him a piece. It tasted like heaven. He put his face in front of hers, and with his lips just inches away from hers, he waited for approval. Robin's smile invited him to proceed forward... slowly. As Noah's lips gently pressed against hers, she accepted his gesture by kissing him back. As if a switch inside her brain were suddenly triggered, memories of loving Noah came flooding back. With butterflies in her stomach, her heart racing, and her eyes fixated on his, there was no one else on earth but Noah.

Sensing the intense connection, Noah asked with a suggestive smile, "Do you surrender?"

"I surrender," she concluded, her eyes twinkling seductively.

"It was as if that one kiss somehow wiped out all of the events that had taken place over the past year, as if nothing had ever changed. Surely the angel I had seen stretching across the sky that day must have answered my prayers and sent her back to me. In any case, we were back together again, and that was all that mattered."

The door to Noah's house burst open as Noah carried Robin over the threshold, kissing her passionately as he carried her up the stairs into the bedroom, setting her gently on the bed.

"I love you," he announced as he slowly started to undress her.

"I love you too," she murmured, ripping the buttons off his shirt.

Hours later, they were still making love, gently, slowly, intensely. Noah was holding back, pleasing her for as long as she could stand it. With the words "I surrender" muttered from her weary lips, they collapsed in each other's arms, falling asleep from exhaustion.

The sun was shining brightly when Noah awoke, alone in his bed. "Was it all just a dream?" he questioned, looking around at the clothes tossed about on the floor. "No... it was no dream," he said, picking his shirt up off the floor and feeling the knots where the buttons used to be. He pulled his shorts on and walked down the stairs to look for Robin. She was sitting outside on the deck, drinking a cup of coffee and wearing his navy robe.

"Good morning, sleepy-head," she said with a pleasant smile.

"Good morning, sweetheart," he replied, walking behind her and kissing the side of her neck as she reached up to touch the back of his head. He sat down in the chair next to her and looked at her.

"Last night was wonderful. I had to pinch myself to make sure I wasn't dreaming."

"It was no dream, Noah."

"So, what are you going to do now, Robin?"

"I don't know," she said, gazing out over the bay. "What do you think I should do?"

"You really don't know?"

She smirked at him.

Noah took her hand and looked into her eyes. "Well... I think you should just put your head on my shoulder."

"That's it?" she said with a confused look, dissatisfied with the answer. "I should just put my head on your shoulder?"

"And keep it there until Polaris is no longer the North Star," he added, eliciting a smile from her. "I think you should marry me again, so we can raise a family together. And I think we should find a house that you feel safe in — one that you can call *home*. So if you're asking me what I think... I think you should stay."

As Robin thought about what he had just said, Noah got up from the chair and knelt down in front of her. "How about I give you three reasons... morning, day, and night."

She narrowed her eyes.

"Stay... so every morning when I open my eyes you'll be the first thing I see. Stay... so every day when I'm with you I can show you all over again exactly how much you mean to me. And stay... so every night when you lay your head down next to mine, you'll know... you'll know just how much you're loved."

Her eyes drifted to the water as she thought for a moment, returning to look deep into Noah's eyes.

"Okay, Noah... I'll stay."

Testing The Waters

"I wouldn't listen to your parents if I were you. If your heart's set on buying the lighthouse, then just do it," Robin advised, stretched out in Noah's arms on the teak deck of Noah's boat, anchored out in front of the old lighthouse on a lazy summer day. "I can definitely picture us getting married there," she continued. "It's such a pretty spot. You know, it's too bad they don't make you wait a year to get divorced. Otherwise, we'd still be married right now, and we wouldn't have to go through all that paperwork again just to get remarried. Speaking of paperwork, when are you planning on having me sign another one of your stupid prenups?"

"There's not going to be a prenup this time. I guess I'll just have to take my chances, that's all."

"But what about your parents?"

"What about them? You're marrying me, not my parents."

She smiled and continued with her list. "I want to have another child," she announced.

"Of course, I'd love to have a child with you... but what kind of child exactly are we talking about?" he joked.

Robin laughed. "I've always loved the name Olivia — if it's a girl, that is."

"I think Olivia's a beautiful name for a girl," he said, eliciting a smile.

"Oh, and one more thing..." Noah looked at her closely. "I don't want to be a social worker anymore. I've always wanted to be an X-Ray tech."

"I think you should do whatever makes you happy, Robin."

"Well, it would mean quitting my job and going back to school full time for a year until I get my certificate."

"So when can you start?"

A big smile stretched across her face. "You're the greatest. I love you, Noah Hartman," she said, leaning in for a kiss. She stood up and dipped her foot into the water, testing it.

"Now that I had Robin back in my life, there wasn't anything I wouldn't do to keep her in it. I was a different person now. I had learned my lesson, and the only thing that mattered to me was Robin. And so, with her encouragement, I started my new job as a boat broker..."

Noah and Neil were wearing khaki pants and white polo shirts that read *Newport Yacht Brokers*. They were standing in the cockpit of a fifty-foot Sea Ray Sundancer that had a *For Sale* sign on the transom. Neil was wearing a bad hairpiece and was smoking a cigar while he wiped a smudge off the fiberglass with a microfiber cloth. Noah unsnapped the canvas around the cockpit, keenly aware that he wouldn't get paid unless he sold a boat. But that didn't bother him; he just loved being around boats. After three weeks of working for Neil, he was still looking for his first sale. Perhaps today would be his lucky day.

A husband and wife walked down the dock holding hands. As they stepped onto the boat, the man gave it a once over and remarked, "What a gorgeous day for a sea trial !"

"Hey, guys. How ya doing?" Neil greeted them, looking up with a salesman's smile painted on his face. "Well, you're certainly buying the right boat, that's for sure. It's a lot of boat for the money," he told them as he started up the engines and pointed at Noah.

"I meant to ask you about the starboard engine," the man asked Noah as he untied the lines. "It looked freshly painted."

"Yeah, that's right," Noah answered honestly. "There was a rebuild on it last year. Piston seized up. But it's running fine now."

"WHAT?" Neil yelled, trying to eavesdrop over the sound of the engines. "No there wasn't. Noah's new here; he doesn't know what he's talking about. It was routine maintenance, that's all, just routine maintenance."

Realizing that the wool was being pulled over his eyes, the man looked at Neil suspiciously. "You know what? Today's not such a nice day for a sea trial after all," he remarked, taking his wife's hand and stepping off the boat, leaving Noah holding the lines.

Noah soon came to the realization that he'd never be a good used boat salesman — he was just too honest. He could never betray the faith bestowed upon him by his trusting customers.

"You're so fired," Neil said, shooting him a nasty look as he shut down the engines.

"And when I wasn't working, we were either sailing on the bay or searching for that perfect home..."

It rained for several days while the realtor took them all around the state, showing them one house after another. However, after visiting dozens of houses throughout the weekend, Noah and Robin were disappointed that none felt like home.

The majestic cliffs on the northeast side of Block Island welcomed Noah and Robin as they sailed toward Old Harbor. There were always plenty of mopeds to rent on the island, and soon after, Robin was sitting on the back of one, wearing a Block Island T-shirt with her arms wrapped tightly around Noah's waist as they zoomed up a hill. They walked the 150 wooden steps down Mohegan Bluffs to the rocky shoreline below. Holding hands as they walked along the beach, they passed several sunbathers and surfers until they came to a bend, whereupon they suddenly found themselves all alone on an empty stretch of beach. With steep cliffs rising two hundred feet behind them, and the expansive ocean stretched out before them, they melted into each other's arms and were at one.

Later that day, several people on the boardwalk were jumping onto a motorboat to go parasailing. Robin hopped into the boat and motioned for Noah to join her. Afraid of heights, Noah waved her off, suggesting horseback riding instead.

As their horses sauntered along the beach, Noah looked at Robin and smiled, the lethargic trail horses being a much safer bet.

"And — as I'm sure you can imagine — finding my niche in Rhode Island's vast boating industry was turning out to be a little harder than it looked..."

As scores of boats crisscrossed in every direction in front of Warwick Point Light, a twenty-six-foot Bayliner express cruiser was being towed around the peninsula on a short tow by a red BayTow towboat with its yellow lights flashing. Wearing a red BayTow t-shirt, Noah smiled as he took in the fresh ocean air, looking back to check on the people in the Bayliner as he navigated through the congested waterway. What was supposed to be a fun day out on the bay had turned out to be a slow, boring ride home for this young family of four who had encountered engine trouble. It wasn't boring for Noah, though. He loved being out on the water, not to mention getting paid for it this time.

Skip was also wearing a red BayTow t-shirt. He had a scruffy, white beard that seemed to illustrate his many years of service out at sea. He was on the bow of the towboat, talking to the family in the cockpit of the cruiser as Noah tied the spring lines nice and tight, attaching the cruiser to his starboard hip just outside the entrance to their marina. As Noah tightly maneuvered the two boats down the narrow fairway, the man in the cruiser pointed out his slip to Skip.

"Put it over there," Skip commanded Noah, pointing in the direction of a small, empty slip wedged in between two large boats. Noah put the boat into neutral and attempted to look around the cruiser attached to his starboard side. As the boat started drifting to port, Noah had no idea where the slip was because he couldn't see it.

Skip wasted no time as he jumped into the cockpit, pushed Noah out of his way, and took control of the helm. He threw the boat hard into reverse, spun the boat on a dime, and maneuvered it into the cramped slip. With an austere look on his face as he brushed past Noah, Skip grabbed the release form and stepped onto the dock.

Not long after, Noah was replaced with a more experienced tow captain.

A long dirt road meandered through the woods, ending at a small cabin with a *For Sale* sign out front. The two-bedroom cabin had a cute front porch with white, carved columns and balusters, and a back porch with a white wooden swing that overlooked a private pond. Along the edge of the pond, a stone's throw from an old tool shed, an enormous maple tree stood guard at the foot of a small dock that was barely big enough to accomodate a rowboat. Noah's six-bedroom shingled house on the ocean seemed like a castle compared to this modest pond-side cabin in the middle of the woods. But then again, who needs a castle when you've got love?

As the realtor placed a *Sale Pending* topper on top of the *For Sale* sign, Noah and Robin embraced at the end of the dock, *Noah + Robin* ∞ carved inside a heart in the bark of the maple.

The next day, a *Sale Pending* topper was placed on top of the sign in front of Noah's house in Jamestown.

"By the end of the summer, everything was falling into place. We had found the perfect home with the best of both worlds — the woods and the water. Robin started school, and she even started seeing her psychiatrist again to help put things into perspective. We lived happily... but would it be our ever after?"

Three Strikes You're Out

As the burgers sizzled beside them on the outdoor grill, Noah swigged a Michelob with Jake and touched the cold bottle to his sweaty forehead. Inside Robin's apartment, Robin put her glass of Gallo Chablis down on the counter to help Julie set the kitchen table. Pregnant again, Julie now had a wedding ring around her finger as she picked up her one-year-old baby boy, Jake Jr., and set him down into the highchair. Robin carried a large plate of corn on the cob over to the table as Jake and Noah entered with platters of grilled food.

"So what are you going to do for work?" Jake asked Noah, sitting down at the table with everyone.

"I'm kind of just winging it right now. Since the summer's almost over, I suppose I could always charter my sailboat next summer. Other than that, I'm not really sure what to do the rest of the year."

"How about that lighthouse idea of yours?" Robin suggested, taking a bite of corn.

"Yeah... well... I guess some things in life are just not meant to be," Noah responded sadly.

"Hey, Noah, a little birdie told me you have a big birthday coming up this week," Julie announced.

Noah nodded. "The big four-'O'. But please... no surprise birthday parties. A romantic dinner for two will do just fine," Noah said, winking at Robin. "Oh... here are the pictures of our new house. We close on Monday," he said, handing a yellow Kodak envelope to Julie.

"It looks so peaceful there with the pond," Julie said, shuffling through the pictures and passing them on to Jake. "So, when does Brittany get back from Virginia?" she asked Robin.

"Next week. I can't wait to get her back. I miss her so much."

"So Robin, how's school going?" Jake asked, handing the pictures back to Noah.

"Great, I love it. Except we have midterms starting already on Tuesday," she grimaced.

"Yeah, Robin left early this morning to go to some study group at the school, and I didn't hear from her again until it was time to come here for dinner," Noah added.

"Oh, right... one of those all-day nude study groups," Julie joked. "I've heard of those before. I think they call it an orgy, ha."

As everyone laughed, Robin shot Julie a dark look. *What's that about?* Noah wondered.

The following evening, Noah walked into the bedroom as Robin was slipping into a dress.

"So, where do you want to go for dinner?" he asked her.

"Oh... I forgot to tell you: I'm going out with Julie tonight — dinner and a movie," she said, spraying both sides of her neck with perfume. "I'll be back around ten. Love you," she said, giving him a peck on the lips as she left the room.

Noah watched from the bedroom window as she got into her car and disappeared down the street.

"I found it a little odd that she'd just run out like that. I had assumed we'd grab a bite to eat somewhere together, like we did every night. Even though I trusted her, I couldn't help but wonder if it had anything to do with her disappearance the day before."

Robin's spur-of-the-moment decision to go out with Julie left Noah home alone and hungry on a Saturday night. He sat down on the sofa with a hot Swanson TV dinner and turned on the Red Sox/Yankees game.

When the game ended at 10:30 p.m., Noah rolled over in bed, turned off the TV, and shut off the lights, turning them back on again an hour later since he couldn't sleep. He tried reaching Robin on her cell phone, but she didn't answer, so he propped himself up on pillows and turned the TV on, channel surfing.

As soon as the clock hit midnight, Noah hit the Redial button on the phone, but Robin still didn't pick up. He dialed a different number this time.

"Hello," Jake answered, half asleep.

"Hey, Jake. It's Noah. Sorry to call so late. Did Julie and Robin get back from the movies yet?"

"Are you drunk or somethin'? Do you know what time it is?"

"Jake, I'm not drunk. Robin hasn't come home yet, and she's not answering her phone. I'm worried that something bad might have happened to her."

"Noah... Julie's been home with me all night watching the game. I have no idea where Robin is. Good night." Noah heard a click followed by the dial tone.

"I don't usually act obsessively — unless of course there's a good reason to. However, that night I had several good reasons to."

Noah redialed, listening to Robin's phone ring six times before going to voicemail. He redialed continuously for a half hour until his call went straight through to voicemail. He dialed the number again and got the same response. Apparently, Robin had shut her phone off.

The clock read *2:53 AM* when Robin tiptoed into the dark bedroom, dropping her clothes to the floor and slipping quietly into bed. Noah was lying there motionless, wide-awake and staring at the clock, the phone still gripped in his hand.

"I'm sorry," she exclaimed the next morning, throwing her clothes into a blue suitcase while Noah looked on. "I know I must have hurt you last night, and I know I'm not treating you fairly. I don't know what's compelling me to do this, but I have to leave," she said, walking into the closet.

"I don't understand. What's happening here? Why are you leaving?"

She came back out with a bunch of shoes in her hands, dumping them into the suitcase. She looked down in the suitcase and removed a clear shoe that was missing its heel, studying it for a moment before tossing it into the trash.

"I promise I'll call you in a couple of days after I sort things out," she said, zipping up the suitcase and looking at Noah. "Please don't worry. I probably just need to talk to Tony about all of this," she said, rolling the suitcase toward the door. "I'm sorry, but that's the best I can do right now," she said callously, leaving the room.

As he heard the front door slam behind her, Noah collapsed on the bed in a fetal position.

I can tell that Scott, Sharon, Brittany, and Josh all feel bad for me at this point. I roll out of the fetal position in my hospital bed and sit up, looking at Brittany. "You were away at your dad's house that whole summer. Your mom moved in right after you left, and she conveniently moved out right before you came home. You never even knew that we had gotten back together, did you?"

Brittany's sad eyes look down at me as she wipes a tear.

"What the hell happened, Britt? What was she just... just testing the waters?"

Brittany looks away, tears flowing down her face as she walks toward the door.

"Wait, Britt, I'm sorry. I didn't mean to upset you."

She turns around and looks back at me. "I gotta go check on Mom. A little fresh air wouldn't hurt either."

We all watch as Brittany leaves the room.

"Well anyway, everything was going so well and we were so happy to be back together again," I explain to my audience. "Not a day went by that I didn't thank God for bringing her back into my life... for giving me a second chance at making things right. A lot of good that did me. Thanks, God," I say sarcastically, glancing up. "Thanks for nothing."

"Well?" I say expectantly, watching Josh shuffle through the robes in his cart, not paying attention to me.

"Unbelievable... all these robes and yours is nowhere in sight," he exclaims.

"Sometimes I think that God just isn't listening to me," I say, watching curiously as Josh rummages through the pile.

"I'm sorry... did you say something?" he says, looking up at me.

I give him a funny look. "And where was God when I needed him, anyway? He seems to be there for other people — or so they say — so why not me?"

"My God, what is going on over here?" Josh says, looking down at the robes. "Everybody gets a robe except for Noah? Now that's just not right," he says, picking up a bunch of robes all at once, examining them.

I lift my head, trying to see what's in his cart. "Just give me any one; it doesn't matter," I say, reaching out.

"Of course it matters, Noah. You wouldn't be happy with just any one. Why, it wouldn't fit you right," he says, pulling one robe up after the other.

"WILL YOU JUST FORGET ABOUT THE STUPID ROBE ALREADY ! If you don't see it, then it's obviously not there."

"Oh, is that so?" Josh exclaims sarcastically, looking over at me with a challenging look. "Sometimes you just have to have faith, especially when you can't see what you're searching for. But don't worry; if your robe isn't here, I'll make sure to stop by with it later, I promise."

"Yeah, whatever..." I say apathetically. "I'll be here if you need me."

"Well, that's comforting to know," Josh quips under his breath, looking down at his cart.

"What did you just say?" I ask suspiciously.

"Well I'll be... here it is," he says, surprised, holding up my robe to show it to me. "Right in front of my eyes, and I didn't even see it, heh heh." I lift my head, trying to get a look at it. "Look... it's even got your name on it," he says proudly, pointing at the embroidery as he hands it to me.

"Thanks, Josh," I say as I get out of bed to unfold it. "I like it," I say, admiring it as I hold it out in front of me.

"Anyway, the summer was coming to an end, just days before Brittany was due to come home," I say, lowering the robe, my smile fading, "when Robin just packed up and left. I had no idea why, but I was going to find out..."

Noah stood near the entrance to the large brick building that read *Community College of Rhode Island*. He watched as a flood of young adults poured through the large glass doors. Among them was Robin, holding hands with some tall, lanky guy with long, wavy blonde hair and a goatee.

"Robin," Noah called out.

Robin turned, shock registering as she spotted Noah. "Hold on a sec," she said to her companion.

"What the hell are you doing here, Noah?" she said, grabbing him by the arm and pulling him aside.

"I've been calling you for the last two days, and you haven't returned any of my phone calls. I deserve to know what's going on."

She looked hard at him. "Okay, we can talk for a minute... in your car."

Noah trailed behind her as she marched toward his truck. Clambering in, she stared straight ahead.

"So who is this guy? A student in one of your classes?"

"He's a teacher... what does that matter, anyway?"

"This doesn't make any sense. So you've known him for what, two... maybe three weeks now? He's pretty much a stranger, don't you think? How do you know he can love you like I love you? For that matter, how do you know he's even going to stick around a month or two from now?"

Robin sat in stony silence.

"Three days ago, we were planning a wedding, a child, growing old together. I'm selling my house for you, for God's sake ! And that charming little cabin we found in the middle of Nowhereland... Well, guess what? We bought it yesterday. I don't understand. Why are you doing this to me?"

"I'm sorry. I didn't plan on any of this. It just happened," she said defensively.

"How? How could this just happen?" he asked in frustration. "Never mind, I don't care how it happened. Let's just go home. I'll forgive you. We can talk about it another time. Just tell him you — "

"No, Noah..." she said, shaking her head. "I choose Frank," she said, opening the door.

"Frank? Is that his name? Frank? Well, you don't even know Frank. And you can't really mean that," Noah pleaded, his voice shaking and tears rolling down his face as she slammed the door behind her.

Frank offered her a cigarette as they walked across the parking lot together, while Noah collapsed across the seats, crying like an infant.

Noah grabbed the last carton from the back of his pickup truck and slammed the tailgate shut. Carrying the box labeled *Kitchen* into his new house, he plopped it down on the pine floor and grabbed a Sam Adams from the refrigerator. He savored the first cold sip as he pushed open the screen door and flopped down on the white swing overlooking the pond. Taking a deep breath as he gazed at the colorful skyline, he took the phone out of his pocket and hit *Redial*.

"Will you please stop calling me, Noah?" Robin snapped. "What's so important, anyway?"

"Tomorrow's my fortieth birthday, and I'm having a really hard time with all of this. All I want for my birthday is to see you, just for one minute, just long enough to get a hug. Please Robin, after all I've done, after all I've been through, can you please see it in your heart to give me a hug for my birthday?"

"I don't know... maybe. I'll call you tomorrow and let you know. But please, stop calling me. I'll call you, okay?"

He closed the phone and stared at the silhouette of the maple tree. After a moment, he shut his heavy eyes, and when he reopened them, it was morning. He heard a couple of birds chirping in the maple tree.

"Did I tell you it was my fortieth birthday, and all I wanted for my birthday was a hug? Oh, right, I said that already. And so I waited..."

With the phone clutched in his hand, Noah sat on the porch swing for the rest of the day, staring wearily out toward the pond. Oblivious to the sweltering heat, he watched as the blue skies darkened and the clouds thickened. The maple was soon swallowed by darkness with the arrival of night.

"I waited that is... until I couldn't wait any longer."

A boom overhead jolted Noah out of his trance. He flinched at a flash of lightning that was followed by another crack of thunder. With the abrupt drop in temperature and increasing winds, Noah was shivering as he took a deep breath and flipped open the phone. Hitting *Redial*, the call went straight through to voicemail.

A red robin swooped down in front of him, settling on a branch half way up the maple tree. Noah set the phone down and stepped off the porch into the rain. As he approached the tree, he could make out a nest and a second robin.

Blinded by a burst of light, Noah was thrown to the ground by a thunderous explosion, and the old maple tree came crashing down onto the dock. Picking himself up, he walked cautiously over to the severed trunk, running his hand over the jagged edge and the remaining words *Robin* ∞. Miraculously, the two birds fluttered down, landing back on the fallen tree. Looking down, he saw the empty nest at his feet, and he picked it up.

The door to the tool shed flew open as Noah stormed in and grabbed a handle off the wall. With the sound of distant thunder and the sky lighting up above his head, Noah began striking the tree with an axe.

The next morning, Noah drove over to Robin's apartment and parked his pickup truck behind her Range Rover. *Good, she's here,* he thought as he rang the doorbell. However, no one answered. He looked back at her car and rang again, this time testing the door handle, which turned in his hand.

"Robin? Are you here?" he called out, poking his head inside. There was no response, so he took one step inside the apartment and stopped. "Robin?" he called out, looking around the room, spotting clothes scattered about the floor. "Robin, if you're here, please answer me. I need to tell you something."

He walked toward her bedroom door. "You in here? Robin?" he said, tapping lightly at the door. "Are you okay?" he asked, reaching slowly for the doorknob, grasping it... turning it...

"GET OUTTA HERE, NOAH ! Get outta here right now," Robin yelled from behind the door.

Noah dropped his hand and backed away from the door. "Of course... I'm leaving right now," he called back nervously. "But I was wondering if I could just talk to you before I go. I need to say good-bye to you in my own way, one last time. So many times you never get a chance to say good-bye to the ones you love. Please, Robin, all I need is one minute."

"Just wait for me outside, okay? I'll be right out, and we can, uh... we can talk."

Noah was sitting on the front steps, rehearsing his emotional farewell, when a police cruiser came flying around the corner, its lights flashing as it came to a screeching stop.

"Oh, shit," Noah muttered as the police officer came running at him, tackling and handcuffing him.

"Officer, this is a big misunderstanding. I didn't do anything wrong."

The officer deposited him in the back seat of his cruiser. "You're under arrest for breaking and entering."

"But the door was unlocked. I only came over to say good-bye."

"You're the ex-husband of the woman who lives in this building, correct?"

Noah nodded.

"The law doesn't differentiate whether or not the door was locked or unlocked; it's still considered breaking in. Your ex-wife was afraid you were going to hurt her."

"That's ridiculous. I'd never hurt her — I love her. She told me to wait outside so we could talk. Look, if I knew she was calling the police, do you really think I'd be sitting out here, waiting for you to come and arrest me? I was set up !"

Another cruiser pulled up with its lights flashing. As the second officer strolled over, Noah continued to explain. "A few days ago we were planning on getting remarried and having a child together. I was even buying her the house she wanted, out in the woods. Then, out of the blue, she packs up and leaves without any explanation. I just came over here to have closure, that's all."

As Robin came out of the apartment, the officers approached her to get her statement. Noah watched as Frank, wearing jeans and a white ribbed tank top, moseyed over to them, smoking a cigarette. Noah could tell that he was talking calmly to the officers, telling them what had happened. Robin pointed angrily at Noah sitting in the police car and screamed, "But I want him arrested."

While one officer tried to calm her down, the other officer walked back to the car to talk to Noah. "You're lucky that guy happened to be in the apartment to corroborate your story. State laws on domestic abuse are not in your favor, pal. If I ever catch you back here again, if I ever catch you so much as driving by the neighborhood, I'll throw your ass in jail so fast you won't even know what hit you. Are we clear on this?" Noah nodded, and the officer pulled him from the car and removed his handcuffs.

"Your wife asked me to give this back to you," he said, handing him an orange foam keychain with his house keys attached. "Now get the hell out of here."

"It was as if I had been bitten by an animal that I had cornered. It's only after you've been bitten do you learn to keep your hands to yourself. Whether I wanted to or not, it would be the last time I'd ever try to reach out to her."

Noah's Arc

Two blue foam rafts floated lazily in a kidney-shaped swimming pool just outside the picture window as Noah sat at the dinner table at his parents' summer house in Newport, gazing out. He took in the winding waterfall-slide that ran through the rock garden and emptied out into the pool, along with the brightly striped towels tossed about the stone deck in between the Jacuzzi and the swim-up bar. Beyond the deck was a sweeping, three-acre lawn that dipped down to the ocean, and in the center of the manicured lawn sat a sleek, black helicopter.

Miriam and Jerry were sitting at the table in their bathing suits as Rosa started clearing the dirty plates from the table. With traces of a beard and rumpled clothes, Noah was slouched in his chair as he continued to stare out the window. Piled behind him was a stack of unopened presents, and piled in front of him was a plate full of food.

"Noah, will you please answer me?" Miriam begged.

"What was that?" Noah asked, breaking from his stupor.

"Will you please eat something? Rosa is already clearing the table."

"I'm not hungry."

"Well, you have to eat."

Noah sat there, unresponsive.

"So tell me, Noah, what exactly are you planning on doing for work?" Miriam asked. "You've been screwing around all summer, jumping from one petty job to another. Don't you think you should get a real job that pays real money? And why not give the company one more chance? Who knows, maybe you'll even like it there this time, now that you've had a chance to sew your oats. Besides, your father needs you there to take over the reigns for him someday. He's not going to work forever, you know?"

"Sorry to disappoint you, Mom, but I can't do that."

"But what do I tell the ladies at Spring Valley? They keep asking me about you, and I have no idea what to say to them. 'Oh, Noah's doing just fine, thanks. He's actually really happy at his new job — as a professional bum!'"

"You can tell them that your son, who is only *temporarily* unemployed, is searching for a career that will provide him with happiness and fulfillment," Noah explained calmly.

"CAREER?" Miriam called out. "What career? You're not even working," Miriam commented with disgust.

"Well, it's not an easy thing to figure out at my age, but I'm working on it. I have a question for you, Mom. Please answer this honestly, okay? Are you ashamed of me?"

"No, Noah, your father and I are not ashamed of you. We're just very disappointed in you, that's all. You keep making bad decisions. I hate to say 'I told you so', but I knew your marriage to Robin would end in disaster. Then you come up with this bright idea to quit your job and trade in the oceanfront home that your dear grandfather left you in his will for a shack in the woods. And for what reason? So you can *not* know what to do with the rest of your life at your age?" she said, throwing her hands up in resignation.

"Well, I could always buy that lighthouse I told you about, and run it as a bed and breakfast, but you won't let me do that."

"Forget it, you're not buying that lighthouse, so just get over it already," Jerry interjected. "Now look, here's the deal. If you come back now, I'll give you your old job back, no questions asked. It'll be like you never even left. However, once I fill your position, the deal is off the table, and you'll have to fend for yourself. Even though you're my son — and I love you very much — I refuse to hire freeloaders. So what's it going to be, Noah? This is your last chance."

Noah looked at his father, considering his proposition. He was about to speak when Scott, Sharon, and their two boys came charging into the room, wearing bathing suits and carrying a cake with the numbers "4" and "0" lit on top, singing **Happy Birthday**. They placed the cake in front of Noah, who just sat there staring at it despondently.

Noah packed his presents into the back of his truck and drove away, his leftover food stuffed into a brown paper bag on the passenger seat. Heading up the ramp to the highway, he ended up at Village Liquors. He peered into the store, squinting to see around the neon Narragansett Beer sign. Looking up and down the street, he crossed into an empty park and stopped beneath a gazebo where a man was lying on a bench.

"Harry?" Noah asked.

"Yeah, that's my name. Don't overuse it," the man said, sitting up. "Do I know you?"

"No... I don't think so. But I know *you*," Noah said, handing him the brown paper bag.

Harry was sitting in the passenger seat, eating the last bit of food as Noah pulled up in front of Emergency Family Services in downtown Providence. He crumpled up the tinfoil and tossed it back into the paper bag. "Thank you," he said, handing Noah the bag and opening the door.

"Actually, I should be the one thanking *you*," Noah retorted.

Harry exited the truck without saying a word.

"You're welcome," he responded, ducking his head back in and smiling, his teeth crooked and yellow. Harry was just standing there, looking at Noah as if he was waiting for something.

"What is it, Harry?"

"You passed the test, Mr. uh... what'd you say your name was again?"

"The name's Noah."

"Oh, right... like in that book."

"You mean the Bible?"

"Yeah, that's the one..." Harry shot back. "The one where everybody thinks building an ark is such a crazy idea — everybody except for Noah. But Noah don't listen to nobody, cuz he has faith."

"Yeah, I guess he did."

"He sure showed them, huh?"

Noah nodded.

"Can you imagine how he must have felt when it finally started raining?" Harry remarked with insight in his eyes, giving Noah the once over and walking away.

As he reached the building, it started to drizzle. "Hey, Noah," he called out, turning around with his palm extended. "Looks like rain."

"I can see that," Noah responded with a laugh, shaking his head as Harry entered the building and was greeted warmly by Theresa. Noah sat for a moment thinking about what Harry had said before pulling away from the curb.

A thick cloud of dirt enveloped a burgundy Rolls Royce Silver Spirit as it bumped down the country road. The dusty automobile came to a stop next to a dirty, black Ford pickup in front of the cabin. The door to the Rolls opened, and two shapely legs in high heels swung around and settled themselves onto the rough surface. "*Oy vey*," Miriam muttered, taking in the scene as she stood up.

As she teetered toward the cabin, a heel on her Chanel shoe snapped. Swearing under her breath, she took off her shoes and continued down the rocky path toward the hammering sound emanating from behind the building.

"Hi, Noah. I brought you a house warming gift," she said, holding out a bottle of Dom Pérignon to her son, who was building a boat out of maple in front of a newly repaired dock.

Noah didn't acknowledge his mother. Instead, he continued hammering away without looking up.

Miriam took a deep breath and looked back at Noah's modest house. "It's... it's very nice," she said reluctantly.

Noah glanced up at her. "Oh, thanks, Mom. You can put it over there," he said, gesturing his head toward the stump next to the dock where the maple tree once stood. He put the hammer down and grabbed a planing tool.

"I've been talking to your father a lot lately, and guess what I got him to agree to?" she said, watching him as he planed the boat. "It wasn't easy, but you now have a brand new office waiting for you in the executive building... right next to your dad's office."

Noah switched to a block of sandpaper and started sanding, uninterested in what his mother had to say.

"And guess what the sign on the door says? Noah Hartman, Assistant Vice President of Real Estate Development. Congratulations, Noah, you earned it. And are you ready for the best part?" she said with a dramatic pause. "Your promotion comes with a fifty thousand-dollar-a-year pay raise !"

Noah continued to sand his boat without looking up.

"So, what do you say? Will you come back and help your dad run the company? He really needs you there," she said, stepping closer to push his hair from his eyes.

She paused, looking hard at him. "You know, Noah... you look different to me somehow."

Noah glanced at his mother, touching his beard. "Oh... the beard. I've just been lazy, that's all."

"No... no it's not the beard, it's something else. I can't put my finger on it, but you've changed," she said, looking down at the boat Noah was building. "So, what's this?"

"It's an ark," he announced.

"*Noah's Ark?*" she snickered. "I'm sorry, but it looks more like a dinghy to me."

"Yeah, ark, dinghy... same difference."

"Well, I hate to break it to you, but you're not going be able to fit too many pairs of animals in that little ark of yours. Well... maybe just one pair — " she said, stopping as the meaning sank in.

"That's right, Mom. It's an ark built just for two — Robin and me. Don't ask me how, but I swear God told me to just have faith and build it. So someday when she returns, we can get in it together and be carried off to some faraway place, someplace new where we can start life all over again..."

Miriam looked sympathetically at her son. "God told you this?" she asked doubtfully. She took a deep breath and stepped closer to him, wiping a tear from his eye. "I know how much you must have loved her. And I can hardly imagine how much pain you must be going through right now. If I could somehow take that pain away from you, transfer it all to me, and bear that burden in your place, I'd gladly do that for you... without hesitation."

"She even promised," Noah continued, tears welling. "When the day comes when Polaris can no longer guide me back to her, on that day, she and I will simply sail away... And this is the ark that's going to get us there," he said, collapsing onto his creation as his mother reached out to catch him.

With tears in her eyes, she gently stroked the nape of her son's neck as she hugged him close. "I'm so sorry," she whispered softly in his ear, trying to comfort him. "I love you, Noah."

"They say everything in this life happens for a reason, and even though she was gone, I now knew the reason why Robin had come in and out of my life — to save it. The least I could do was to start living it."

Looking down from the scaffolding surrounding the old lighthouse, Noah exhaled and cautiously moved away from the rail. "Thanks for helping me."

"No problem," Mike replied as he painted alongside of him. "Anything for you, buddy. Everybody at the office misses you. You should stop by sometime and say 'hello'. It's just not the same without you."

"So, what do you think?" Noah asked, breathing in the fresh air.

"It's going to be beautiful when it's all done. Lots of luck with it."

Noah nodded. "It's my dream come true."

"So what does Jerry think about your dream?"

Noah glanced at him without answering.

"Oh... I wouldn't worry about it too much if I were you. He'll get over it. He's got bigger fish to fry. Hey, pass me that rag, will ya?"

As Noah tossed him a bag, he thought about his parents for a moment, then lifted his paint bucket and moved on to the next section.

While Mike pasted wallpaper in one bedroom, Noah hung up curtains in another. They replaced rotted planks on the dock, planted flowers in the garden, and carried several kayaks and a paddleboat over to the clearing by the dock. They maneuvered a small piano into the first-floor parlor and dragged dressers upstairs into the bedrooms. Noah put used books onto the shelves in the parlor and placed a large sand dollar on top of the fireplace mantel. Lastly, he and Mike pounded two posts into the ground and nailed on a sign.

A few weeks later, two couples sat next to their luggage, enjoying a pleasant ride in a Venetian water-taxi as Noah proudly captained his first passengers toward the lighthouse. The sign on the post read *Lighthouse B & B — now open for business.*

"For the first time in my life I felt as though I was living my life — not my parents'. I did what I had to do to pursue my dreams. It remained to be seen if they would actually follow through with their threat to disinherit me. Whether they did or didn't, I still loved my parents, and I was at peace with my educated decision."

The Hidden Secret

"It had been seven years since I had last seen or heard from Robin. It was as if she had vanished off the face of the earth... and died. If I ever wanted to see Robin again, it would have to be in my dreams. And so, while I slept, my soul searched endlessly for her, desperately trying to reach her..."

$\mathcal{F}$orty-seven-year-old Noah was standing in a strange classroom with other adults whom he didn't know. On the other side of the large room was Robin, standing on a stage. Noah called out to her, but she didn't hear or see him. As he tried to make his way toward her, the more desks and people there were in his way. He forged on, desperate to reach her, but it seemed to be taking all night. He suddenly stopped. The desks were stacked on top of each other, forming a wall that reached the ceiling, and there were no longer any people in the room. The room was silent, and Robin was gone.

Waking in a sweat from his dream, Noah curled up and started to moan, tears flowing from his eyes.

"Even if I couldn't remember what I had dreamt about by the time I woke up, I'd have a strange feeling, a lump in my throat and a pit in my stomach, and I'd know — I'd know that Robin's ghost had visited me."

"Why was it so hard to get over her?" I say, repeating Josh's question. *"That's what I wanted to know. So I made an appointment to see Gabe Shapiro, a renowned psychologist at Butler Hospital — to get answers."*

"Isn't there some prescription I can take to prevent dreaming?" Noah asked Gabe. "Because I keep having the same recurring dream. And in that dream, I'm old and lying in a bed — my deathbed, I think. There's an attractive nurse trying to take care of me, but she's only in the way. I try to hang on, hoping to hear her say it one last time — you know... before I die."

"Hear what?" Gabe asked.

"And then, out of nowhere she's there. She came back for me."

"Who? The nurse?"

"No... Robin. She's old too, with silver hair, but she looks beautiful to me."

"Oh, of course... you're talking about Robin again."

"The nurse is visibly upset. She walks away... down a dock — at least I think it's a dock."

"And then what?"

"She leans over me, looks into my eyes, and tells me she loves me."

"Noah, you realize this is just some self-indulgent fantasy, right? And in this fantasy of yours, you want Robin to love you all over again. *Why?* Because you want everything to go back to just the way it was before. But while you're stuck in the past, everybody else is moving forward with their lives in the present — everybody except for you, that is."

"I get all that, but I think there's a deeper meaning here. Hear me out. When Robin severed our relationship, it all happened so fast, and it was so senseless. I realize now if I'm ever going to have any closure, if I'm ever going to rest in peace... I need to hear her tell me she loves me one last time."

"Noah, let's be realistic here. You know that's never going to happen. When was the last time she even spoke to you?"

"Seven years ago, on my fortieth birthday... when she tried to have me arrested," he said, his voice trailing off.

"Unbelievable. And then she just vanished off the face of the earth as far as you're concerned. Am I right?"

Noah looked away, nodding reluctantly.

"Noah, come on now; can't you take a hint? She doesn't want to have anything to do with you. She has moved on, and you should too. You're a good-looking guy, only forty-seven. Go find somebody else. There's plenty of fish in the sea."

"Yeah, that's true, there are a lot of fish out there... except the one that got away was the one I loved the most. I could never love like that again... not to that intensity anyway. When she was around me, I became a better person. I'm telling you, she's my soul mate — I just know it."

168

"Okay, I get it. Let's just say for the moment that she really is your soul mate: the only person in this world with whom you were meant to be. You found her, quite an achievement, and your soul connected with hers on a level like none other."

"EXACTLY."

"Good, then we understand each other. There's just one problem with that, Noah. Although she may in fact be *your* soul mate, you, on the other hand, do not appear to be *hers*."

"But I am... I'm telling you. She just lost sight of it. I don't know how else to explain it. And she might as well have joined the witness protection program, because I don't even know her telephone number or where she lives anymore, and I'm fine with that. But what was my crime? Wanting to love her and take care of her for the rest of her life? And what did I do that was so bad to receive a life sentence?"

"I think you just answered your own question. You obviously loved her very much and committed no crime, so stop second-guessing yourself."

"If she could just pick up the phone and call me once in awhile, just to say hi or maybe to see how my life's going, I'd be able to deal with it so much better than cold turkey."

"Noah, you're acting delusional. Face the facts: she doesn't want to talk to you... not now, not ever."

"But why? I mean... I promised to love her in sickness and in health. You'd think that'd mean something — anything at all."

"Well, perhaps it didn't mean the same thing to her as it did to you."

"You don't understand... I loved her more than I loved myself."

"Well in that case, maybe it's time to start loving yourself. Have you ever considered that?"

"All in all, it's strange how things turned out. I still don't really understand it. Somehow, it was just really easy for her to have me in her life one day, and out of her life the next day, like I never even existed. I wish I could just say to her, 'HEY, remember me? The guy who loved you? The guy who married you? Well, here I am... I STILL EXIST!'" he said, raising his voice.

Gabe waited for him to calm down, and then said quietly, "I bet there are a lot of things you'd like to say to her."

Noah thought about it for a moment. "Yeah, now that you mention it, I guess there are."

"If you could say just one thing to her right now, what would it be?"

"Just one thing?"

Gabe nodded.

"I'd say, 'Robin... I still love you... I never stopped, and I always will.'"

"But why?" Gabe asked gently. "There's a pattern here, and it doesn't look good. You tried, time and time again, and it didn't work out. There's no reason for you to think that things could ever be any different with her. What was it about her that makes it so hard for you to let go?"

"You mean besides the way she used to look at me... gazing deep into my eyes, deep into my soul, like I was the only other person on earth?"

"Yeah, that's right. There's got to be more to it than that."

Noah thought for a moment. "She was overflowing with life, something I could never have," he said, leaning forward earnestly, "not until she taught me how. The ironic part is that I somehow thought I was her guardian angel, you know, put on earth to take care of her and love her. I didn't realize it at the time, but I had it wrong. You see, I wasn't *her* angel... she was *mine*. Right up until that senseless night I threw it all away, tossing my wedding band into the ocean. I had no idea how fragile she was. If I could just go back in time, I'd —"

"Listen, Noah, you're not making any sense. You may not want to hear this, but here it is, the brutal truth: she wasn't any good for you. Don't you get that?"

"Of course I get that. I don't want to feel this way about her, but my heart loves whom it loves, and I have no control over it. Not a day goes by that I don't think about her. And what I need to know is, how many more years is it going to take? Because I don't want to *think* about her anymore, I don't want to *dream* about her anymore, and I don't want to *miss* her anymore. And so I'm asking you, I'm begging you, what do I have to do to let go of her? Just tell me what to do, and I'll do it," Noah pleaded, looking at Gabe hopefully, but Gabe didn't respond.

Noah leaned in with tears in his eyes, and emphasizing each word, he asked, "What's the medical procedure for extracting her from my heart?"

"Noah, you know there's no medical procedure..." Gabe said gently, subtly shaking his head, "but I do know a psychological one that might help. Here's what I want you to do..."

Inside the secluded cabin, Noah knelt in front of the fireplace and touched a match to the newspaper, watching as the kindling wood ignited. He sat down at his desk as the fireplace started to blaze.

"Noah, get a pen and piece of paper," Gabe's voice said inside his head as Noah took a sheet of blank paper from his printer. "Now write down everything you want to say to Robin. Don't leave anything out. Write it all down. Dig as far as you can into the depths of your heart and pull out your deepest feelings."

As the words formed on the paper, tears formed in Noah's eyes. "I know it's hard, but that's okay — you're supposed to cry," Gabe's voice continued sympathetically.

Noah finished writing the letter and picked it up, staring at it. "Now that you've written everything down, how does it feel? Pretty good, huh?" Gabe's voice said encouragingly. Noah looked over at the roaring fireplace. "Okay... now burn it. Stick it in the fire and burn it. This is how you get rid of her, Noah. Embrace how you feel about her... then let go."

Noah walked over to the fireplace, clutching the letter. Hesitating a moment before holding it up to the fire, he stopped just short of it. He took a deep breath and extended it into the flames. As the corner ignited, Gabe's voice nudged, "Now let go, Noah... let go."

Noah yanked back on the letter, patting out the flames and singeing his hand.

"I just couldn't do it. I couldn't let go — not yet, anyway."

The blackened letter was on the desk in front of him as he typed away at his computer, posting his letter in the *Missed Connections* section of Craigslist. It was crazy to think that Robin would randomly come across it online, but then again, stranger things have happened.

TO ROBIN FROM NOAH

I'm posting this letter knowing full well that you'll probably never read it. Just the same, I'm hoping that it will somehow help me have closure. Even though it has been seven years since I last saw you, I still miss you like it was yesterday. I even dream about you. In fact, I'll probably go my whole life without ever getting over you, and there's nothing I can do about it. I guess it was just the way you looked at me that made me love you so much. Whether I like it or not, you'll always be the one who got away.

Just so you know, I don't blame you for leaving me. If anyone's to blame, it's me. I screwed up, and now I'm forced to live my life in the shadow of my mistakes. When we were together, I did the unthinkable. I shattered your sense of security and the fragile trust you placed in me. I didn't treat you the way you deserved to be treated, and when you spoke, I didn't listen. And so I'm writing to say I'm sorry; please forgive me.

I want you to know that I still love you, I never stopped loving you, and I always will love you. I can't help but take a piece of you with me wherever I go, as your memory is indelibly inscribed in my heart.

If someday you should ever think of me and miss me, know in your heart that I'd want you to find me once again. No matter how distant in time or space... FIND ME.

"Shit," Robin said, grabbing the padlock on the front door of her ranch house, pulling on it hard and banging on the door.

"Why can't we go into our house, Mommy?" asked six-year-old Olivia.

"I don't know, sweetie," Robin said, ripping off the orange notice stapled to her door. "I don't know," she repeated, reading the words on the paper — *BANK FORECLOSURE AUCTION Monday, September 7th, 2004 at 9:00 A.M. Do not remove under penalty of law.*

She crumpled up the paper and sat down on the concrete steps, cradling her head in her hands. She hated to bother him after all this time, but what choice did she have? Out of options and out of time, she desperately needed to protect her daughter. She took out her cell phone and started dialing a number. Halfway through, she lowered the phone and stared at the sweet, brown-haired girl sitting beside her. *Maybe this isn't such a good idea after all,* she thought, pausing before dialing the rest of the number.

"Nope... nothing from Robin," Noah said, closing the mailbox and shuffling through the mail as he walked back to his cabin. Even if she or one of her friends happened to read his posting on Craigslist, it didn't mean she'd ever respond to it.

He threw the mail on the table and sat down on the sofa, flipping through the latest issue of Sailing magazine that had just arrived. Just then, the phone rang, and not willing to be disturbed, he listened as the answering machine picked up.

"Hi, this is Noah. I'm not in right now, so please leave your name and number at the sound of the tone, and I'll get back to you as soon as possible. Thanks."

"Hi, Noah. It's me... Robin —"

Noah dropped the magazine and scrambled to pick up the phone. "OH MY GOD... Robin. How are you?"

"Oh, hey," she said with surprise in her voice. "I didn't think you were home."

"I can't believe I'm actually talking to you. I can't believe you read my letter."

"Letter? What letter? I didn't read any letter."

"You didn't see my posting on Craigslist?"

"I have no idea what you're talking about. What's Craigslist?"

"Then why are you calling me?"

"Sorry to bother you, Noah, but you're the only one left I could turn to. Frank lost his teaching job a year ago, and he hasn't been able to get another job since. I've had to work three jobs just trying to make ends meet. I leave the house in the morning, and I don't get home until late at night. I don't get a day off, and I hardly ever see my six-year-old."

"You have another child?"

"Yeah, her name's Olivia," she said, looking at her little girl, exchanging smiles with her.

There was silence on the other end. "So what do you want from me?" Noah asked cautiously.

Robin hesitated. "Twenty thousand dollars."

Noah opened the playground gate and spotted Robin standing next to the slide, where a cute, little brown-haired girl was sliding down. Robin smiled at him as he approached. It was the first time he had seen her in seven years, and at thirty-seven she looked more beautiful than ever to him.

"Olivia," Robin said, taking her daughter's hand at the bottom of the slide, "I want you to meet a good friend of mine. His name's Noah... Noah Hartman."

"Hi," she said sweetly.

"Hi, Olivia. Nice to meet you," Noah said, bending down and shaking her hand.

"Hey, mister," she said, running over to the swings. "Give me a push... will ya?"

Noah obliged, pushing her several times before turning to Robin. "So what's this all about?"

"They're gonna foreclose on our house if we don't come up with the money by Friday," she said, looking down and rubbing her foot in the dirt.

Noah was silent, waiting for her to continue.

"We'll be homeless, Noah."

"So why can't your husband help out?" he asked, waving at Olivia on the swing.

"Because he doesn't have any money, and neither do I. We're dirt poor."

"I can't believe you finally called me, not to see how I'm doing, not to say hello... but to ask for money," he said, shaking his head and looking away.

"I wouldn't have asked you if I wasn't so desperate. You're my last resort. Please, Noah, I'll be eternally grateful."

"Why? After all these years... why should *I* help you?"

Robin hesitated. "Because Olivia's your daughter."

Noah pulled up fast to Robin's old apartment, running up to the door and banging on it several times.

"NOAH... HI !" Julie greeted him excitedly, a baby in her arms.

"Hey, Julie," he said flatly.

"Come on in. Long time no see. What's goin' on?"

Noah stepped into the apartment and looked around. Three other children were running around the house. "Wow, I see you've been really busy."

Julie nodded. "That's Jake Jr., Joey, John, and this is little Emily. I had to keep trying 'till I got a girl, and I got one !"

"Julie, they're all so beautiful. Congratulations."

"Thanks, Noah. Can I get you something to drink?"

"Oh, no thanks."

"So how've ya been?"

"I ran into Robin the other day," he said, getting right to the point. "Told me Olivia's my child. Is that true?"

Julie looked hard at him for a moment. "Yeah, it's true. But Frank thinks Olivia's *his* kid."

"Why didn't she ever tell me? She should have told me."

"Yeah, you're right, she should have. But she was scared... scared that it would tear her new family apart. All she could think of was protecting her baby. Why turn her little world upside down if she didn't have to? In a strange way, I kind of agree with her."

"So she kept the secret from me and from her husband," he said incredulously. "Are there any other secrets I need to know about, because she just asked me for twenty thousand dollars?"

"WHAT? I can't believe she asked you for money. What a bitch ! I haven't seen her in five years. Do you believe that? After she married Frank, she dumped me. Wouldn't even return my calls. After all I did for her, letting her and Britt stay in my apartment rent-free for all those years. She was my oldest friend, since second grade. What did I do to deserve that? Screw her; don't give her any money," she said, setting the baby down, and reaching for a cigarette. She looked at her kids running around and put it out without smoking it.

"But you were her best friend. That doesn't make any sense. Why would someone abandon their best friend?"

"Turns out she's got a little problem... called Crossing The Border Disorder — or something like that. She never told you? The psychiatrist prescribed pills for it, but it only made things worse. What was that shrink's name again? Oh yeah... Tony."

"Please try to remember," Noah said, sitting on the edge of his chair in Tony's office. "Her name's Robin, Robin Hartman, but you might know her by her maiden name, Jaworski."

"Well, the name does ring a bell, but I still don't remember her. I have hundreds of female patients just like her," Tony bragged, sitting back in his chair, fidgeting with a little blue box.

"She was my wife. I haven't heard from her in seven years... that is, until yesterday."

Tony opened the little box and peered inside at the sterling silver Tiffany heart necklace. He opened a drawer in his desk and tossed it in with all of the other little blue boxes, all of them filled with sterling silver Tiffany heart necklaces.

"Mr. Hartman, I'm really sorry," he said, shutting the drawer.

"Why are *you* sorry? You didn't do anything."

"No... no of course not. That's... that's not what I meant," he said nervously, twirling his gold wedding band on his finger. "I'm really sorry..." he continued, "but I'm afraid I can't help you. It's against the law for me to discuss a patient without their consent," he stated, standing up and extending his hand. "Good-bye, Mr. Hartman."

"But she and her six-year-old daughter are about to become homeless."

"And I had nothing to do with that, either," Tony blurted.

"Look, you've got to help me or — "

"OR WHAT?" Tony said loudly. "You'll report me to the medical board?"

Noah looked at him, confused. "Or she'll lose her house," he explained. "Please, Tony, you treated her for years. If you can help me understand what makes her tick, maybe I can come up with a solution to prevent her and her family from becoming homeless."

Noah picked up a frame on his desk. It was a picture of Tony standing next to a pretty woman with long dark hair and two handsome boys. "Nice looking family. You all look so happy..."

"Thanks."

"How long you been married?"

"Fifteen wonderful years," he announced proudly.

Noah nodded and set the picture back down on the desk. "I had a family once..." he said sadly, slouching in his chair.

Tony sat back down and looked at Noah, sizing him up. "So, you really have no idea what went on here?"

Noah shook his head.

"And after all these years, after everything you went through... you actually still have feelings for this woman?"

Noah nodded.

"Remarkable," Tony muttered, puzzled. "Well, like I said, it's against the law for me to discuss her condition with you without her consent." Noah's head slumped. "So... let me put it this way," he continued. "I once had a *patient*, you wouldn't know her, pretty redhead chick as a matter of fact," he said, turning off the voice recorder hidden on his desk. "I want to be completely clear about this. I'm talking about a completely different person, definitely not your Robin, got it?" he said with a twinkle in his eye.

Noah perked up in his chair. "Yeah, got it. So what can you tell me about... *this patient?*"

"She had what I'd like to call a little hidden secret... called Borderline Personality Disorder. People with BPD have a problem with object relations and constancy." Noah looked confused. "They regard people in their lives as objects, and when they have no use for them anymore, they simply discard that object along with any associated feelings attached to it. Think of it like... like a switch going off."

"What are you talking about? What switch?"

"Borderlines have trouble holding onto their relationships with their friends, spouses, jobs, even their care givers. When it's convenient for them, this switch in their brain goes off, and people they previously viewed as *good* are suddenly devalued and viewed as *bad*. When this happens, no matter how much history there is between them, it all becomes... irrelevant."

"I've never heard of this before."

"That's okay, you're not alone, a lot of people have never heard of it, even though it's actually a relatively common disorder. It's widely believed that up to two percent of the adult population has this. But no one knows for sure, because so many people go undiagnosed without ever realizing that's there's anything wrong with them. It occurs mostly in young women, ages eighteen to about thirty-five. For some reason, after thirty-five, the symptoms sometimes go away all by themselves. Perhaps by that age, some Borderlines finally realize the importance of maintaining stability in their lives, but who knows?"

"I don't believe this. This is crazy."

"As of now, there is no cure, and medication rarely helps. And it's not so crazy. For most people like you and me, we are who we are today based on all the steps we took along the way to get us here, right? And associated with those steps are all the emotions that go along with it. These experiences form the basis of our character. But it's different with Robin, I mean... *this patient.* If you ask me, I'd say there's more to it than just BPD. She describes remembering the technical steps she took along the way, but once her brain devalues someone due to her illness, she can no longer remember how she felt toward that person. Somehow the emotions become conveniently erased, as if they never even existed, enabling her to discard the object without remorse. It's almost as if she falls victim to some kind of amnesia... emotional amnesia. It's really not her fault; she has no control over how her brain is programmed. I've got to give her credit though, she tried desperately to fight it, even writing herself a letter once."

"A letter?" Noah repeated, remembering the mysterious red envelope.

"Yeah... a letter. I told her not to write it, but she insisted on it anyhow. Turns out I was right after all; it was just a waste time. Because no matter how hard she'd try to hang onto her emotions, once that switch was triggered, she'd lose; and she'd lose every time. That's when her brain simply switches gears, and she finds herself just going with the flow, floating off, like a... caterpillar turned butterfly. It's kind of ironic, really."

"What do you mean?"

"Her affliction... in a way it's both a curse and a blessing at the same time. The same defect that causes her brain to unfairly cast people aside is the same defect that enables her to be a free spirit and live in the moment."

"So what you're telling me is... while Robin was off having a good time, she happened to forget that she ever loved me."

"No, not exactly. Let me put it this way: even though this patient is completely aware of the fact that she once loved this other person in her life, she has no recollection of *what it was like* to love him. All she knows is that whatever feelings she once had for him, they're no longer there. They're gone, buried deep inside her brain, where she can't access them. I'm sorry to tell you this, Noah, but she'll never remember how much she once loved you... never."

"How can you be so sure that Robin even has this?"

"Well, I call it a *hidden* secret, because it's not so obvious. Unless you start piecing together her long-term pattern of behavior, and how it affected her past relationships, you'd never even know she has it. Her life would otherwise seem pretty normal. I kind of feel bad for her. She's going to have a tough life. By the way, that beautiful red bird of yours that you loved so much... was never meant to be caged. It was never a question of *if* she was going to fly away. The question would always be *when* was she going to fly away. Consider yourself lucky it happened early on."

Noah's eyes shifted as he tried to digest all of what Tony had just said.

"Let me ask you this. The cause of BPD is relatively unknown, but many would suggest it's directly related to traumatic events that took place during childhood. In my opinion, what makes her particular case so remarkable is how her brain seems to automatically shift into some kind of adapted memory suppression. I've never seen that before in any other Borderline. To me, this suggests a particularly severe trauma. Aside from her father abandoning her and her mother when she was just a child, do you know of any other traumatic events that may have happened to her? Perhaps occurring at an early age, during the critical stages of her brain's development?"

Noah started to shake his head, but then remembered something Robin had once told him...

Three-year-old Robin was held tightly in her mother's arms, her eyes wide open with fear, her mouth covered by her mother's hand. They were hiding in back of a riding lawn mower in a dark, cluttered garage, as the bay door squeaked open. High-beam lights from an old station wagon were bright and blinding. The shadow of a man holding a gun flickered on the wall in back of them as the gunman walked into the garage, stopped, and looked around. "*Robbie Robin...* come out, come out, wherever you are..." the toothless man said in an eerie, raspy voice. With the sudden crack of a branch outside, the man went running out.

Carrying her child in her arms, Mary was running as fast as she could through the dark woods. As Robin stared back at the dwindling house, she heard the sound of a car speeding away over her mother's heaving breathing and the snapping of tree branches. Robin's delicate face was suddenly cast in yellow and orange as the house exploded, and her mother collapsed to the ground, cradling her precious cargo. As she struggled to catch her breath, Mary kissed her daughter's head repeatedly and began to cry.

"It's a beautiful yacht you got here, Noah," Neil said, getting a tour of Noah's sixty-foot sailboat. "I'm pretty sure I can get you your asking price of half a million. Just give me until next summer to find a buyer."

"Next summer? I don't have that kind of time. I need the money now."

"Whoa, hold your horses there, cowboy. I'm not God, ya know — I can't work miracles. I'll tell you what. I'll give you two hundred thousand for it right now. We could sign the papers today, and the money could be wired to you tomorrow."

"But I thought you said it's worth five hundred thousand."

"Yeah, if you got lots of time, which you ain't got. And I don't do no charity work neither. I have to make a profit, too, ya know."

"But the mortgage alone is two hundred thousand," Noah said, contemplating his offer. "Okay... make it two twenty, and you got yourself a deal."

"Are you sure you want to do this? I thought you love this beauty more than anything else in the world."

"Yeah, you're right... I do love her more than anything else," Noah replied, thinking of Robin. "And I've never been more sure of anything else in my entire life."

"Okay, then," Neil said with a sly smile, shaking Noah's hand on the deal.

"I suddenly realized that not only was it the last time I'd ever own a big, beautiful boat like that, but it was also the last time I'd ever make a sacrifice for Robin."

Noah was sitting at Dunkin Donuts, sipping a cup of coffee and clutching the partially burned letter, when Robin walked in.

"Do you want a cup of coffee or anything?" he asked her.

"No thanks," Robin replied, shaking her head and sitting down. "I have to be back at work in twenty minutes."

He sipped his coffee while Robin watched anxiously. "Hey, I was just wondering... what was in that red envelope you once handed me in the foyer, remember? You gave it to me for safekeeping and told me never to open it."

Her eyes drifted for a moment, and then she shook her head. "Don't remember."

"That's okay, never mind. It doesn't matter anymore," he said, setting the coffee cup down. He took out a check from his wallet and handed it to her.

"Thanks, Noah," she said, looking at a check for $20,000. "I promise to repay you, even if it takes me the rest of my life."

Noah nodded. "Are you sure I can't get you some coffee?"

"Sorry, I really do need to get back," she said, rising and tucking the check into her purse as she walked toward the door.

"WAIT !" Noah called out.

Robin paused, and turned to look at him.

"Before you go, there's uh, something I need to tell you," he said, picking up the letter and gathering the courage to read it.

"What is it, Noah? What do you need to tell me?"

He looked up from the paper and swallowed. "I uh... just want to say that I hope you find happiness in your life, that's all," he said, forcing a smile, and stuffing the letter into his pocket.

"I just couldn't do it. Even though I could move my lips, I couldn't manage to move my words."

"Thanks, Noah. That's really sweet of you. I hope you do too."

"I'd like to see Olivia from time to time — if that's okay with you. She'd never have to know."

"I think I can arrange that," Robin said, sending him a smile. She stared at him for a moment, and then walked back toward him.

He looked up at her as she approached. "What?"

She held out her arms, and without hesitation, Noah stood and walked into them.

"Good-bye, Robin," he said softly with tears in his eyes. "I'm going to miss you."

"And so, I finally got that hug I wanted for my fortieth birthday. Even though it arrived seven years late, it was still exactly what I needed."

Moving On

"Well, I must admit, for an eighty-year-old guy, this robe fits pretty good," I say, admiring it in the mirror, turning and checking out the back. I turn the faucet on and cup the cold water in my hands. What was it about that ark I built, anyway? Something happened on it, that I know for sure. It's all starting to come back to me now. Let's see, I was rowing out on the pond... a beautiful yellow butterfly, not unlike the one I'd seen years ago... Maybe it was all just a dream? No... definitely not a dream. What happened next? Think, Noah, think. Oh yeah...

> "Noah?" she called out, stepping closer to the water's edge.
>
> Noah looked back at the silver-haired woman in the yellow cardigan.
>
> "NOAH !" she screamed, running toward him, her coffee mug shattering as it hit the ground.
>
> *Something urgent to tell her now...*

Splash! goes the water into my eyes, dripping down my face. I turn off the faucet and grab a hand towel to dry off, looking at myself in the mirror. And it all goes blank from there.

"Noah, you okay in there?" Josh asks, knocking on the bathroom door.

"Just fine and dandy. I'll be right out," I say, focusing on the small, white bandage taped to my forehead. I grasp the edge of the tape and lift up, slowly.

Oh my God, I think to myself, looking beneath the bandage. *There's nothing there — not a scratch.*

As Noah veered the Venetian water taxi toward the lighthouse with his brother's family onboard, he told Scott all about Robin and Olivia.

"Maybe now that you've seen her, you can finally have closure and move on with your life," Scott suggested.

"Yeah, I guess you're right. It's funny, though; I never realized how fragile she really was until it was too late," Noah said, shaking his head. "And it was all my fault. After all, I was the one who threw the ring away. I broke her, and she never could recover from it."

"Listen to me," Scott demanded. "NOAH, LISTEN TO ME ! It was NOT all your fault, you hear me? It always takes two... remember that." Scott stared at his brother. "You know what your problem is? It's really easy for you to forgive everybody — everybody except yourself, that is. Don't you think it's about time to forgive yourself?"

"YES... yes it was time... time to replace blaming myself with loving myself, time to let my open wounds heal, and time, once and for all... to let go of Robin."

Seeing Noah overcome with emotion, Scott reached out to him and gave him a hug. "Let's change the subject before I start welling up," Noah suggested, wiping a tear from under his eye. "So, how's your screenwriting coming along? Have you sold a screenplay yet?"

"Apparently, Hollywood isn't making Westerns anymore these days, and they couldn't care less that I won the Nicholl Fellowship. Producers and directors have all told me how great my work is, but without financing or attaching actors, it's just sitting there, dead in the water."

"I've got a great idea for a movie. I even have a name picked out for it already: Sand Dollar, a story of undying love. Want to hear it?" Scott nodded. "We can write it together, you and I. Have you ever heard of Borderline Personality Disorder?"

"No, what's that?"

"Well apparently, people with that disorder can have a kind of switch in their brain. Now imagine that the switch goes off, and a free-spirited woman casts her soul mate away, essentially forgetting what it was like to ever love him. For her in particular, it's kind of like... emotional amnesia. But this guy could never get over her, you see, because she was the only one to ever make him feel alive. Now rewind to the beginning of the movie: a man and a woman are scuba diving on their honeymoon, when the man spots a lone sand dollar sitting undisturbed on the ocean floor below..."

As Scott and the rest of his family stepped off the boat onto the dock at the lighthouse bed-and-breakfast, Noah continued telling his brother about his great idea for a movie.

"As it turned out, I wasn't the only one in the family with a knack for expressive writing, huh, Scott?" I say, sitting down on the hospital bed in my new linen robe. "Can you believe our little screenplay actually got turned into a major motion picture? Ha. We made a pretty good team together, didn't we, Scott?"

Scott doesn't respond.

"Who'd have thought that the missing ingredient for the two of us would be each other?" I say, laughing to myself, thinking about it. "I guess we both had to learn to trust each other and not try to do everything by ourselves, huh, Scott?"

Hearing a distracting noise in the hallway, Scott and I both look toward the door and then back at each other.

"So I kept trying different doors until I found one that opened," I continue, turning to Josh. "Then, I had to be brave enough to walk through it."

"I've got to give you credit," Josh tells me. "Even though you never knew where the road was going to take you, you always had faith."

"Yeah, I did, didn't I?" I say proudly.

"Tell me something, Noah. Whom exactly did you have faith in?"

"Well, it wasn't in God, if that's what you mean. SO... anyone know what's taking so long?" I ask, taking a deep breath as I look at the three people standing around my bed. "I'd like to go home already, if you don't mind. *Home*... now that's a pleasant thought," I say, adjusting my pillow as I lie back down. "Where the soft morning light filters through the sheer curtains of our bedroom..."

Noah opened his eyes and smiled with contentment as he stared lovingly at the silver-haired woman sleeping peacefully beside him. He kissed her head lightly as he quietly left the room, leaving a pink envelope beside her on the pillow.

"It's coming back to me in pieces. Which reminds me — you know what today is?" I say with my hands nestled behind my head, looking up at my sister-in-law. "It's our anniversary. Now if I could only remember what I needed to tell her that was so important..."

"Do you think he can hear us?" Sharon asks her husband as though I'm invisible.

"In my heart, I just know he can," Scott responds, his eyes watery.

"Ha ha, very funny," I say sarcastically.

"I love you, Noah," my sister-in law says softly, kissing my forehead. "Life just won't be the same without you."

Just then, Doctor Feldman enters my room and walks straight over to greet my brother and sister-in-law. "Mr. Hartman," he says to him, holding out his hand, "may I please see Noah's living will?"

Scott takes a document out of his pocket and hands it to the doctor.

"Living will? Hey, Scott, what's this all about? Why does he want to see my living will?" I ask, sitting up to get a closer look.

"Okay, good," the doctor says, handing my brother a clipboard with a form on it. "Now please sign here at the bottom, instructing us to take Noah off of life support."

"LIFE SUPPORT? What the hell are you talking about? There's nothing wrong with me. I don't even know why I'm here," I say, jumping off the bed and looking over Scott's shoulder. "That's what it says, all right... *life support*. This doesn't make any sense. What's happening here?"

My eyes drift off the clipboard to the equipment in back of my bed that I hadn't paid much attention to until now. On the wall in back of my bed is a large glass monitor projecting a three-dimensional image of a pumping heart, along with a three-dimensional contour map of the heart's continuous electrical activity. Also on the large glass monitor is a three-dimensional image of a brain, shown in black and white, with the number *00.000* and the words *No Brain Activity* beside it.

"What the hell is that thing, a ventilator?" I exclaim, jolting backward, pointing at a silver box on wheels. It has a flat-panel display on top displaying an animation of a bellows travelling up and down a cylinder, making a swishing sound.

"It's okay, Noah... relax," Josh says, trying to calm me. "Everything is going to be fine. You're in good hands, trust me."

My eyes sink slowly to the bed. "Josh..." I mutter nervously. "Who is that in the bed?"

"It's you, Noah. *You're* in the bed," Josh explains gently.

Lying in the bed, comatose with a small, white bandage taped to his forehead, is my carbon copy. An aluminum, dome-shaped frame positioned on his head has red lights along the perimeter and electrical sensors along the interior, wirelessly transmitting electrical brain activity to the glass monitor. Sitting on top of his chest is a smooth, graphite half-sphere device with a green LED light flashing quickly around it, wirelessly transmitting electrical heart activity. He has a breathing tube coming out of his mouth that's connected to a silver box that I presume is a ventilator, keeping him alive. An IV tube keeps his blood nourished.

"I don't understand. If that's me in the bed, then how could I be standing here talking to you?"

"Noah, your *body* is in the bed. Your *soul* is standing here, talking to me."

"How could that be?" What, am I dead or something?" I say with a nervous laugh. "You can't be serious?" I say, staring into Josh's solemn eyes, my face turning grim. "NO... no, it's not true. Look... over here, on the monitor. I have a heartbeat and everything. No way, I'm not dead. I'm dreaming, right? Tell me I'm dreaming."

Josh folds his arms, not answering.

"*I* know... they gave me too much morphine, right? I'm hallucinating, that's all."

"Noah, you're not dreaming, and you're not hallucinating. There's nothing to worry about; trust me. Your soul has merely been separated from your body in preparation."

Tears form in Scott's eyes as he stares at the document on the clipboard, which is now shaking in his hand.

"Give me that thing," I say, lunging for the clipboard, my hand passing right through it. I stare at my hand in disbelief. "What was that you just said about preparation?"

Josh walks over to Sharon, resting his hand on her shoulder. "Sharon, Scott needs you right now. Tell him everything's going to be okay."

Sharon holds her husband's hand tenderly to stop it from shaking. "Don't worry, honey, everything's going to be okay," she says, putting her arms around him.

"Josh, or whoever you are, please tell me... in preparation for what?"

186

"Look, Mr. Hartman," Doctor Feldman says to Scott, "you're making the right decision. Your brother's brain is dead, and there's nothing we can do to bring him back to life — it'd take a miracle. The quality of his life would be no more than that of a vegetable. He'll never see, hear, smell, taste, or feel anything ever again. He can't ever have emotion, and he certainly would never know that you're standing right here next to him. The only thing he can do now is exist in a coma, and nothing more."

"But I do know you're standing right here next to me," I whisper.

Josh walks over to me, his eyes piercing deep into mine. I feel calmness come over me, a familiar feeling of peace and tranquility that I used to only feel out at sea.

"In preparation for your entry into heaven," he says compassionately.

"Scott, everything is going to be okay," I say, placing my hand on my brother's back. "My life may be over, but my love will live on forever."

Scott nods, reluctantly signing the form and handing it back to the doctor. "My brother was a kind soul," he explains, tears welling in his eyes as he looks up at the three-dimensional image of the heart beating on the large glass monitor. "You have such a big heart, Noah. No wonder why you always followed it. I can still feel your love, even now. Good-bye, Little Brother. I'm going to miss you."

"I never realized," I say to Josh, reflecting.

"Realized what, Noah?"

"How much they all loved me."

The doctor puts his hand on my brother's shoulder. "It won't be long now before Noah's soul moves on to a better place."

A New Chapter

"We're live here in Newport, Rhode Island for the premiere of the new movie **Sand Dollar**, filmed right here in Rhode Island and written by fellow Rhode Islanders Scott and Noah Hartman," said Ginger, who was dressed in a black sleeveless sequined gown and speaking into a handheld microphone while a Channel 10 cameraman filmed her. "As you can see in back of me, the stars have just arrived on the red carpet to a tremendous crowd of people, who have turned out this evening to get a glimpse of stardom, and who knows, maybe even go home with an autograph or two. I'm one of the lucky ones to actually receive an invitation to tonight's premiere, and I'll report back on it tonight at 11:00. Back to you, Tom."

Fifty-year-old Noah was all smiles as he stood on the red carpet in a black tuxedo. He shook people's hands and hugged some friends who had come to support him. Scott and Sharon were also on the red carpet, talking to people they knew in the crowd.

Sarah, a beautiful thirty-four-year-old woman with long, dark hair and Mediterranean looks, was wearing an elegant Armani dress as she stood behind a rope at the front of the crowd.

"Congratulations on your new movie, Noah," she said with a radiant smile. "May I have your autograph?"

"Thanks. To whom do I make this out?" he said, accepting her pen.

"You can make it out to Sarah... Sarah Schwartz."

He stopped signing and looked up from the paper, her grin indicating that she knew something that he didn't. "*The* Sarah Schwartz? The Brown Med School student?"

"The one and only. Except I'm no longer a student; I'm a pediatrician."

He signed the rest of his name and handed it back to her. "I was just wondering..." he said, taking in her shapely figure and beautiful face, "how'd you like to go to the movies with me tonight?"

Sarah smiled.

Doctor Feldman removes the breathing tube from the body lying in the hospital bed as Josh, Scott, Sharon, and I look on. The door opens, and sixty-four-year-old Sarah rushes into the room with Zachary, our twenty-seven-year-old son.

"Are we too late?" Sarah asks, out of breath.

"Hi, Sarah," Scott answers. "No, the doctor is doing it now."

The doctor turns off the power to the ventilator and quietly leaves the room.

"I love you, Dad," Zach says, putting his arms around the body in the bed.

"Zach wanted to say good-bye to his father one last time," Sarah explains.

"Isn't there anything I can do for my son?" I ask, turning to Josh.

"Go ahead... speak to him. He won't be able to hear you, but maybe he'll feel your spirit deep inside."

"Zach, can you hear me?" I ask, walking over to him. "I love you, Zach," I say, placing my hand on his head. "Don't worry about me, okay, buddy? I'll be just fine."

With tears in his eyes, Zach looks up at Sarah and says, "Mom, this seems so surreal. I feel like at any minute Dad's going to give us all a big hug and tell us he'll be just fine."

Above them on the large glass monitor, Noah's heartbeats grow farther and farther apart.

"I was starting a new chapter in my life — a happy chapter, with Sarah. She was not only my best friend, but she also loved me very much. And so two years later, it was time to move on to the next level..."

An opened pregnancy test box sat on top of a French vanity in her brick colonial on the East Side. "Oh my God, I don't believe it," Sarah gasped with a sigh of relief, the stick in her hand revealing a *plus* sign. She checked it again just to make sure — definitely a *plus* sign. She flushed the toilet, turned the hot water on to the large, heart-shaped Jacuzzi, and left the room, smiling.

Downstairs in the library, Noah was sitting at an antique roll-top desk, writing on notepaper. He tore off the note and attached it to a DVD of his new movie, **Sand Dollar**, slipping it inside a padded mailer and addressing it to Robin. He sealed the envelope and placed it face down on the desk, closing the tambour.

Stretching as he stood up, he walked across the room and pushed open the two sliding French pocket doors. Glancing down at his feet, red rose petals were scattered on the floor, forming a trail that traveled down the hall and around the corner. He followed it into the kitchen, where it passed over a bottle of Roederer Cristal Champagne that was immersed in a sterling silver bucket of ice next to two Waterford crystal Champagne glasses. He picked up the bottle and glasses, and continued on his expedition, following the trail through the butler's pantry, the formal dining room, and up the stairs to the second floor, ending at the door to the master bathroom. He pushed the door open slowly.

Soaking in bubbles, Sarah looked up from the Jacuzzi, the glow from a dozen candles flickering in the dimly lit room. Noah smiled as he walked over to her, sitting on the pink marble platform and kissing her while she unbuttoned his shirt.

"So, what's this all about?" he asked, taking a sip of Champagne as he eased into the hot water across from her.

"What?" she responded coyly, holding the glass of Champagne in her hand without drinking it. "Can't a woman take a bubble bath in peace without being accused of wanting something?"

"So that's it... you want something..."

"*Maybe*," she said sweetly, setting the Champagne glass down and crawling over to his side of the tub. "Let's get married," she said enthusiastically. "Don't you see how perfect we are for each other? We like the same things, laugh at the same jokes, share the same values, the same background, the same religion, and we almost never argue. We're the perfect match for each other."

"I don't know, Sarah... I guess I just don't want marriage to ruin a good relationship. After all, you're my best friend."

"And who says that best friends can't marry each other? Besides, our parents have been friends forever, and you know your parents are crazy about me. Even our friends think we're perfect for each other. So what's the hold up? If you're waiting for the right moment to propose, this is it."

"Sarah, you're a wonderful woman, but it's not you, it's me. You know I never fully got over Robin. You deserve better, that's all."

"I'm so sick of hearing that lame excuse from you all the time. When are you going to finally let go of that ghost from your past, and start living life with me in the present? The truth is, Robin's not coming through that door, not now, not ever. She's moved on, and you should too. Look at me, Noah. I'm no ghost. I'm real, I'm right here right now, and I love you."

"Sarah, you're a great friend, and I love you too — you know that — but I just don't think it would be fair to you if — "

"How do you feel about having a child? I mean... wouldn't it be great to have one?" she said, sitting back and picking up her Champagne glass, staring at it.

"What do you mean by that?"

She exhaled and looked at him. "I'm pregnant, you big dummy," she said, scooping a clump of bubbles collected between her large breasts and tossing it toward him.

"Wow... I didn't see that one coming."

"Maybe you're right; I wouldn't want marriage to ruin a good friendship," she said self-consciously.

"No... no, it's a good idea. You're right, let's get married... absolutely."

Sarah let out of scream of joy. "Really? You want to get married?"

Noah nodded as he tried to sip his Champagne, spilling it as she tackled him in the tub, kissing him all over his face. He tried to smile as they hugged in the water, but all he could think of at that moment was Robin's face, casting a shadow on Sarah's.

Revelations

$\mathcal{F}$orty-two years old and wearing prescription eyeglasses, Robin opened the padded mailer that had just arrived in the mail, and she was surprised to pull out a DVD of **Sand Dollar**. She hadn't been to the movie theater in years, and she knew nothing about Noah's involvement... until now. She read the attached note.

Dear Robin,

For what it's worth, even though my life has moved on without you, I want you to know that I will always take a part of you with me. Although we live separate lives, time has proven that my love for you will never die. Enclosed is a movie I wrote about us. I hope you enjoy it. And most of all, I hope your life is filled with happiness and love.

Love always,
Noah

Frank had aged poorly. He had gained a considerable amount of weight over the years, and his hair, which was now cut short with a bald spot on top, was offset by a goatee on the bottom.

"Hey, Robin, bring me another beer," Frank demanded from the basement.

Robin put **Sand Dollar** into the DVD player in the den and pressed *Play*. She left to go into the kitchen, taking out a container of pineapple ice cream from the freezer and putting a small scoop into a bowl. Back in the den with her ice cream she went, sitting down and watching the movie while ignoring her husband's command.

As the movie unfolded, she realized that the love story playing out before her eyes was actually her own. Everything was in it — getting butterflies when she stared at Noah driving his car, Noah taking her hand and pointing it up at the North Star, the amazing kiss in the foyer, and the tumultuous waves crashing onto the beach as she and Noah made love for the first time. Tears started rolling down her face as memories of loving Noah floated back to the surface.

"Hey, where the hell's my beer already?" Frank shouted up from the basement, annoyed.

Robin got up, blew her nose, and left the room just as her film character was opening a mysterious manila envelope. She went into the kitchen and opened the refrigerator door, staring at shelves stuffed with Budweiser. She closed the refrigerator door without taking one, opening the freezer door instead and eating directly out of the container of ice cream with a large serving spoon.

Sarah, very pregnant and wearing a coat over her scrubs, was carrying a baby toy wrapped with a blue ribbon as she opened the front door of her brick colonial and stepped inside. Upon entering the foyer, Noah surprised her with a long, passionate kiss.

"What the hell has gotten into you?" she said, pushing him away. "There's a time and place for that. Can I at least take my coat off first?"

"I'm sorry," Noah said, looking dejected. "I uh... just missed you, that's all."

"I missed you too, but geesh, cool your jets."

Noah couldn't help but compare that disappointing foyer kiss to the unforgettable one he once shared with Robin. Of all the things Sarah could be, there was one thing she could never be — Robin.

"Here..." she said, handing him the present as she hung up her coat. "Will you please put this in the basement with the other baby shower gifts? Thanks."

"Come on upstairs," he said, setting aside the present and taking her hand. "I want to show you something."

She followed him up the stairs to the spare bedroom that would soon become Zach's nursery. "TAH DAH," he exclaimed with a big smile, turning on the lights.

"What do you think you're doing?" she said, worried, looking around the room at the blue wallpaper with whimsical sailboats. "Don't you know it's bad luck to prepare the nursery *before* the baby's born? What if something bad happens?"

"Nothing bad is going to happen. We both saw the ultrasound this morning. He's perfect, all eleven fingers and all nine toes," he joked, putting his arms around her.

"I know you had good intentions," she said, breaking free from his hug, "but please don't do anything like this again without checking with me first, okay?" She shook her head as she turned the light off and left the room.

Disappointed yet again, Noah had hoped Sarah would have been more appreciative, like Robin was when he fixed up Brittany's room. Noah retrieved the present and ambled down to the basement. Sitting on the berber carpet with baby presents stacked around him, Noah wiped off a dusty box and opened it.

"Ahem," Sarah said, standing behind him with her arms crossed.

"Oh, hi, hon," he said, looking up, sliding the wedding pictures of him and Robin back into the box and closing the lid.

"I'll take those," she demanded, holding out her hand.

"What?" he said, putting his arms around the box, shielding it. "They're just a bunch of old pictures. They don't mean anything to me."

Sarah stood there, tapping her foot, her hand still out. Noah grudgingly handed the box over to her. He followed her back upstairs and into the kitchen, watching helplessly as she threw the box into the garbage can.

"What did you do that for?"

"I did it for Zach," she said, standing between Noah and the garbage can. "He's going to need a father that loves his mother, not some... ghost."

"But I don't love her anymore... I love *you*," he said, putting his hands on her shoulders, looking into her eyes. "Besides, that was ages ago, and Robin's happily married with a child. Just keep showing me love like you always do, and her memory will disappear into the distant past, I promise."

Sarah tried to smile as Noah gave her a hug and stared sadly past her at the garbage can.

Noah was tossing and turning in bed, dreaming while Sarah slept soundly beside him, snoring. In the dream, the small sailboat that Noah once built was sailing on the pond. Back at the dock, Noah was lying in a hospital bed, old and dying. A young nurse was taking his blood pressure as a bellows travelled up and down a glass cylinder, making a snoring sound as it pumped air.

The sailboat pulled up to the dock, and Robin stepped off. She was old too, with silver hair, but she still looked beautiful to Noah. Walking away down the dock, the nurse's face was now visible beneath her hood. The disappointed face was Sarah's.

"Here I am, Noah. I came back for you," Robin said, gazing lovingly into his eyes. "And this time, I'm here to stay." Noah couldn't believe his eyes or ears. "I remember now, and I'm so sorry. Please forgive me," she said as a tear rolled down his face. "I love you, Noah," she said softly, taking his hand and leaning over him. She closed her eyes and gently placed her lips up against his.

"I love you, Noah," her voice echoed as he awoke from his dream, sobbing quietly as his fiancée slumbered peacefully beside him.

In Robin's dream, she was making love to Noah, riding him. Outside, the ocean was turbulent as large, white waves pounded the beach in a violent storm. Lightning lit up the room, projecting the silhouette of her shapely body rocking back and forth on the wall.

Noah looked up at her and smiled. With his mouth open and his eyes dilated, his face displayed sheer ecstasy. She removed his hands from her slow-moving hips and placed them together over his head on the bed, pinning his wrists down with her hands. The more he tried to resist, the more pressure she used to hold them down. Her hair and breasts brushed lightly across his skin as she kissed her way down his arm, then his forehead, both eyes, cheeks, lips, chin, and neck. Releasing his hands, her moist lips continued ever so slowly downward, savoring every inch of his succulent, toned body, which quivered when she reached his lower abdomen.

There was a faint crash outside, and Robin turned her head. As lightning lit up her naked torso, she walked across the room toward the large, arched window. With rain rolling down the window, obscuring her view, she wiped the fog off the glass and peered outside.

"Oh my God, there's something out there," she exclaimed, observing what appeared to be a boat in distress. She looked back toward the bed and was surprised to see Tony lying in it, shirtless and smoking a cigarette.

She cupped her hands around her eyes as she pressed them back against the glass. "NOAH !" she screamed, spotting him in the water, clinging onto a rock beside his capsized boat as a large wave broke over his head. "Here I am, Noah," she yelled in vain, banging on the glass.

Another wave broke over his head, and he was gone. "NOOOOO !" she screamed as Tony pulled her away from the window toward the bed, snickering.

Sitting up abruptly, Robin awoke in a sweat, her heart racing and her breathing heavy. She looked beside her and saw that Frank had not come to bed yet. Realizing that she had no clothes on, she arose and slipped a nightgown over her head. She walked into the living room and picked up her wedding album with Noah from the shelf, browsing through it.

Just then the front door burst open, and Frank stumbled in with a crushed can of Budweiser in his hand. Robin shut the album and shoved it back onto the shelf beside a dusty manila envelope.

"Come on, woman, time to make yourself useful," he demanded, grabbing her arm and pulling her into the bedroom.

"Leave me alone, Frank, you're drunk," she said, trying to free her arm.

He slammed the bedroom door behind them, locking it. "Been staring at titties all night long at the Foxy Lady, and it's time I get me some ass," he said, shoving her onto the bed and dropping his pants.

"No, Frank, I don't want to," she said, struggling to break free.

"Where do you think you're goin'?" he growled, tossing himself onto her.

"GET OFF OF ME !" she screamed, her nightgown pulled up to her neck.

She slapped him across the face, screaming when he slapped her back.

"Mom, are you okay in there?" she heard coming from the other side of the door. "MOM?" Olivia yelled, banging on the door. "MOM?"

"Yeah, I'm fine, sweetie. Go back to bed," she called out calmly while her husband humped away.

As Robin's eyes rolled to the back of her head, her mind drifted off to some faraway place, and the memory that had eluded her all these years finally revealed itself.

The neon sign on top of the Art Deco style building that read *Zeke's Diner* went off with a click. Inside, Robin was helping to clear tables in the empty diner. The retro wall clock showed that it was 10:21 p.m.

"I gotta go pick up Zeke from his night job. Are you sure you're okay closing up all by yourself?" asked Mary.

"Mom, I'm sixteen. I'm not a child anymore. Stop worrying about me; I'll be just fine," she said, wiping off a table with a wet rag. She looked up and saw her mom still standing there, staring at her. "GO... go already. Dad's waiting for you. I'll see you at home in a little while," she said, picking up a broom and sweeping it toward her mom.

"Love you," her mother said, kissing her on the cheek and setting the keys to the diner down on the counter.

"Love you too, Mom," she said, the bell on the door jingling as her mother left.

A minute later, the bell on the door jingled once again, and Robin let out a grunt of frustration. "Mom, why are you —" she said, turning around to face the door, surprised to see a man standing there with a scruffy beard and a long trench coat.

"Coffee, please," the man said in a raspy voice.

"Sorry, sir, we closed at ten."

"So, you must be Robin."

"Yeah, how'd you know that?"

"Says it right there on your tag," he said, pointing at her name badge.

Robin glanced over at the coffee machine and saw that there was still some coffee left in the pot.

"Okay, whatever... But you have to take it to go. I have to lock up and get out of here. I have school in the morning," she said, setting the broom down and walking behind the counter to get the coffee. She removed her name badge and read it — *Mary Jr.*

Suddenly the lights went off. She turned around and jumped, dropping the coffee pot to the floor, where it shattered. The man had come around the counter and was standing way too close to her.

"What's the matter, Robbie Robin? Don't you recognize me?" he asked, cornering her. She shook her head. "I've been searching for you and your mom for quite some time now, but you seem to be avoiding me for some reason.

197

Don't you know that hurts my feelings? And look at you, all grown up and everything," he said, licking his lips as he stared at the zipper resting at her cleavage. "I bet all the boys at school fight over who's going to be the first one to get into your pants, don't they? But, you don't want a boy, do you? What you want... is a *man*."

She threw the Styrofoam cup of coffee at him and ran to the door. She rattled it hard, but it was locked. Looking desperately at the counter, she realized with horror that the keys were no longer there. With a toothless grin, the man walking toward her was holding the keys in one hand and a long knife in the other.

As Mary drove her Ford Taurus down the street, she looked in her rear-view mirror at the diner. *That's strange*, she thought to herself, noticing that the inside lights were off. *Robin knows to always leave the security lights on.* She slammed on the brakes and opened the glove compartment, revealing a .22-caliber snub nose revolver. Her tires screeched as she hastily made a U-turn in the middle of the street, cutting off an oncoming car.

The man grabbed Robin by the neck and threw her on top of a booth, pinning her down as he unbuckled his belt and dropped his pants. As Robin's eyes rolled to the back of her head, she began to black out. The last thing she heard before everything went blank was the odd sound of a bell jingling on a door, followed by the harsh sound of bullets.

The Wedding

$\mathcal{T}$ ormented by memories from her past, Robin had gained fifty pounds in the year that followed. She was torn between loving Noah in her previous life, and the harsh reality she was now living with an abusive husband in her current life. Looking back, she had married Frank because he was the polar opposite of Noah — a safe bet. Robin knew that Frank would never abandon her, but she wasn't so sure with Noah. And so she had done to Noah what she had always feared Noah would do to her. There was just one flaw in her thinking: Noah never would have left her; he worshiped her. But there was nothing she could do about it now. It was ancient history.

She realized that she had misjudged Noah and made a terrible mistake in ever allowing Tony to influence her. The sad part about all of this was that Tony had not only abused his professional influence to exploit her on one occasion, he had done it on two. The first occasion took place when he persuaded Robin to divorce Noah so he could sleep with her whenever he wanted. But that arrangement was short lived when she got back together with Noah a year later, ruining his setup. That's when Tony seized the opportunity to do it again, this time convincing her to leave Noah for Frank. He figured if he was ever going to sleep with her again, he had to get Noah out of the picture once and for all. Robin finally realized what a creep he was when he continued to hit on her even after she was seeing Frank. Only then did she start thinking that she might not be the only patient with whom Tony slept.

And so thirteen years later, Robin's longtime suspicions about Tony were finally confirmed at her kitchen table as she sat in her robe drinking hazelnut coffee and reading the Providence Journal. Tony's picture was plastered all over the front page, the headline reading — *Prominent Psychiatrist Indicted On Charges Of Sexual Misconduct.* Apparently, having sex with your patients was illegal in the state of Rhode Island. The laundry list of female patients lined up to testify against him supposedly gave the prosecution a cut and dried case. Not finding him at any of his usual places, the police eventually discovered him hiding out in his mother's attic. That's where they arrested him.

As Robin read the article, she was disgusted by his total disregard for the lives he ruined — including her own — and the wake of personal devastation he left behind. She took a sip of coffee and turned to the *Classifieds*, where she started circling jobs that interested her.

"Hey, Robin, get me some coffee, will ya?" Frank yelled from across the house.

She put the paper down on the table and stood up, suddenly noticing the feature article on the cover of the *Lifebeat* section. It was a picture of Noah and Sarah, the headline reading — *Noah Hartman, Co-Author Of Sand Dollar, To Wed Today In Newport*. She picked up the article and started reading it as she moseyed over to the coffee maker. She picked up the pot and put it back down without pouring any, engrossed in the article as she returned to her chair.

"What, are you deaf?" Frank said, stomping into the kitchen, grabbing the coffee pot and a Father-Of-The-Year mug. She quickly hid the article underneath the rest of the newspaper and resumed searching the *Classifieds* for a job.

"Yeah, that's right," he said, taking a sip of coffee as he looked over her shoulder, "time to get your fat ass back into a job already. What was wrong with the last job you quit, anyway? Ya know what? Forget the frickin' job, just walk the streets and sell your body," he said, gawking at her overweight figure, disgusted. "On second thought, what jerk would be stupid enough to pay money for that? Me, that's who."

"Asshole," she said softly into her coffee mug, drinking the last sip and standing up to get more.

"EXCUSE ME?" he said with an intimidating voice, following her over to the coffee maker. She poured herself another cup and walked over to the refrigerator without acknowledging him. "What did you just say to me?" he asked, trailing her.

She opened the refrigerator door and took out the half and half, ignoring him. "Look at me when I'm talking to you, goddamn it !" he yelled, knocking the carton out of her hand and on to the floor, where it spilled. "Here..." he said, handing her a mop. "Clean it up," he ordered as he stormed out of the house.

She was mopping up the spill when she heard a car's engine starting. "Hey, it's my day to use the car," she screamed, running to the doorway with the mop as Frank drove away, his middle finger extended out the window.

Robin walked back into the kitchen and put the mop down. She pulled her wedding picture off of the refrigerator door, looked at it for a second, and then tore it right down the middle, throwing Frank's side of the picture into the trash. She uncovered Noah's article and covered up Sarah's side of the picture with her own. As she stared at the composite image of the two of them, she noticed the Staples advertisement sticking out from underneath the rest of the newspaper. It featured a box of 100 manila envelopes for $4.99. "What was so important about manila envelopes?" she mumbled, trying to remember.

Robin ran over to the entertainment center in the living room and started rummaging through the collection of DVDs, flipping them onto the ground one at a time until she came to the one she wanted — **Sand Dollar**. She hastily put the DVD into the player and fast-forwarded it to the part she was looking for.

In the movie, the actor playing Noah rang a doorbell and left, leaving behind a manila envelope. The actress playing Robin opened the door and looked around, not seeing anyone. She picked up the manila envelope and went back inside, shutting the door behind her. Emptying the contents onto the coffee table, she discovered a mysterious red envelope sticking up from the pile of old photographs that had fallen out. As she read the letter that was inside, she ran to the door, screaming, "Wait... Noah, come back!"

Robin paused the movie and took a deep breath, looking over her shoulder across the room at the bookcase. "Holy shit," she said, spotting the unopened manila envelope sitting in plain view on the shelf with the rest of the photo albums. She ran over to the bookcase and grabbed the manila envelope, ripping it open and dumping the contents onto the floor, a bunch of old photographs dropping out. She reached her hand inside the manila envelope and slowly pulled out a red envelope. On the front, it read *Deliver to Robin when the time is right.* On the back, it read *Noah, you promised never to open this.* She hesitated and then opened it, finding a letter that had turned yellow over time, written on butterfly-themed stationery. It was dated fifteen years earlier.

To my future self,
November 15, 1995

I hope I never find myself reading this letter, but if I do, it means that the switch inside my head has erased the memories I once had of loving him. Please, God, help my brain search the depths of my heart to rediscover the love that has since been lost. Give me the courage to follow my heart and the strength to fight for the only man I have ever truly loved, my soul mate, Noah.

Robin

Inspired by her own words, she picked up the phone and dialed a number. Noah was tying a white bowtie when his cell phone started ringing. "Hello," he said into the phone, not hearing anyone. "Hello," he repeated, hearing a clicking sound. He looked at his phone curiously and then put it away in his pocket, attending to his bowtie. After all, he didn't want to be late for his own wedding.

Robin picked up the phone again and started dialing a number. "Hello, Orange Cab Company? How soon can you get here? I live at 2267 Hope Street..."

Robin was in an orange taxicab, stuck in traffic on Farewell Street in Newport. "What's the hold up?" she inquired.

"Apparently, some horse and buggy is in the road up ahead, slowing everything down," the driver said, looking at her in his rear-view mirror. "It's part of that fancy wedding they're having today at Touro Synagogue."

Inside the oldest Jewish synagogue in North America, the room was filling with people wearing formal attire. Large, white stone pillars supported an ornate stone balcony that wrapped around the entire second floor of the interior. Large arched windows on all sides added to the beauty of the architectural design.

Two white horses pulling a white stagecoach drew up in front of the building. Stepping out of the coach and looking absolutely gorgeous in her custom-made Vera Wang wedding gown was Sarah. Apparently, working with a personal trainer three times a week after giving birth had paid off, and she looked great. Six bridesmaids in wine-colored dresses held up her ten-foot train as they headed up the red-carpeted granite steps.

An orchestra could be heard playing Pachelbel's **Canon In D** as the orange taxi pulled up in front of the building. Robin jumped out of the cab and ran up the steps. As she tugged open the heavy wooden door and ran in, the orchestra began playing **Here Comes The Bride.** The audience gasped, with all eyes falling upon her as she stopped dead in her tracks. And speaking of brides, there happened to be one standing right next to her only a few feet away, a look of horror on her face behind her sheer, white veil. Across the synagogue, Noah was standing on the *bema* in a white tuxedo with tails, staring at her in astonishment. The music came to a grinding halt.

Robin turned around and ran back out the door as the audience began to chatter and the orchestra resumed playing **Here Comes The Bride.** Noah ran out after her, dashing down the red-carpeted steps and past the line of white stretch limos.

"Hey... what the hell are you doing here?" he exclaimed, grabbing her arm, catching up to her as she walked briskly down the sidewalk.

"I'm sorry, Noah," she said, wiping a tear from her eye, turning around to face him. "I never should have come here. I'm such a fool," she said, shaking her head, glancing at the white stagecoach. "Go back to your fairy tale wedding," she insisted as she turned and crossed the street.

Noah dodged traffic and caught up with her on the other side. "HEY !", he yelled, grabbing her arm again. "You still haven't answered my question. Why are you here?"

"It's not your fault... There's no reason why we couldn't have stayed married. The medication... the psychiatrist... God, I don't even know where to start," she said, covering her mouth and looking off.

"I don't believe this," Noah said, shaking his head. "Don't tell me *you're* the one who needs closure, because if you do — "

"No... no, that's not it. I made a big mistake... I never should have left you."

"Let me get this straight. You came all the way down here just to tell me you made some kind of big mistake?" She nodded. "A mistake," he repeated, throwing his hands up in the air. "A mistake?" he questioned, looking for confirmation. "Don't you think I know that already? Huh? I wanted to hate you so bad, but I couldn't stop loving you long enough to hate you. If there were any way I could have erased your memory from my brain, I would have done it in a heartbeat. But not a chance of that... not with my heart refusing to let go. I would have given my *left lung* just to hold you in my arms for one more day, just one day. Thirteen years... and not a day gone by that I didn't pray you'd come back, look into my eyes... and hear the words that you just said to me," Noah said, looking across the street at Sarah and the rest of the wedding party filtering out of the building. "NO... No, I can't do it. Sarah's a good woman and a good friend. She'd never leave me; she loves me. I'm sorry Robin. You're too late. In case you haven't noticed, I'm getting married today."

Noah walked away from her and stopped at the corner, waiting for a few cars to pass so he could cross the street and rejoin his bride waiting for him on the other side.

"Wait, don't go," Robin said softly, watching as her soul mate was about to leave her life forever. A voice inside her head spoke. "Give me the courage to follow my heart and the strength to fight for the only man I have ever truly loved, my soul mate, Noah."

As the last car passed in front of him, Noah's foot left the curb.

"I REMEMBER !" she screamed, running toward him.

"What did you just say?" he asked, his foot landing back on the sidewalk.

"I remember," she repeated, reaching him, trying to catch her breath.

"You remember?" he said, shaking his head. "What could you possibly remember?"

The beauty from within her soul shined brightly through her loving eyes as she looked deep into Noah's eyes.

"I remember I love you," she said softly.

As Noah heard these cathartic words, tears filled his eyes.

"There it was... she said it. She actually looked me in the eyes and said it. After all these years... CLOSURE."

Noah let out a scream, turned, and walked straight out into the street in front of an orange taxicab, which came to a screeching halt.

"GODDAMN YOU !" Noah screamed at her, slamming the hood of the taxi with his fist.

"HEY !" yelled the taxi driver out the window.

"How do you do that?" Noah asked her. "How do you just stand there and tell me you love me? Like... like the last thirteen years never existed. Like you somehow traveled back in time to when I last held you in my arms, and... and everything is still the same, just the way you left it. What do you expect me to do, Robin? What do you — " The lump in his throat prevented him from speaking any further. He shook his head and looked away as Robin opened the door to the taxi and jumped in.

Noah stood in the middle of the road not knowing what to do. He looked at Sarah on the other side and then looked back at Robin sitting inside the taxi, crying.

We all turn our heads as seventy-year-old Robin bursts into my hospital room crying hysterically, her body shaking. She is followed by Brittany and thirty-nine-year-old Olivia. Sarah doesn't look happy to see Robin there.

"I'll be with you soon, Noah, I'll be with you soon," Robin cries out, making her way over to the comatose body in the hospital bed. The three-dimensional mapping on the glass monitor shows my heartbeats growing ever so far apart.

"Here I am, Robin... right over here," I say to her, standing in back of her. "I'm not dead yet. I'm still alive."

"She can't hear or see you, Noah — you know that," Josh says to me.

I turn to face him. Glancing down at his photo ID card hanging around his neck, I read the name — *GOD*.

"Please, God... send me back. I'm not ready to go yet."

Doctor Feldman runs into the room, reaches right through me, and grabs hold of Robin. "Come on now, Robin, let's get you back to your room, so you can rest," he says, pulling her away from the bed and back through my image as she struggles to break free. The glass monitor starts flickering, and my eyes are drawn to the screen where the heart activity is barely active.

"I beg you, just one more minute with Robin," I say, getting down on my knees, tears rolling down my face as Josh looks down at me. "Please, God... there's something I need to tell her."

Robin breaks free from the doctor's grasp and runs back to the bed. "Here I am, Noah, right over here," she whispers, kissing both eyes on the lifeless body.

The doctor pulls her away from the bed and whisks her out of the room, followed by Brittany and Olivia. Robin reaches back hopelessly toward the room as she is taken down the hallway, screaming, "Stop, don't do it. NOOOOOOOOOOO..."

Noah was standing in the middle of the road in front of the orange taxi as cars beeped their horns. Inside the taxi sat the only woman to ever hold the key to Noah's heart. Her face painted a picture of helpless vulnerability. Noah's gentle smile and warm eyes told her that everything was going to be okay. She wiped a tear from her eye, attempting to smile.

Noah turned to look at Sarah standing across the street. The grief and sadness in his eyes told her everything she needed to know. Her forced smile turned to disappointment as she shook her head and looked down at the ground. She knew that she'd never really have a chance so long as Robin still lingered in his heart. There'd never be room for anyone else. Sarah had always been a loving friend to Noah, and in the end, she just wanted him to be happy and loved. She took a deep breath and looked back up at him. The warmth radiating from her eyes told him she'd always love him. Noah's eyes reflected the same warmth.

A photographer flying in a red helicopter took photographs of a bride and groom standing arm in arm on the outside walkway at the top of Noah's lighthouse. Below, a group of people began taking their seats in white folding chairs set up in front of a white wedding canopy.

The people getting married that day were Noah and Robin, who were now standing under the canopy putting wedding rings on each other's fingers and kissing each other passionately. The small audience stood up and cheered, and the exuberant judge belatedly added, "You may now kiss the bride !"

Noticeably absent were Jerry and Miriam.

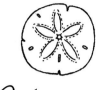

Redemption

*I*t had been five years since his parents last spoke to him. It was bad enough that Noah disobeyed their wishes and bought the lighthouse to spite them. But humiliating them and all of their country club friends at the half-million-dollar wedding that they had paid for? That was the last straw. Noah had heard from Scott that their father was sick, but up until then he didn't know exactly how sick.

Enjoying their ride over to the lighthouse, three couples were sitting in the Venetian water taxi with the wind blowing through their hair, when Noah's phone started vibrating in his pocket. He took it out and read the display — *Big Brother.*

"You better get over here right away," Scott said on the phone. "It's Dad, and he needs to talk to you."

Noah abruptly turned the water taxi around.

Jerry, who was now eighty-five years old, was lying in a hospital bed when Noah came running into his hospital room. Scott, Sharon, and Miriam were by his bedside. Miriam stepped away from the bed to greet Noah as he entered, giving him a hug and a kiss on the cheek.

"I'm really sorry about the way I treated you all these years," Miriam said, looking into his eyes, resisting the temptation to fix his hair. "All I ever wanted was to see you succeed. It's what gave purpose to my life. I couldn't bear to stand by on the sidelines and watch you fail, so I tried to detach myself. But no parent can ever truly do that. And you were always so stubborn, never understanding how important it was for me to see you make good decisions in life. So I said things to you I didn't really mean. It was the only way I knew how to steer you in the right direction. I guess I was just afraid to let go and see you fall. But you didn't fall, did you? You stayed on your feet and walked on your own. I was wrong, Noah... you always did make good decisions, because you always stayed true to your heart."

Noah took a deep breath and looked across the room at his father lying there. "I may have a funny way of showing it," Miriam concluded, "but I really do love you. Please forgive me."

"It's okay, Mom, I understand, I really do," he said, giving his mother a hug. "And I forgive you."

"Come on, let's go outside," Scott said to Sharon and Miriam, "so Dad and Noah can have privacy."

"Hey, Mom..." Noah blurted as she walked through the doorway, turning around to look at him. "I love you too," he said, trading smiles with his mother as the door closed in front of her.

"Noah... You're here," Jerry said, reaching out to him.

"Yeah, Dad... of course I'm here," he said, holding his hand.

"There's something I need to tell you."

"If you're going to tell me you love me, I already know, and I love you too, Dad."

"Will you just shut up for a second and let me speak?" They both laughed. "There's something I realize you've waited your whole life to hear from me, but for some reason I could never get myself to say it to you. It's not that I didn't feel it...because I did."

"What? What did you feel?"

Jerry coughed and started to slip away. As he regained consciousness, he looked back at his son. "I want to tell you — "

Jerry coughed again.

"What... what, Dad?"

"I want to tell you..." he said, looking directly into his eyes, "I'm proud of you, Noah," he said, smiling as the life inside of him faded away.

"I'm proud of you too, Dad," Noah whispered, kissing his father's lifeless hand as tears streamed down his face.

"My entire life, the only thing I ever wanted to do was to make my parents proud. Instead, my entire life was spent thinking I had somehow let them down... until now."

Noah was standing at his deceased father's bedside, holding his hand, while Jerry's unseen soul was right beside him, wearing a white linen robe with his hand lovingly placed on his son's back. Josh quietly left the room pushing his cart, undetected.

The Miracle

*N*oah and Robin watched as a pair of red robins flew in and out of a birdhouse hanging from a small maple tree that Noah had planted fifteen years earlier at the base of the dock where a much older maple tree once stood. In the shade of the tree, a tarp concealed the resting place of what had been sitting there undisturbed since its creation. While Robin stood by and watched, Noah brushed the branches off of the pile and proudly removed the ragged tarp, uncovering his labor of love, a dusty, old twelve-foot sailboat he had built but never used. He cleaned it up, and before long, they were out on the pond. Noah gave her a kiss as she snuggled into his arms, the small boat sailing off. The name on the transom — *Noah's Ark*.

"And so, Robin and I spent the next twenty-five years of our lives together. We were inseparable. We enjoyed biking together and even went jogging on the beach from time to time. It wasn't long before she lost the weight and felt great. She did it for her — not for me. I didn't care what she looked like; she'd always be beautiful in my eyes."

"And we did things together I never would have dreamed of doing before, like taking a pottery class, traveling across the country in a camper, and going for a ride in a hot air balloon. That's right... you heard me... a hot air balloon. It was both scary and exciting at the same time... just like life. As it turns out, I wasn't actually afraid of heights after all. What I was afraid of... was living."

"As far as my career goes, the Hartman Brothers continued to write successful screenplays, and Robin and I enjoyed running the bed-and-breakfast together. Britt, Zach, and Olivia even helped out too. We only kept as much money as we needed to live comfortably; the rest went to our favorite charity. Oh... which reminds me — just in case you're wondering — my parents didn't disinherit me after all. And I have a funny feeling they might even be proud of how I spent my share of all their millions: establishing the Miriam And Jerry Hartman Foundation To End Homelessness, a

large non-profit organization dedicated to helping families get back on their feet, out of shelters, and into affordable housing so they can live with pride and dignity. I even got Scott into the act, getting him to donate materials and equipment from Hartman Enterprises to start construction."

"You see... Robin had made me a better person. She had taught me what really matters in life, and for the last twenty-five years of my life... I felt alive."

As the sun rose over the trees, a soft light filtered through the sheer curtains of their humble cabin in the woods. Noah opened his eyes and smiled with contentment, staring at the love of his life, the silver-haired woman sleeping peacefully beside him.

"As I lay there watching Robin sleep beside me, I realized that she was right all along. I didn't need to live in a castle — a shack in the woods with her would do just fine. And for that matter, I didn't need to be prince of the ocean either, because with her by my side... I was king of the pond."

Noah eased out of bed and walked quietly over to the dresser to get dressed. He opened the top drawer, revealing the only memento he had of her for all the years she had been gone — the clear, heelless shoe. Pushing it aside, he lifted out the pink envelope that was resting underneath it, along with his pocketknife. He placed the envelope on the pillow beside her and kissed her head ever so gently, being careful not to wake her.

Noah picked up the frame that was sitting on the nightstand beside her bed. It was the letter that Robin had written to herself over forty years earlier. It was torn and faded, but still legible. She had framed it so she could read it every morning and every night, so never again would the only man she ever truly loved be forgotten. He looked at it for a moment and then set it back down carefully.

He pulled an old picture off the mirror and held it in his hand. It was the picture that Robin had taken on their honeymoon, the one with Noah holding out the sand dollar underwater. As he stared at it, memories of the sand dollar exploding replayed in his head. *Life sure is fragile,* he thought to himself, tucking the picture into his pocket and raising his head to look at his reflection in the mirror. He was now eighty years old.

Freshly carved in the bark of the maple was a heart with the inscription *Noah + Robin* ∞. Noah tucked his pocketknife away as he made his way down the dock.

He stepped into the small, wooden sailboat he had built, untied it from the posts, and dropped the lines onto the dock. There was no wind that tranquil morning on the secluded pond, so he began to paddle.

"I guess what I'm really trying to tell you is... we loved each other's souls, and as long as we had each other, we were happy. And in the end, that's all that really matters."

Seventy-year-old Robin lifted her head up off the pillow and looked at the empty space in bed beside her. Spotting the envelope, she grabbed her reading glasses and pulled out the card.

To my beloved wife,

> Once upon a time, there lived a broken man who had everything a man could possibly need, or so he thought, anyway. Then one day, the most beautiful red bird happened to be flying by. She glanced down at him and saw he needed help, so she decided to swoop down and fix him, saving his life. That's when the man realized that the only thing he really needed was the beautiful red bird.
>
> Robin, I'm so lucky you swooped down into my life. I'm the happiest man alive. After all these years, you still give me butterflies.

Happy Anniversary.
Loving you until the end of time,
Noah

As Robin tilted the envelope, a small object slid out into her hand. It was the butterfly broach that Noah had given his mother for her birthday — the priceless costume one with rhinestones from his childhood.

A ceramic sand dollar sat protected in soft cotton batting inside a small, white box. The words stenciled around the edge — *To my darling soul mate, Happy Anniversary. Noah + Robin forever.* She placed the cover over it and tied a blue ribbon around it, licking an envelope and placing it with the present on the kitchen counter.

The screen door slammed loudly behind her as she stepped out back, the rhinestone broach pinned proudly to her yellow cotton cardigan. She sipped coffee from her mug and gazed out over the pond, smiling with contentment.

A spotted, yellow butterfly hovered peacefully over a rose bush on the rocky bank of the pond. Entranced, Noah paddled over to it. He bent down as he staggered across the small boat. As he leaned against the side, he reached out his index finger toward the butterfly, and the boat listed starboard. The butterfly was just out of reach.

Robin put her hand above her eyes, concerned as Noah paddled closer to the edge. He reached out again and put his foot on the gunwale, stretching out over the water as far as he could as the boat continued to list, smiling when the butterfly made a soft landing on his finger.

"Noah?" she called out, stepping closer to the water's edge.

He turned his head and looked back at her... slipping off.

"NOAH !" she screamed, her mug shattering on the ground as she ran toward the bank of the pond. "Noah?" she yelled, charging through the thicket. But Noah didn't answer.

When she reached him, he was floating face down in the water, with blood dripping from the gash on his forehead where it hit the rock. "NOAH !" she screamed, jumping into the shallow water and turning him over. "HELP !" she screamed, crying hysterically with Noah lying motionless in her arms. "SOMEBODY HELP ME !" she pleaded, her words echoing across the isolated pond as she tried desperately to drag him out.

With Josh nowhere in sight, Noah was lying comatose in a hospital bed at Mount Sinai Hospital, a breathing tube coming out of his mouth and a white bandage taped to his forehead. An aluminum dome-shaped frame with red lights around the perimeter was positioned on his head. A smooth, graphite half-sphere device sat on top of his chest with a green LED light flashing around it. The old, wavy picture of Noah holding out the sand dollar underwater was sitting inconspicuously on the table next to a box of Kleenex.

Scott and Sharon watched as Brittany, who was overcome with emotion, walked across the room and out the door. She passed Doctor Feldman in the hallway on her way to check on her mother, who was resting comfortably in another room, having been sedated for hysteria.

The doctor entered the room and walked over to greet Scott and Sharon, who were standing next to Noah's unconscious body in the bed. "Mr. Hartman, may I please see Noah's living will?" he requested, holding out his hand. Scott took the living will out of his pocket and handed it to the doctor. "Okay, good," the doctor said, reading it and handing him a clipboard with a release form on it. "Now please sign here at the bottom, instructing us to take Noah off of life support."

As Scott attempted to read the form, tears welled in his eyes and the words blurred on the page, which was shaking in his hand. Sharon walked over to him and held his hand tenderly to stop it from shaking. "Don't worry, honey, everything's going to be okay," she said, giving her husband a hug as he wept on her shoulder.

"Look, Mr. Hartman, you're making the right decision," the doctor said gently. "Your brother's brain is dead, and there's nothing we can do to bring him back to life — it'd take a miracle. The quality of his life would be no more than that of a vegetable. He'll never see, hear, smell, taste, or feel anything ever again. He can't ever have emotion, and he certainly would never know that you're standing right here next to him. The only thing he can do now is exist in a coma, and nothing more."

Scott looked at the lifeless body in the bed and realized that Noah's soul no longer occupied it. Scott nodded and reluctantly signed the document on the clipboard, handing it back to the doctor. "My brother was a kind soul," he said, looking up at the three-dimensional image of Noah's heart beating on the large, glass monitor hanging on the wall in back of the bed. "You have such a big heart, Noah. No wonder why you always followed it. I can still feel your love, even now. Good-bye, Little Brother. I'm going to miss you," he said sadly, looking down at Noah's sunken face.

"It won't be long now before Noah's soul moves on to a better place," the doctor said, putting his hand on Scott's shoulder. "Your brother must have been a very caring human being," he continued, looking over at the body in the bed. "Just the fact that he elected to donate his organs to give the gift of life is in itself a testimonial to his selfless nature. I wish more people were like your brother. Due to his age, however, we can't use his heart, but we can use just about everything else. Pretty soon, some fortunate people will be benefiting from your brother's ultimate gift of kindness. I'm deeply sorry for your loss, I really am. Before I turn off life support, would you like me to call the chaplain in to say a few words?"

"No, that won't be necessary. Besides, over the years, Noah stopped believing in God. Claimed God was never there for him," Scott sadly admitted.

"I understand," the doctor said, walking over to Noah's body and pulling the breathing tube out of his mouth.

"Are we too late?" Sarah asked, rushing into the room with Zack.

"Hi, Sarah. No, the doctor is doing it now," Scott answered.

The doctor touched a small circle on top of the silver ventilator, turning it off and quietly left the room. The illustration of the bellows traveling up and down the cylinder slowly came to a stop along with the swishing sound. Without air going into his lungs, his heart would no longer function. The intervals between heartbeats on the three-dimensional glass monitor started getting longer as Noah's heartbeats slowed.

Doctor Feldman was reading the document on his clipboard as he passed Robin, Brittany, and Olivia in the hallway.

"Please, Mom, let me take you back to your room," Brittany insisted as she and Olivia chased after their mother. "I never should have told you we were taking Noah off of life support."

"Yeah, Brittany, why'd you have to go and tell her that anyway?" Olivia complained childishly.

The doctor looked up from his clipboard and looked back over his shoulder.

"She's too smart. She forced it out of me," Brittany claimed, following Robin as she burst into Noah's room.

"Hey, come back here," the doctor yelled, running after them, wondering why the extra dose of sedative he had given Robin earlier for her nervous breakdown wasn't working.

Crying hysterically as she entered the room, Robin stopped and looked across the room at Noah's lifeless body in the bed, his heartbeats growing ever so far apart on the large, glass monitor.

"I'll be with you soon, Noah. I'll be with you soon," she cried out, her body shaking as she approached his bedside.

Just then, Doctor Feldman ran into the room and grabbed hold of her. She tried to break free from his grip, but it was no use, he was too strong.

"Come on now, Robin, let's get you back to your room so you can rest," he said, pulling her away from the bed as the glass monitor started flickering.

Unseen and unheard, tears roll down my face as I kneel before Josh, my desperate eyes seeking refuge in his eyes as the doctor pulls Robin past me in another dimension. "Please, God... there's something I need to tell her." His compassionate eyes provide safe harbor for mine as his hand slowly reaches out toward me, touching the tip of his forefinger against the teardrop clinging to my face.

As she was being swept across the room, Robin looked back one last time at Noah's body, and she suddenly noticed tears rolling down his face. Looking down at the table, something caught her eye next to a box of Kleenex, and she wondered how it ever got there. It was the picture of Noah holding the sand dollar right before it exploded, as if he was holding it out to her again now. With newfound strength and determination, she managed to break free from the doctor's grip and ran back to the bed.

"Here I am, Noah... right over here," she whispered, kissing each of Noah's tearful eyes before being yanked away by the doctor and whisked out of the room, with Brittany and Olivia following close behind.

"Stop, don't do it. NOOOOOOOOOO..." she yelled, reaching back hopelessly toward the room that was getting farther and farther away.

"Robin, please try to relax," the doctor said, pulling a hypodermic needle out of his pocket and squirting it. "You're having another nervous breakdown."

"But Noah's not dead. HE'S STILL ALIVE !" she screamed in desperation.

Turning his attention back to his brother, Scott noticed tears rolling down his face, and the small LED lights on the dome on his head were now flashing green. He glanced up at the glass monitor and saw the three-dimensional image of Noah's heart beating away as fast as ever. The three-dimensional black and white image of his brain now had yellow, orange, and red colors flowing freely into each other, constantly changing form while increasing numbers flashed beside it. The words *BRAIN ACTIVITY DETECTED* flashed across the screen in large letters. Noah's left index finger started to move.

"You've got to see this !" Scott exclaimed, running out to the hallway and grabbing the doctor. "It's a miracle !" he said as they ran back into the room.

Noah was conscious and looking around the room. He gazed at Robin as she approached him.

"I love you, Noah," she said softly, taking his hand and leaning over him, like she had done in his dream.

"Robin, I want you to know... my love for you will never die."

"Me too, Noah. Me too," she said, wiping a tear from her eye.

As the glass monitor flickered, Noah heard Josh's voice saying, "Noah, your minute's almost up."

"But I haven't told her yet," Noah replied, looking around for Josh.

"Better tell her now," Noah heard him say.

"Remember Polaris?" Noah said, looking up at Robin. She nodded. "Don't forget what I told you: when the day comes when Polaris no longer leads me back to you... on that day, you and I —"

Noah gasped, unable to breathe. The intervals between heartbeats on the glass monitor started getting longer as his heartbeats grew farther apart. With a sense of tranquility, Noah's loving eyes stared deep into Robin's eyes for as long as he could keep them open.

"Will simply sail..." Robin said softly as his eyes began to close. "Away," she whispered to herself, placing her lips ever so gently against his as his eyes shut for the very last time.

On the large monitor in the background, the image of Noah's heart stopped pumping, his heartbeats went flat, and the alarm sounded. With tears in their eyes, Robin, Scott, Sharon, Brittany, Olivia, Sarah, and Zach stood solemnly around the bed, mourning the passing of a man whose love would never die.

Sailing Away

"So that was my life's story..." I say to Josh, "a story I really needed to tell. I refused to allow it to be defined by heartbreak. On the contrary, my life's story... was defined by undying love."

"It was a beautiful story, Noah. Extraordinary. Thanks for sharing it with me. Well, I'm off to the next room," he says, pushing his cart. "Got another story to listen to — as if I don't already know what it's all about," he says, winking at me.

"Yeah, I'm sure you've got lots of stories to listen to, all of them unique, all of them special. Thanks, God... for listening to *mine*."

Josh bows his head in silence.

"You know, it's funny how things have a way of working themselves out in the end. That whole time Robin was gone, I never stopped missing her, and I never stopped loving her. Having her back in my arms again made it all worthwhile. I wasn't perfect, and I made my mistakes. But I learned from them and became a better person for it. I always followed my heart, and most of all... I loved. I loved with every ounce of my being. I guess the best love story ever written is the one we write for ourselves," I say, putting my hand in my robe pocket, surprised to feel something wedged inside. I take it out and stare at it. It's some kind of oddly shaped key.

"Oh, better push that *top* button," Josh says, pointing his finger. "You don't want to accidentally push the bottom one."

I turn around, surprised to see an elevator behind me. As instructed, I push the top button — the one with the up arrow. The elevator doors open, and I step inside.

"I guess that's what life's all about... why we're here," I say, turning around in the elevator. "It has nothing to do with dollars. In fact, it's totally free, isn't it? Life's greatest gift. And the best part is, the best part, this gift we give to others... we get it back. It's what makes the journey so worthwhile... it's LOVE."

"You got *that* right," Josh says, nodding as the elevator doors start to close. "Hey, Noah..."

I press a button, and the doors open again.

"I'll be here if you need me," he tells me reassuringly.

I let out a smile. "Yeah. Somehow I always knew," I say, nodding my head, feeling as if I've known him my whole life. "I just never admitted it... until now."

The elevator doors shut in front of me, and I insert the key in the keyhole.

Josh is all alone in an empty hospital room. He picks up his clipboard hanging on the side of his cart and puts on his glasses to read the next name on the list. He hangs the clipboard back up and pushes the cart out of the room and into the hallway, passing Doctor Feldman who now looks twenty years older. He stops at the next room and knocks lightly on the door, waits, then knocks again, this time louder.

"Please come in," says the sweet voice of an elderly woman.

Josh pushes the door open with his cart and enters the room, taking a tray of food out from underneath it and placing it on a table extended out over a ninety-two-year-old woman, who is sitting up in her hospital bed.

"Thank you so much," she says in a kind voice. "It's exactly what I wanted," she says, looking down at the dinner on her tray.

"My name's Josh... Josh Numen," he says, handing her a cup of wine. "What's yours?"

"Robin..." she says, taking a sip of wine. "Robin Hartman," she says with a pleasant smile. "Would you like to hear my story?"

The elevator doors open, and I'm blinded by a bright light. I put my hand over my eyes as I step off, attempting to see. Nineties music is playing, and I can barely make out something or someone. As my eyes adjust to the bright light, the image comes into focus. It's Robin, looking young again, exactly the same as she did on the night I first met her, except she's wearing a white linen robe just like mine. By the look of my youthful hands, I must be young again too. I walk over to her as she dances in heaven with her arms up in the air. She sure looks beautiful to me.

"I have a present for you, Noah," she says, handing me the sand dollar. "Remember this?"

I take it carefully in my hand and stare at it, amazed. It's the same sand dollar that had exploded on our honeymoon, except all of the pieces have somehow been put back together. I look at her and smile.

I Will Be Here starts playing, and in the glistening water before us, the small sailboat I once built awaits us. We look down at it and then back at each other. I get in first, reaching out my hand to help her in. She gazes affectionately into my eyes. More than words, her warm eyes speak volumes to my soul, and I know she loves me. The sail fills with air, and the small ark carries us off toward the distant horizon. Robin cuddles up into my loving arms as we disappear into the light.

THE END

A Note From Sebastian Cole

SAND DOLLAR is best classified as a romantic fantasy. Although there are a lot of readers out there who enjoy a good fantasy, I realize that there are others who prefer to keep things real. So for those romantics out there who only want to read *real* love stories, consider this: Noah is actually a real person in real life, and his love for Robin, the one who got away, is real too. The real-life Noah is convinced that he'll never get over his one true love, blaming himself for taking her for granted and for throwing away his wedding band during a senseless argument — a mistake he's forced to live with for the rest of his life. His fantasy is that one day before he dies, perhaps even on his deathbed, Robin will come back and tell him that she loves him once again.

Rather than waiting indefinitely for this to happen, the real-life Noah decides to tempt fate by writing a screenplay about their lives together. His dream is that someday his screenplay will actually get made into a movie, and perhaps then — and only then — Robin will watch the movie and remember how much she loves him. In the mean time, Noah novelizes the screenplay into a book — a book that you've just finished reading — called *SAND DOLLAR*.

So perhaps *SAND DOLLAR* is not so much a fantasy as it is a dream — Noah's dream — that some day his long lost love will once again return to him. But only you, the reader, have the power to make dreams come true. And so, on behalf of the real-life Noah, I thank you for playing a supporting role in whatever happens in the next chapter of his life.

Until then, I leave you with these thoughts: Perhaps you know someone whose heart clutches onto the bittersweet memory of the one who got away. Someone who secretly bears the weight of this imperceptible burden wherever he or she goes, every day of his or her life. Someone who'd gladly travel back in a time machine to a day when paths diverged, to mend together that which has been torn apart, setting destiny back on its rightful track — if only he or she could. Perhaps you know this someone better than you think. And should this someone happen to be you, may you find strength and support in the millions of others who shoulder this burden with you, and may you be reintroduced one day to true love... in this lifetime and whatever comes after.

Acknowledgements

Now that I've started this journey, I look forward to the challenges that lie ahead. First and foremost, I'd like to thank *you*, the reader, for supporting me in my newfound endeavors as an author. With a little luck and a lot of hard work, I hope to continue bringing you the kind of novels you love to fall in love with.

I'd like to thank so many people in my life who've helped me, but I'd be remiss if I didn't start with my parents, to whom I owe a debt of gratitude. Without their love and support, I wouldn't be the person I am today. I love you both.

To the dozen friends and family members who read the first drafts of my manuscript and provided me with valuable feedback. Thanks for not holding back and for giving it to me straight.

To Sondra, the first person to ever read *SAND DOLLAR*. Her comments on every page of the first draft became my introduction to better writing. Sondra, you're my inspiration, and thanks to you, look how far I've come ! To my friend Judy Pelkey, for taking the time to mark up the pages of the manuscript with helpful advice. To Stuart Horwitz from Book Architecture, whose critique of the story proved to be invaluable. I can't praise him enough for his insight, professionalism, and expert recommendations. To Melissa and Chad Oman, who provided me with useful coverage.

To April Eberhardt, who, in a sea of literary agents who are far too quick to dismiss new authors, was the one — and only one — to rescue me. And she did it with congeniality, kindness, and compassion. Thanks, April, for showing me the way.

To Jan Kardys, a friend who taught me a thing or two about the meaning of romance. To Deborah DeWit, whose romantic pastel drawings grace the first cover of *SAND DOLLAR*. To Ainsley Bonham, whose cute sand dollar illustration bookmarks the beginning of each chapter. To Daniel Middleton from Scribe Freelance, whose creative formatting and cover design far exceeded all of my expectations.

I encourage everyone to pursue his or her dreams — that's what I've done. Like the sand dollar, life can change in a heartbeat, so better do it now while you've still got the opportunity. Now that I've started this journey, I can't see what lies ahead on this unfamiliar road, but I know one thing for sure: when I look behind, I see the things that I've accomplished... and I smile with pride.

CPSIA information can be obtained at www.ICGtesting.com
Printed in the USA
BVOW070609170912

300455BV00001B/5/P